I0831762

The Independent

by

Dana L Turk

2 Turk Books

ISBN-13: 978-1547258307 (CreateSpace-Assigned)
ISBN-10: 1547258306

CONTENTS

FROM THE AUTHOR

Throughout our nation's history, there have been several independent presidential candidates as well as write-in candidates.

George Washington could be considered an Independent, because in 1776 there were no official political parties and he was appointed to the Presidency, a job he did not want, by a Congress he did not feel comfortable supporting.

Although, the Continental Congress was split in their beliefs of how the country should be governed, it wasn't until the end of Washington's tenure as President that the parties began to appear.

Theodore Roosevelt came close to winning as an independent when his progressive party had more electoral votes than the republican candidate. However, in the end the democrat, Woodrow Wilson, would soundly defeat him.

Since the beginning of the presidential debates in the nineteen sixties, only one independent candidate has been invited to participate.

We have had Congressmen and Women and Senators who belonged to Independent parties, but, we have never had a President who carried the "Independent" label.

What would happen if an independent candidate gained enough support from the voting public to win the election? Not someone from an Independent Party, like the Tea Party or the Green Party, but someone who was truly Independent: with no party ties whatsoever. Which members of the two-party House of Representatives or Senate would support him or her? What would be the highest hurdles and toughest challenges they would face?

The Independent would have to explore the possibility of a non-party-affiliated individual and would have to express an ideology so brash it would draw the attention of a global audience — an audience that is frustrated by a government which is blind to the wants and needs of the people they serve — an audience that would demand respect and a reformation of basic human rights – an audience that demands accountability from their elected representatives.

D. L. Turk

INTRODUCTION

Buffalo is a small, peaceful hamlet in the heart of the Powder River Valley in north central Wyoming. It is located at the junction where Interstate 25 intersects with Interstate 90.

If you enter the town from either end, exiting from the Interstates, the streets slope downhill toward Clear Creek. After crossing the creek, the streets rise uphill toward the other Interstate. Buffalo, with its forty-six-hundred population and single main street down the center of town, is quite literally a dip in the road. If you don't take either of the exits from the interstates to tour the scenic drive down Main Street, you might blink and miss the entire town at seventy-five-miles-per-hour.

Buffalo is also the County Seat of Johnson County, a ranching and farming community with a significant history. Buffalo and Johnson County aren't just some backwoods part of the country. They have an historical background and were the scene of the greatest war between cattle ranchers, sheepherders, and farmers in the history of the United States. The Johnson County War, between the affluent cattle barons and the poorer dirt farmers and sheepherders, ravaged Johnson County for four years between 1889 and 1893. Johnson County is also home to the wagon box fight and the Fetterman Massacre, the incidents which drew General Custer and the Seventh Cavalry into the area and resulted in the massacre at Little Bighorn.

Yes, Buffalo and Johnson County have a history; but, that isn't the only history the Town and County have -- Buffalo was also home to Sam Waters.

Sam was a common man -- husband, father, and Veteran. He was fifty-six years old, just a little over six feet tall with black, slightly graying, short-cropped hair and was very muscular from years of construction work. He and his wife, Kate and their children, Toby and Lauren, lived in a small ranch-style log home just off Main Street on the North side of town.

Sam owns a small construction company in Buffalo that pays his bills, gives the family a couple of weeks of vacation each year and buys a few luxuries, but not much more. He pays his taxes and complains about the government like everyone else. And, like everyone else, he votes and hopes this candidate will be better than the last one. He was well liked by everyone in the community because of his friendly even temperament and willingness to lend a helping hand to those in need.

In April of 2016, the unthinkable happened! The Mayor and City Counsel of Buffalo put an issue on the ballot -- a tax. Not just a tax, but a new sales tax. The six percent sales tax applied specifically to sweetened beverages and sugary drinks. These beverages ranged from sport drinks, carbonated soda, and soft drinks to Kool Aid products.

Sam felt people were already taxed to the limit, between Federal, State, County and City taxes and surcharges. The part of this new tax, which was especially aggravating to Sam, was the use of children to stress the claims.

The proponents of the new tax used the children as the reason to tax soda drinks. With slogans like "By taxing soft drinks, people will buy less of them and there won't be such a high rate of child-onset-diabetes and obesity." Or, in the alternative "The tax dollars would provide affordable pre-schooling to families who can't afford it."

Opponents were firmly entrenched by the fact that the State Government already gives money to the Board of Education as does the Federal Government so why was it necessary to place yet another tax burden on the people.

There were several other issues pro and con on the tax, and each issue would build on the ire of the people of Buffalo, creating a rift between the people and their elected representatives.

Sam felt it was such an outrageous example of political dishonesty and greed, he needed to act. He carefully drafted a letter to the editor of the Buffalo Bulletin, the local newspaper:

To Whom It May Concern:

A recent item placed on the election ballot has raised the question: who do our representatives represent? The Soda Tax, which our Mayor and City Counsel added to the ballot in April, defines the fact that our Elected Officials, DO NOT represent the people. The Tax also emphasized the fact that our representatives will go to any lengths, including using our children in an attempt to deceive us. It would seem the government isn't satisfied with taxing most of what we purchase and most of what we own, they now want to tax the kitchen sink as well.

We have watched as our City, State, and Federal Governments continue to spend like there is an endless river of money to bail out Big Corporations, Big Bank, and Big Insurance Companies for the benefit of these entities. We have watched our representatives line their pockets at the expense of the people they serve in this country and I'M TIRED OF IT. We have watched as legitimate small businesses must pay increasingly higher financial homage to the Economic Development Departments and Programs.

From small towns to large cities, at all levels of Government, those businesses which don't line the pockets or 'pay the homage' fail within a couple of years. They fail because their Representatives refuse to act on their behalf. Yet, our City, County, State, and Federal Governments continue to support those corporations who will funnel the manufacture of their products overseas and import them back to the United States at a premium price to the consumer.

Why won't our Representatives support innovative companies which develop home grown, Made-in-America, products, and businesses.

We watch the news daily as inquiries and investigations bring out fact-after-fact about the corruption of the individuals who are supposed to represent the people. What we never see is the punishment when those people are found guilty – they are pardoned by the President and never serve a day in jail for the crimes of which they were found guilty. Guilty of treason. Guilty of insider trading. Guilty of pandering and prostituting America for their own personal gain. Guilty of bribery and accepting bribes. Guilty of failure to abide with and uphold the Constitution in accordance with their oath of office.

GUILTY!

I'm tired of paying thirty percent of my income for criminals to become wealthy. Our elected representatives are not above the law. They are not exempt from those laws they pass for the People. And they are not exempt from being punished for their crimes.

I'm tired of seeing my government sending billions of dollars in Foreign Aid to countries which would see this country destroyed while our own cities become cesspools of poverty and despair.

I'm tired of watching our nation's homeless crisis become epidemic while the fat cat politicians look the other way

.

I'm tired of watching the major parties fight over party lines leaving the people without representation. Our elected officials cannot represent all of the people if they are constantly split by party lines and agendas.

I'm tired of seeing more and more of our military bases closed and our military strength downsized while we have threats against us from foreign governments and extremist nations around the world.

And I'm tired of watching as our citizenry become so overly dependent on our Government, that we allow the wolves to regulate us into third world status by passing laws which restrict growth, which restrict innovation, which restrict the people from being represented as our Constitution intended.

It's time our Elected Representatives show respect for those who put them in office. It's time for change! It's time for a reckoning! It's time for the people to come together and unify against those in our governments who are gradually, but with ever-increasing vigor, sucking the life out of our great country.

Sincerely,

Sam Waters
Buffalo, Wyoming

The Bulletin published Sam's letter and he received praise and accolades from his friends and the people he knew and worked with in Buffalo. Everyone thought it was a great letter; however, no one knew what lay in store for the small Wyoming town.

The citizens of Buffalo were unaware that Sam's two brothers: Mike, in Washington, D.C. and Jim, in Los Angeles, watched the Buffalo paper on line to keep up with hometown events. Mike and Jim saw the letter by their brother and copied it and sent it to their local papers. Jim sent it to the L.A. Times and several other West coast papers and Mike sent it to the Washington Post, NY Times, and several East coast papers. As odd and rare an occurrence as it may be, the letter was picked up and published by all the editors.

Because of the number of large papers which printed the letter, it was picked up by the Associated Press and United Press International. It became an article in many more major city newspapers like the Denver Post, Chicago Sun-Times, and the Dallas Morning News.

People from all over the country read the letter, copied it, and posted it online, sharing it with their friends and family who in-turn shared it with their friends and families.

When Sam's letter was posted and shared on the internet, it went viral on social media getting over a million hits per day and being shared five-hundred times per hour.

The sweetened beverage tax measure was defeated in the November election, but the letter remained and continued to circumnavigate the globe at an amazing rate.

1
FIRST CONTACT

It had been an extremely stressful Friday. The city building inspector had been several hours late and Sam's crew had been standing around with their hands in their pockets looking for something to do that would at least allow them to earn their pay while they waited.

Sam could hear the phone ringing in his home office as he entered his back door into the kitchen. After a long week and longer days putting the final trim and accents on a new house for the City Attorney, he wasn't sure he wanted to answer it. Sam was more than a little irritated with the situation with the building inspector and it could be heard in his voice as he answered the phone.

"Waters Construction." Sam briskly answered in his customary greeting.

"Is Sam Waters available?" queried the voice on the other end.

"Speaking" Sam replied, then continued as he does for all solicitors, "Whatever you're selling, we aren't buying. Whatever you're giving away, we don't want any and whatever you're asking for, we aren't giving any. Take this number off your call list." Sam started to hang up the phone.

"I'm Jerry Cummings with Channel Five News." The man rushed to get his name out, expecting the next sound he would hear would be the dial tone. When he didn't hear the tone, he continued "I'm not a solicitor Mr. Waters. I would like to do an interview with you for the news this weekend."

Sam had stopped to listen when he heard the name. He watched the news and listened to Jerry on Channel Five every night.

"Mr. Cummings, I'm sorry, you have me at a loss. What could you possibly want to interview me about?"

"Mr. Waters, may I call you Sam?"

"Sure, that's my name."

"Sam, about six months ago you wrote a letter to the editor of the Buffalo Bulletin. Do you remember that letter?"

"Yes. I remember being really pissed off at our Mayor and the city council and was voicing some of my frustrations with government. Why?"

"Well, Sam, it seems your letter was picked up by a lot of people and it has been flying around the press, the internet and social media and getting a lot of attention from some very important people. I have been assigned to interview you and do your story and more or less assess your political views."

"That will be a very short interview, Mr. Cummings, and we can do it right here on the phone. I don't have any political views. I don't belong to any party and, like I said, I wrote that stupid letter because I was pissed at our Mayor. End of story."

"Sorry, Sam. I can't let you off quite that easy. I will be in Buffalo tomorrow. Do you have some time we can meet?"

"I usually take my kids out to Lake De Smet on Saturday, but it's supposed to turn cold overnight and rain tomorrow. If you agree to buy lunch for my family at Pie Zanos, I'll give you your interview."

"Deal. Does noon work for you?"

"Better be closer to one. Saturday's are always busy about noon because a lot of folks take their kids out for pizza."

"One it is then. See you tomorrow."

"See ya then."

Sam hung up the phone and turned to see Kate, staring at him. Kate was forty-five, a pretty redhead and slight in stature. She could be gentle as a newborn lamb or mean as a junk-yard dog at the flip of a switch; but she loved Sam and her kids and would stand by them no matter what.

"That sounded like an intimate conversation. Secret meetings with bribed kids to keep them quiet. Who was that on the phone?"

"You're not going to believe this, honey. That was Jerry Cummings from Channel Five News and he wants to interview me about that stupid letter I wrote to the Bulletin a while back. We're meeting him tomorrow at one over at Pies."

"Really? The news wants to interview you about that letter? That ought to stir the town up a bit. I better do some laundry and ironing, so we will look presentable." Kate turns and heads off toward the door to the basement.

“Are we going to have dinner tonight, baby?” Sam asks.

“Oh shoot, can we order something delivered?” Kate queries as she looks around the kitchen and realizes she hadn’t started dinner and it was seven o’clock.

“Tell you what baby, since we're having pizza tomorrow, I'll just throw some burgers on the grill. The kids will like that -- two junk meals back-to-back.” Sam wasn’t a health nut, but he believed that eating right resulted in good health - mentally and physically.

Sam yelled for his son. “Toby, come help me get some burgers on the grill.”

***

At one o’clock Sam, Kate, Toby, and Lauren were seated in a booth near the middle of Pie Zanos restaurant when the Channel Five news van pulled up in front of the building. Jerry entered, and Sam met him halfway to the counter.

“Mr. Cummings, I’m Sam Waters and it's a pleasure to meet you.”

“Please Sam, call me Jerry, and believe me when I say the pleasure is all mine.”

Jerry was a typical news reporter. Tall, handsome, well dressed, well groomed, fit, and polite.

“My family is right over here. We can order a pizza for them and then go to another table for the interview.”

“Sam, I'd like to do the interview with your family near you if that's okay. Then afterwards, we can sit and eat without the camera rolling.”

“You’re the man in charge.”

“Great! I'll be right back.”

Jerry went out to the news van where a crowd was already beginning to gather. The few people who were in the restaurant when Jerry walked in were already texting their friends that Jerry Cummings was in Buffalo at Pies.

Jerry returned to Sam’s table with his camera crew, two guys who, with their beards, blue jeans, and t-shirts, looked very out of place next to the well-groomed Cummings. Peter placed the camera on a tripod and set up some lights to illuminate the dimly lit table.

Jeff clipped a microphone to Sam's shirt and set up a couple of microphones on the table for the rest of the family.

"Are we ready?" Jerry asked his crew.

Getting thumbs up, Jerry turned to Sam and his family.

"Okay, guys this is what's going to happen: I'm going to ask some questions and I want you all to be as detailed as possible in your answers. If you need me to repeat the question, please don't hesitate to ask or if you don't understand a question, just ask me to explain anything that isn't clear. The interview will take about thirty to forty minutes and there will be some stuff which will be edited out once we are back at the studio. The interview will be broadcast as a special feature and will run about eleven to seventeen minutes on the ten o'clock edition of the news tonight. All set?" Everyone expressed they were ready and Peter cued Jerry for the interview.

"Three, two, one." Peter pointed at Jerry

"Good evening. I'm here on assignment in Buffalo, Wyoming with what is possibly the biggest story since the Johnson County War, because tonight I'm talking with Sam Waters, the man behind the letter. Also with us are Mrs. Waters --"

"Kate, and this is Toby and Lauren" Kate interrupted.

"Okay, Kate, kids – It's nice to meet you.

"What did you guys think of your Dad's letter?"

"I thought it was kinda lame." Toby stated as Kate gave him a quick and stern glance. Toby was thirteen and had an average teenage attitude. He was almost as tall as his dad and handsome enough to have many of the teenage girls in town swooning over him.

"How about you Lauren, did you know your Dad wrote a letter to the newspaper?"

"Yes, we all talked about it; but that was a long time ago. Why are you talking about it now?"

"Well, Lauren your dad's letter is news and that's my job, to talk about news."

"Well, okay, just seems like old news." Lauren was nine and pretty typical of a young girl - quizzical and unashamed about expressing her opinion.

"Sam, can you tell us a little bit about what drove you to write the letter to the editor of the Buffalo Bulletin?"

"Not much to it, Jerry. The Mayor and City Council put a sales tax issue on the ballot that would specifically tax sweetened drinks. Then they tried to use children's health and pre-school as the reason. I got pissed. Oh, sorry can I say that?"

"You're fine, Sam. We will edit the interview before it airs."

"Kate, how did you feel about the letter your husband wrote?"

"Sam and I have been married a long time and I know he can get pretty passionate about things like that tax. Heck, it had the entire town up in arms. I seriously thought we were going to tar and feather the Mayor and run him out of town on a rail."

"I can understand where that might happen; but, how did you personally feel about the letter?"

"Sam's letter was a breath of fresh air around here. Something that has been needed to be said for a long time. Buffalo has been growing and our city officials have been taking advantage of that growth without regard to the consequences of their actions on the people. Sam hit the nail on the head when he said it's time for change and I agreed with every word."

"Thank you, Kate. Sam, do you have any aspirations to run for Mayor or city Council?"

"Oh, Hell No! Sorry. No, I don't, I have no desire to run for any kind of political office. Too much BS and you are always on the wrong end of someone's stick."

"What if I told you that you are on the radar to be a candidate for a high-level position in the next election?"

"I would have to say that whoever's radar I'm on is out of order. I told you, I'm not interested in any office. I wouldn't even run for dog catcher. I'm quite happy with my little construction company, my family, and my pets. I don't need anything else."

"Sam, I told you on the phone that your letter had gained the attention of some pretty important people. I just mentioned you are on their radar for a high-level position. What if I told you those people think you should take a shot at the White House."

"Wow, our dad in the White House. Now that's cool" Toby burst in echoed by Lauren.

"The President? Now I know your people are whacko. What would I do in the White House? Fix the paneling in the Lincoln bedroom or remodel the Oval Office. Come on, look at me. I'm just a disgruntled nobody contractor who wrote a letter to the editor of a Podunk newspaper in a Podunk town in Podunk Wyoming. Don't misunderstand me. I love Buffalo and our little local newspaper, and I love Wyoming, but it's not Washington D.C and the Post, or New York and the Times or Wall Street Journal. I told you on the phone, I have no party affiliation. Not Republican, Not Democrat, Not Green or Tea or any of the other independent parties. I'm just me. One person. One vote, not even a drop in the political bucket."

"Sam, everything you've said is true, but you are not a nobody. You are better known than President Obama was, and he came out of absolute obscurity to be the President for eight years. You have a degree in business with a minor in accounting. Because you have no party ties and have never registered to vote with any party affiliation, every single party wants you, both major parties and all the independents. Have you been contacted by any of them yet?"

"No, and if they do call --"

"Actually," Kate interrupted, "the Republican Party called yesterday while you were at work. Barry Simms from the Republican National Committee here in Buffalo wanted to talk to you. I thought he wanted to contract some work on his house, but now his comments make sense. He said he had some big plans for you."

"Well, I've got some big plans for him too. I'm going to tell him to forget it. I'm not running for any political office. Period. End of discussion and the end of this interview!"

"Thank you, Sam and Kate. Ladies and Gentlemen, Sam and Kate Waters with their children, Toby and Lauren. Could we be looking at the next First Family? Apparently not if Sam has anything to say about it. Jerry Cummings, from Buffalo. Cut and out"

There was a large crowd which seemed like the entire population of Buffalo either in the restaurant, peering in through the large plate glass windows or gathering on the street. They started applauding, whistling, and yelling loudly and chanting "Waters for President. Waters for President." Some were laughing at the idea, but you could see in their faces their belief that Sam would be fully capable of the task.

“Thank you, Sam that was great. Now, while Peter and Jeff put our gear away, let’s order some pizza. What do you guys like?”

Pizza and drinks were ordered and the news gear all packed up. Jerry and his crew joined Sam and his family in the oversized booth.

“Off the record guys, what are your thoughts on a run for the White House?”

“On or off the record, I think I was pretty clear on the answer to that. Pizza and soft drinks aren't going to persuade me otherwise.”

“You have a pretty large following here in Buffalo already. Are you sure you don't want to take a shot?”

“On a true scale of things, Jerry, even if every one of the forty-six-hundred or so people in Buffalo voted for me, it would be like trying to drain the Pacific Ocean with an eye dropper. No, I don't think so.”

For the next hour, while the group ate and chatted about Buffalo and Sam’s business, Jerry attempted to influence Sam to change his mind.

“Sam, Kate, kids, it has been a pleasure meeting and talking with you today. Be sure to watch the news tonight at ten. Sam, I've read your letter and I've seen what it is doing on the Internet, I wish you would change your mind and run. If nothing else, you could join one of the independent parties, and give the two-party establishment a run for their money.

2
UNDER PRESSURE

After the interview, Sam and his family were the talk of the town for the six or so hours until the ten o'clock news. The crowd at the restaurant kept talking about President Sam, the town's very own, real-life, Uncle Sam and chanting "Sam for President" and "Sam 2024".

That night Channel Five News did broadcast the interview, but it wasn't the typical ten to seventeen-minute feature. The interview was the focal point of the entire news broadcast and the interview wasn't edited as Jerry had said it would be. The full video of the interview was shown with the people of Buffalo gathering in and around the restaurant; the chanting crowd and even a couple of spot interviews with Sam's neighbors and friends. There was a segment on the Internet showing a social media post of the letter with over thirty-three million views and that was only one of the thousand or so posts, reposts, and shares. Sam turned the channel midway through, but Kate immediately turned it back.

"Kate, I don't want to watch this. I told Jerry, I wasn't going to run, and I meant exactly that. I'm not Running. Period."

"Sam, I know what you said. I just want to watch this broadcast of our interview. It's not every day you get to be a big shot TV star." Kate smirked as she gave Sam a big hug and kiss on the cheek.

"Well, it is kinda cool. Being a big shot TV star." Both laughed.

***

The warm days of an 'Indian Summer' Fall in Buffalo survived the weather forecast for colder temperatures and rain throughout the week. This weekend, Sam was taking the family to the lake to get a bit of fishing in, knowing that when the weather did change to winter, it would be too cold and wintery to go to the lake until mid-June. Since it was already mid-October that change could happen at any moment. Sam had just finished loading the pickup and was hitching up the boat trailer when Barry Simms, the chairperson for the Republican National Committee walked up.

"Howdy Sam, heading to the lake?"

"No Barry, I just thought I'd hitch up the boat and drive it around town for an hour or two." Sam said sarcastically, but with a broad smile on his face.

"Hahaha, that's what I like about you Sam, your great sense of humor. While your pulling the boat around town, let's put a couple of signs on each side saying, 'Sam Waters – Republican for President.' That would sure make a splash around here. No pun intended."

"Barry, not to be rude or disrespectful, but I'm sure you watched the news and saw Jerry Cumming's report last Saturday, and I'm equally sure you watched it right to the end where I very forcefully told everyone who would be watching that I wasn't running. So, why are you bothering me when I'm trying to get away and relax on the lake. You have my answer and I am not going to waiver from it."

"Look Sam, I'm here because you are, or seem to be, the people's choice and I want you in the Republican Camp next election. What do you say?"

"Well, Barry, since I'm the people's choice I suppose I better give you an answer. It may not be the answer you are looking for, but here it is. The people aren't looking for 'me' to run – they're looking for anyone who isn't party affiliated to run. Any independent with real 'dedication' to the people and this country will be the people's choice. Now, with that said, I will give you my answer about running for office. My answer is the same this morning as it was last weekend when I did the interview with Jerry Cummings. It is the same as it was when the interview aired on the news last Saturday night. And, finally, what I'm telling you now. I am not joining any party and not running for any office. Now, please, get out of my driveway!"

"You'll regret this decision, Sam. There are a lot of people who want you to be the next President of the United States and the Republican Party is the backing you would need to get elected. If you do decide to run and run with one of the independent parties, the two real parties of this country will bury you like they have so many independents before you."

"Still not biting, Barry. I have a good life here and I really have no aspirations to be anything more than Sam, the contractor. Now can I please finish getting ready for the lake?" Barry raised his hands up and backed away from Sam and turned toward the alley.

"Kate, kids, let's go."

With everyone in the pickup, Sam was startled as he almost ran over Barry who was still standing behind the hedgerow in the alley at the edge of the driveway. Barry waved as Sam drove off down the alley toward Main Street.

It takes about sixteen minutes to get to Lake De Smet and during the whole trip up interstate 90, people were passing him and honking their horns, waving, and giving him thumbs up. Sam was really getting annoyed by the time they reached the exit for the lake. He pulled up to the boat ramp and Toby ran around to the back of the boat trailer to undo the boat locks.

"Hey, Dad, did you change your mind about doing the president thing?"

Toby had a strange look on his face as he asked the question, so Kate walked to the end of the boat to see what was wrong.

"Toby, not you, too? No! I did not change my mind."

"Well, dear, someone seems to think you have." Kate said as she held up a well-printed sign that read, 'Sam Waters for President.'

"That son of a..."

"Don't say it!" Kate interrupted.

Disgruntled, Sam took the sign and put it behind the seat of the truck.

"Let's get the boat in the water before the rest of the county finds out we're here and comes to pester us."

The rest of the day was filled with people on the lake who would wave and cheer slogans of "Waters for President" or "Our Uncle Sam for President" every time they passed near Sam's boat.

Even with all the people passing by, it was a good day of fishing for most of the family. Toby pulled in a twenty-two-pound pike and Lauren and Kate caught a couple of perch and a few bass each. Sam had hooked a good-sized Rainbow trout and was reeling it in when an idiot steered in too close to Sam's boat and cut his line. That was it for Sam! He threw his pole in the bottom of the boat, gunned the motor, and sped toward the boat ramp. Sam was so furious he ignored the no-wake rules for that end of the lake and came very near beaching the boat on the ramp. He jumped out of the boat in waist deep freezing water and waded to the shore and up the bank to the parking area to get the pickup and back the trailer onto the ramp. Kate slowly maneuvered the boat onto the trailer and Sam pulled it out of the water. Toby locked it down and they took off for home.

3
THE DECISION

At home, everything was as hectic as it was at the lake. People coming by the house to show their support and pressuring Sam to run for President. Some of them, were total strangers that Sam had never seen before, and he knew about everyone in Johnson County. Sam figured they must be leftover actors and crew from some movie that had been filmed in the vicinity or tourists who hadn't headed back to the sun states.

By late afternoon, the weather had turned, and the temperature was approaching freezing. Many people with their kids were camped out in Sam's yard.

"Kate, this is absolutely amazing and totally asinine. These people must not care for themselves or their kids – out there in this cold. Didn't any of them watch the news and hear me say I wasn't running for anything including dog catcher? For crying out loud! How I wish I had never written that stupid letter."

"Well, Sam, you did write the stupid letter and you said what needed to be said not only to the Mayor of our podunk little Wyoming town, but to every podunk little town and big city in this country. I am proud of you for taking a stand and even prouder that your stand has inspired so many to support you. A lot of those people on the lake today were from Sheridan, Story, Ranchester and Big Horn. So, you have more support than just the folks from Buffalo."

"Kate, even if I had the support of everyone in the state I'd only have about six-hundred-thousand votes and three electors. Not even a drop in the bucket of the two-hundred-seventy electors needed to win the White House. I won't change my mind regardless of how many people around here support me. Let's cook up some of those fish we caught and eat, then turn off all of the lights so the morons on the lawn will take their kids home out of the cold."

Kate fried all the fish and after everyone had their fill she put together some meals on paper plates and told Toby and Lauren to take them out to the people still on the lawn.

"Kate, what in the world are you doing? You're just encouraging them to come back. If they can't see their mythical presidential candidate, they'll want the free vittles and we'll never get rid of them."

"You know Sam, if it weren't for all of this political foolishness you'd be helping with the food."

"You're probably right. That's why I love you. Here, let me help with those plates."

"You want to help with something, Mr. President, you can do our dishes. The dishwasher is empty." Kate reached up and gave Sam a quick kiss on the cheek and chased Toby and Lauren out the door with their arms full of food for the rather large group of people still in the yard.

Sam turned toward the sink full of dishes as the phone rang in his office. He believed Sundays were a day of rest and doesn't answer the office phone. As he placed the last plate in the dishwasher, the phone rang in the kitchen.

"Hello." Sam answers.

"Hi, Sam, this is Marjorie Cox, the chairperson of the Wyoming Democratic National Committee."

"Look you're not my best friend and not a close acquaintance, so your informality just cost you any of my time." Sam abruptly hung up the phone and turned to start the dishwasher cycle. He regretted his intolerance with the caller, but had enough of the whole political thing for one day.

"Who was on the phone?" Kate asked, as she came in from the yard and shook off the cold.

"Kate, that was the Chairperson of the Wyoming DNC. Don't these people have any kind of life? Calling at eight o'clock on a Sunday night. There ought to be a law forbidding that kind of crap."

Toby and Lauren came in and Kate shooed them into the den.

"Get to your homework, guys. Your dad and I will be in as soon as we finish the dishes.

"You know, Sam, those people outside really want to see someone run for president who isn't linked to money, special interests or big corporations. They look at your popularity as some sign things are changing in this country and, who knows, maybe the whole Trump and Clinton thing in 2016 and the results of the last election are just the tip of the iceberg. You've always said we should get rid of the Bilderbergers' hold on the government and I think we may be seeing a break in at least some of that hold. You've also said, and I can't tell you how many thousands of times, we need to stop voting the party line and get someone who really cares about the people. The Democrats and Republicans, fighting between themselves as well as with each other, may be the destruction of both. Then we move in with an independent with a real plan of action to make the country whole and a world power again. Not pushing, just saying."

"Maybe, but it won't be me. Let's go see how the kids are doing."

Sam thought about what Kate had said in the kitchen as he helped Toby with his math homework. Kate checked Lauren's spelling and sent her off to get ready for bed. A little while later Toby finished his homework and headed down the hall to bed. At the door to his room, he turned and stated;

"Dad, it would be really cool to be the son of the president."

Sam picked up a small pillow from the couch and flung it in Toby's direction.

***

For the next couple of months, life was more of the same for the Waters family. People were chanting "Sam for President" slogans every time Sam or his family went by and were putting banners in his yard and other yards around town. Sam just shook his head and drove on. There was still a small contingent of people who came to Sam's house and camped in the yard even though the temperatures were near zero degrees Fahrenheit.

Kate searched the internet and found nearly a thousand posts of Sam's letter and looked at the number of views on each. She searched on social media and found another thousand posts, reposts and shares each having well over a million views and each day the number of views, shares and posts grew. She started searching "Sam for President" posts and found another thousand or so posts with large amounts of reposts and shares. She found dozens of pages dedicated to Sam for President. Kate even found numerous posts and supporting pages from foreign countries like England, Australia, Spain, and the Ukraine. It seemed everyone was behind Sam -- not just the local folks from Buffalo and surrounding communities, but world-wide.

After dinner, Kate asked Sam "Have you looked at any of the information I've put on your desk lately?"

"Yes, and then I put it in the appropriate file."

"Which file would that be? The round file, or file 13."

"Actually neither. You have been doing a lot of research and it wouldn't be right for your work to just go into the trash; so, I made a file folder just for your stuff."

"And what would that file be called? My "Ain't Gonna Run file?" Or better yet - "I Wish Kate Would Stop It file."

"No, Kate, I labeled it my "Sam Waters for President File." I've read the research you've given me and although I'm not in any way interested in putting my hat in the ring. It would seem that both nationally and internationally there are a lot of people who want me to do just that."

"Cool! I'm going to be the first kid!" Toby yelled from the kitchen doorway; followed by Lauren's "No, I am."

"Whoa, you two. Nobody is going to be the first anything if your homework isn't done. Lauren, if by chance your dad does decide to run and if by greater chance he should win, then Toby would be first because he's the oldest. Of course, you would be the first girl kid."

Lauren turned and stuck her tongue out at her brother and they raced down the hall to the den.

"Sam, are you seriously considering this election thing now?"

"Not seriously, but it crosses my mind several times a day. Especially when I see your effort, the people freezing on our yard and all the signs around town. Some of the signs are hand written and some professionally done, all with the same message. I just don't know. You know me, I'm never one to disappoint anyone."

"Hmmm. First Lady Katherine Waters. Does have a nice ring to it. What could I be known for? Obama did the White House Garden and child obesity. Bush did children's literacy. There have been numerous drug and alcohol centers since Ford, and various foundations for the children and the poor and indigent. Some have been known for their costing the taxpayers millions of dollars. What does Kate Waters have to offer the world?"

"The same thing Sam Waters has to offer: A fresh point of view and honesty."

"Sam, you know the kids and I are behind you one hundred percent, rain or shine, win or not. If you do decide to run, you know what your biggest challenge is going to be?"

"Deciding which party line to follow?"

"No, I think you should maintain your "no party" stance and run as a total Independent. If you get into bed with the parties, regardless of which one, you will ultimately lose yourself and your self-respect. Your biggest challenge is going to be fighting the money. Every time there has been an independent candidate, the money, the Bilderbergers if you will, have found some way of assassinating their character or forcing them out of the election. Those who have the wealth to fund their own campaigns are restricted, because the money constantly changes the rules for the Presidential debates to keep independents from being heard. They will also fund the party candidates with vast amounts of PAC money to flood all the news media, so you won't get a word in edgewise through media advertising. Of course, the media wants more money and knows it can ask any amount from the party candidates and the parties will pay it. So, that raises the price for advertising beyond the budgets of most independent candidates. How will you fight the money? You know it's going to be a fight and they aren't going to give up easily."

"Kate, I've been fighting and scrapping most of my life. Haven't had a good fight in a long time. Never in my wildest dreams would I have thought it would be one like this. Let's get the kids in bed, have a good night's sleep, and talk about it again in the morning. Maybe by then I will have come to my senses and be more solid in my commitment not to run.

***

"Well, Sam, did your tossing and turning all night long provide any insight into how to win the election or strengthen your commitment to just let someone else bear the weight?"

"What do you mean?"

"Sam, you were a whirling dervish all night and talking in your sleep like you always do when you're stressed about something. You kept mentioning the campaign, so I figured you were dreaming about the pressure of either running the gauntlet or letting someone else carry the torch."

"Yes, Kate, I thought about it last night and dreamed about it all night long, and although I slept, it was the most restless sleep I've had in over ten years. Here's what I came up with. This is the starter plan, which will determine whether I run or not. I want you to go online today to some of those sites you found and announce that I am going to run. Ask for donations of no more than ten dollars from each person who supports me. Let them know that I will not accept anonymous donations. Anonymous contributions will be recorded and turned over to charity. Every donor and every penny received must be identified. Give them the company post office box number."

"Ok Sam, but how is doing that going to help you make your decision?"

"Well, I figure if we receive only a couple of donations, it will show that people really don't want change. They'll talk the talk, without walking the walk. We've seen it many times in my bids for construction jobs. People are all set to have me start a project, until I ask for the deposit check, then it's a whole different story. We need to see who is willing to walk the walk, who is willing to open their checkbook for someone they don't know. If we don't have contributions, we don't have a campaign. There is no way we can afford to finance a campaign ourselves."

"Okay, Sam, I see where your plan is going. How long are we going to give them to respond?"

"That's the part I haven't figured out. Let's get the word out and see what happens and then we can decide on a time limit."

"Sounds good. I'll get on it as soon as I get home from dropping the kids off at school and my morning errands."

"Thanks, Baby, you're the best. I have to do a bid at the Pierce's and finish the kitchen tile at the Clay's then I'll be home to help." With that Sam sets off to work.

Kate returns home from her errands and laughs at the thought of Sam's plan.

"Ok Kate, where do you start?" she says verbally to herself. "Well, the beginning is always a good place, so let's look at the notes

I've been giving Sam. What did he say the file name was? Oh yes. Here it is. Sam Waters for President."

Sam had indeed kept every piece of paper Kate had given him and even kept them meticulously in order, unlike his business files. Kate found the documents on the social media groups and decided to start there.

"If we are going to need the biggest bang for our buck we may as well start with groups who are most active."

Kate identified a couple of groups and pages that seemed like they might be promising and began composing the post.

My Dear Friends

Today I am in search of support for a campaign for President of the United States. If I am to run, I will need support both in words and deeds to make my run worthwhile for everyone. I will not enter the race just to lose.

Here's what I need from you. Just ten dollars, $10. There are three hundred million people in the United States. Of those approximately fifty-eight percent or one-hundred-seventy-four million are eligible to vote. I need a third of that number, fifty-eight million people, to support me in a campaign for the Presidency. With just a mere ten- dollar pledge I can begin to answer your call. Because I promise to personally thank every donor and account for every penny, I cannot accept anonymous donations. Any donations from anonymous parties or persons will be generously divided amongst the various charitable organizations and those organizations who provide help to our Veterans.

Thank you for your Support
You can make donations to

Sam Waters Presidential Campaign Fund
P.O. Box 15820
Buffalo, Wy 82834-5820

Sam Waters

Kate, makes the post and it instantly gets one hundred views. Kate takes a screenshot of the page and then posts on a couple more pages and one more social media site with a couple of pages. The results are staggering. In just a matter of minutes the sites and pages were alive with activity with hundreds of views, shares and reposts. Kate looks at the printouts from the pages and sites and says to herself, "Damn, Sam, I think you are a candidate for President."

When Sam gets home, Kate shows him the sheets.

"Just because there's a flurry of support online doesn't mean it will still be there when they open their wallets and purses. We've seen too many times, even in my business, where the project is just perfect, and everything is great and within budget. Then I ask for the deposit and suddenly, the project is too pricey, or they don't have the money right now. Let's just enjoy the weekend and forget the politics for a while. Why don't we head over to Meadowlark Ski Resort in Tensleep and stay at the lodge? We can ski and ice skate and just relax with the kids for a couple of days.

Kate agrees and when the kids come in from school, they are all packed for the trip. Outside of the occasional pep rally to urge Sam to run, they have a great weekend.

4
WALKING THE WALK

Monday, Kate went about her normal morning errands. She dropped the kids off at school and went to the Post Office to collect the usual business bills and a few payments. This morning, however, she had a surprise. Instead of the usual mail in the Post Office Box, she found a note asking her to come to the counter. As Kate approached the clerk at the counter, he handed her a large mail tub full of letters and asked:

"Kate, is Sam really going to run for President?"

"Eric, what would give you that idea?"

"I don't know, maybe all those letters addressed to the Sam Waters Presidential Campaign Fund. Kind of a giveaway, don't you think?"

"Sam is just doing some research to see what kind of support he might get. Please keep the mail thing under your hat until Sam makes up his mind. We don't need a bunch of people getting all excited if Sam decides not to run."

"No problem Kate. It's against the law for me to talk about someone's mail to a third party."

"Thanks, Eric."

Kate usually sorted the mail on the seat of her Explorer then went to the bank to make the deposits then home to pay the bills and check Sam's schedule for the week. Today, however, she took the mail home to sort it on the table.

She went into the garage and found the cart Sam used for tools when doing small projects around the house. Obviously, he had been too busy to do much around the house because the cart was covered with an inch of dust and cobwebs. Kate cleaned up the cart and dumped the tub of mail onto it. She placed the empty tub at the end of the cart for business mail and put a trash can at the other end for junk mail and started sorting. Kate didn't put much stock in Eric's comment about all the letters being addressed to Sam's campaign. She grabbed a handful of mail and looked at the address on the first piece and saw 'Sam Waters Presidential Campaign Fund.' She dropped the rest of the mail and opened the envelop. There, inside was a ten-dollar bill neatly wrapped in a piece of plain white paper with the words "Good Luck Sam! Samantha Gibson 1023 Edgewater Dr. Gillette, Wy 82717. Kate put the letter in the mail tub and continued to sort through the rest of the mail. When she had finished, she had one-hundred-twenty letters in the tub, five in the business bills and payments box and three junk mail.

Kate retrieved a notebook from the stash of the kid's school supplies and sat on the floor next to the tub of contributor mail. About two-thirds were from husband and wife couples and contained notes and letters of support and twenty-dollars. The rest contained similar notes and letters with the requested ten-dollars. Kate found a name and address either on the letters or cards inside the envelopes or on the return address label. There was one letter from an anonymous donor with a bank counter check for one-thousand-dollars. Kate recorded every name, address, and donation both in the notebook and on a deposit slip. There would be a complete accounting of every cent and who it came from. She made an entry in the notebook for the receipt of the one-thousand-dollars with the counter check number and added a column for the entry of a check number and notation paying a one-thousand-dollar donation to the American Legion.

Kate said to herself, "The local legion will like that one for sure. Thanks whoever you are, for supporting our Veterans." She looked at the envelope one last time for any sign of a name.

That evening, Kate showed Sam the letters, and although excited and thankful, he was forever the sceptic and said that two-thousand dollars is hardly a campaign fund.

"Tomorrow, after you drop the kids off at school and pick up the mail, I would like you to send the announcement to a few more websites and social media. If we have more campaign contributions, add them to the money in the bag and go to the bank and start a new account. Go straight to Ginny and tell her this account must be held in the strictest confidence, absolutely no one is to know about the account. Tell her that if she leaks a single word we will sue the bank."

Kate, again, went about her morning routine and Eric handed her another large mail tub at the post office. This one contained nearly twice as many letters as the one the day before. Kate, went home sorted the mail and proceeded to the bank with the deposit.

“Hi Kate,” Ginny’s boisterous greeting could be heard throughout the bank.

“Hi Ginny, can you help me? I need to open a new account.”

“Sure thing, Kate. Come into my office.”

Even though Ginny had a private office, the acoustics in the century old building carried Ginny’s voice far beyond the confines of her office.

“Ginny,” Kate lowered her voice, so it wouldn’t be overheard. “I need you to keep this account in the very strictest of confidence. There must be absolutely no mention of this account or of the reason I came into the bank today if anyone asks.”

“Okay, I can keep a secret, but what is this all about? You and Sam aren’t having problems, are you?”

“Oh, Ginny, heavens no!”

“I’m so glad. You and Sam are such a nice couple and the whole town loves you, but I see an awful lot of that sort of thing and am always asked to keep the banking business secret. So, what is the name on the new account?”

Kate had wondered why Sam had made the comment about going to Ginny and demanding secrecy at the threat of a law suit. It didn’t make sense to her until Ginny asked for the name on the account. Kate almost blurted out the name before she caught herself and lowered her voice even further.

“Ginny, the name on the account will be the Sam Waters Presidential Campaign fund.”

“Oh My God! Sam’s going to run! Kate, that’s fabulous. Why keep it a secret?”

“Ginny, you have managed our accounts here for years and you know that we don’t have a lot of loose money hanging around, especially not enough to run a political campaign. We are putting out some feelers to see how many people will, as Sam puts it, ‘walk the walk.’ If it looks like we will get the kind of contributions necessary to fund a campaign, Sam will make the decision. We don’t want a big circus going on until we have that assurance.”

“I fully understand, and my lips are sealed: but, I can’t say my excitement may not show. Have you asked for contributions yet?”

"Yes, I posted to a couple of pages on social media on Friday. We're only asking for a ten-dollar contribution per person and so far, it's looking pretty fair."

"Cool. Will this be savings, checking or checking with interest? How much should I transfer from your account for the initial deposit?"

"Checking with a debit card. Can we add debit cards to this account in the future?"

"Of course. Now how much should I transfer?"

"Oh, I'm sorry, we won't be transferring anything from our account."

"Kate, I will need a deposit of some sort to open the account."

"Yes, I know. I have deposit slips with the total campaign contributions received so far."

"Contributions already? When did you say you put out the request for campaign contributions?"

"I put the request out Friday. I had a hundred and twenty letters in yesterday's mail, mostly in-state folks but a few from Billings and Rapid City. We had another two-hundred-ten today. Oh. and two anonymous contributions for eighteen-hundred dollars. Sam doesn't want to accept any anonymous contributions; but these have no return address, so we have no way of returning them. Maybe we should open a separate account for those. We will turn those into donations to Veteran's organizations and charities. We just have to see what this week brings." Kate hands Ginny the two deposits.

"Wow, Kate: fifty-five-hundred dollars just over the weekend. That's incredible. I can't wait to see what happens."

Ginny opened the accounts and although she was obviously excited about something, she promised she wouldn't tell a soul. When one of the clerks asked what had her so giddy, she said she just got news a good friend had given birth to a new baby. Kate thought, yea, right. What do you call having three hundred million babies at the same time?

During the next three days, Kate collected contributions totaling just over one-hundred-thousand-dollars. The next week, she opened another three hundred thousand dollars in contributions. It would appear people were walking the walk.

Over the weekend, after several talks with Kate and the kids, Sam decided to make a formal announcement and toss his hat into the ring for President.

5
UNMASKED

On Monday, Sam walked into the Johnson County Courthouse to see Terry Jacobs the Buffalo City Attorney. Sam knocked on Terry's open door and his secretary looked up from her work.

"Sam, come in. Terry's with another attorney but should be done in just a moment. You know if you made an appointment you wouldn't have to wait."

"Yes, I know, Cheryl, but some things just happen without a real plan."

Sam's rear had just met the cushions of the oversized couch when Terry came out with Tom Meadows, the other attorney.

"Sam, what a pleasant surprise! Or is it? Do I still owe you money on the new house you built for me?"

"No, Terry, nothing like that. Hi Tom." Sam acknowledged his intrusion into the discussion.

"Hello Sam, how's the next President? Tom chided with a Cheshire grin.

"Let's not go there, Tom, but I'm fine."

"Tom, I'll see you in court next Monday." Terry concluded his business with Tom and turned to Sam

"So, what's up?" Terry asked.

"Terry, there's something I need to ask you. Do you have a minute?"

"Sure, Sam." Terry replied and ushered Sam into his office.

"What's up, big guy?"

"Terry, you know all of the hype about me running for President, right? I mean you should. You just witnessed part of it from Tom."

"Yes, what about it? You said you weren't running so I haven't pestered you about it."

"Well, I've reconsidered my position. There are a lot of people out there who really care about this country and are apparently backing me for the job or at least the run. Whether I win or not is going to be a different story; but right now, I'm going to listen to the people and not let them down."

"It's about time. I said I wouldn't pester you, but that didn't mean I wouldn't support you in the race for the White House. I personally can't think of anyone I'd rather see in that position."

"I'm glad you feel that way. Terry, we've been friends for a long time and there isn't anyone in the world I trust more than you. I want you to be my running mate. I want you for my Vice President."

"Damn, Sam, I'm honored, but don't you think it would be better to pick someone who is better known politically? Someone who could help you carry at least some of the electoral vote?"

"That's just it Terry. I'm getting a lot of support because no one knows me, but they all think they know what I stand for. You were elected to be the City Attorney as an Independent, because people were tired of the status quo, good ole boys in our city government."

"No, Sam, I was elected, because Willie Franks was a hundred years old and unable to do the job prosecuting criminals and I was the only attorney who wanted to run against him."

"Look, you're my best friend and have been practically since birth. You're the only person, besides Kate, that I would want by my side in this."

"I'm sorry Sam, I just can't. I can't afford to take the chance of losing my job because I wanted to go off and play caped crusader with you and trust me I do want to go. I have to think about Mary and the kids. I hope you can understand. I guess I'm caught up in my comfort zone and can't make the kind of change you're asking me for. You know I will support you any way I can, just not as your running mate."

"That's okay, Terry. I'm fortunate enough to be able to fall off a roof or construction project anywhere if this goes south. I do need a favor."

"What can I do for you?

"I need the Courthouse on Friday. I want to hold a press conference downstairs to announce my candidacy."

"By all means. I want a front row seat to hear you make the announcement. My best friend, the President of the United States."

"Not yet Terry, and if you can, please, keep this under your hat until Friday. You can have that front row seat only if you agree to introduce me."

"No problem big guy, I'll give you an intro, and your secret is safe with me until then."

"Thanks, Terry"

Sam leaves Terry's office in a funk. Although, he hadn't talked to Terry at all about his thoughts, he had relied on their friendship. He was rather counting on Terry's acceptance of the offer to be his running mate.

"Hell, Sam, what did you expect?" He asked himself. "You, yourself didn't make the decision until this last weekend. Then you spring all of this on your best friend. Would have been nice if he had accepted, but I can understand where he's coming from." Sam kicked himself all the way home for not talking to Terry about the possibility of running before now.

When Sam pulled into his driveway, there wasn't the usual small crowd of people who normally met him. For the first time in the last two months there was no one at his house.

"Maybe they aren't here in the mornings after I leave for work." Sam thinks as he turned off the truck and started inside.

Kate met him at the door.

"Did you get the courthouse and get the conference set up?"

"Yes, Dear."

"Did you talk to Terry?"

"Yes, Dear."

"Well, what did he say?"

"No, Dear. Now can I please come into my house? It's cold out here."

"What? Terry said no?" Kate opened the door and stepped aside so Sam could come in

"Yep, turned me down flat. Can't afford to leave his job and how did he put it? Oh yeah, to go off and play caped crusader with me."

"What a crappy comment! It's not like you're going outside to play as bat man and robin. This is the Presidency for crying out loud."

"He knows that Kate, but it's a cause. One of many I've fought for in my life and you know Terry has usually been right there with me. Terry knows where I stand on big government and he feels that I'm heading into a fight I cannot win. He knows that if he joins me and we don't win or are forced to drop out, he won't have the City Attorney job to come back to and he's not ready to come bang nails with me. Terry also knows the things I want to see changed in our Government and knows the people behind those things won't go down without a battle."

"Still a crappy comment."

"Yes, but right now I need to call some news folks, or I'll be standing in the courthouse on Friday talking to the walls."

Sam went into his office and closed the door. He thought again about Terry's Caped crusader remark. He picked up the phone and called the Buffalo Bulletin, Jerry Cummings at Channel 5 and the few numbers from other news media sources available in Northern Wyoming.

6

MEET THE PRESS

Sam was having second thoughts about declaring his intention to run. The question of who would vote for a nobody from Wyoming, kept running through his mind. He thought about the caped crusades and the pointless waste of time and money this campaign would be.

The lobby and foyer of the courthouse were far too small to accommodate the multitude of people who came to listen to Sam's announcement. Although, everyone who knew about Sam's plans had remained silent, the news had traveled like a wind-driven grass fire through the small community anyway. Again, second thoughts plagued Sam as he looked out of the court house windows at the throng gathered in the snow. "Too late now," he said to himself. "Let's go meet the press." He gave Terry a nod and it all began.

"Ladies and Gentlemen, Ladies and Gentlemen, if you will please quiet down. Most of you know me, but for those who don't, my name is Terry Jacobs and I would like to introduce a great friend, a patriot, neighbor, the man behind the letter and the next President of the United States: Sam Waters.

The applause and cheers were deafening in the large, but confined, space of the Courthouse lobby where some of the town's more elite and governmental officials and workers had gathered. Nearly a hundred or so reporters and most of the residents of Buffalo were gathered in front of the courthouse around a temporary platform and podium. The crowd was so large it spilled off the Courthouse front lawn and onto the snow shrouded grounds around the building and across the street.

Even the weather supported Sam. A warm Chinook wind elevated the temperature into the mid forty degrees, very unseasonable temperatures for Northern Wyoming in January.

Terry had thought of everything: the warm change in temperature allowed him to open the first story windows of the Courthouse and place speakers and monitors so everyone could hear, and some could see the event.

"Thank you, Terry.

"Friends, neighbors, fellow Wyomingites and members of the press. Almost a year ago, I made what I have considered to be a very big mistake and wrote a letter to the editor of the Buffalo Bulletin.

"Today I find that my letter has been the catalyst for change in our representation by our governments. Not just the Government of our township in Buffalo, or Johnson County or the State of Wyoming -- but globally.

"Throughout my life, I have had no interest in joining a political party and even less interest in pursuing any form of public or political office. Yet here I am today, three years ahead of the 2024 election, declaring my candidacy as an Independent for the Presidency of the United States."

Several minutes of cheers, claps and whistles followed until Sam raised his arms to quiet the crowd.

"You the People, have voiced -- no shouted your desire to have a renewed voice in what our Government does and how it represents you. You have shouted your desire for change and you have even more loudly expressed your desire to have me as your candidate. ***I AM ANSWERING YOUR CALL!"***

The crowd again flared with boisterous applause and cheers their approval in a deafening chorus of "We want Sam." As the crowd quieted, members of the press corps started trying to upstage their competitors to ask their questions.

"Mr. Waters, Mr. Waters." Sam looked down and saw Jerry Cummings.

"Jerry, I'll take your question"

"Thank you, Mr. Waters. Jerry Cummings, NBC, Channel 5 News. You stated in my interview a few months ago, and again today, that you had no interest in ever running for public office. What changed your mind?"

"My wife, Katherine, was probably the greatest influence. After the interview, she watched the activity on the internet and social media and would put print outs on my desk every day showing the responses to my letter. That, along with the support shown by the community of Buffalo, started the wheels rolling."

"Mr. Waters, another question. Although it isn't rare for a candidate to show interest in a campaign for President shortly after an election, most wait and don't announce their candidacy until about nineteen months before the election. Why have you chosen to announce your candidacy at double that time frame?"

"Jerry, one of the last things you said to me the day of our interview was that I should give the two-party establishment a run for their money. I don't feel I can give them a real show if I don't take the stage early and seriously. It will take most of the next three years to be a contender in this race."

"Mr. Waters, Mr. Waters" again the press maneuvered for position. Sam called the reporter from the Bulletin.

"Thank you. Ted Woodbyne, Buffalo Bulletin. Sam, isn't it true that you posted your intent to run on the internet and social media several weeks ago? Why did it take so long to have this conference?"

"Yes, Ted, I did post an initial intent letter to social media and various internet sites three weeks ago. It was a test. In the past, I have seen where people in general will verbally support a cause, or action, or candidate. However, when it comes to physically or actively supporting that cause, or action, or candidate -- when it's time to open their checkbook -- that support fails in deed. People will talk the talk but will not walk the walk so to speak. I wanted to be sure I had the support in both word and deed before making my final decision. The support was overwhelming. It was the support I received over the last three weeks that helped me make the decision to run and finalized my commitment to those supporters."

"Mr. Waters. Another question please! What happened over the last three weeks that, as you say, helped you make your decision?" Ted asked.

"When I made the Internet posts, I asked for a simple ten-dollar contribution to my campaign and was very adamant and honest when I said I would not accept any anonymous contributions.

"In the last three weeks, I have received over three-million dollars in contributions all securely held in an account here in the Wyoming Bank and Trust. That was how the support made my decision."

"Mr. Waters. Mr. Waters."

"You in the red hat."

"Thank you. Steven Booker, MSNBC. How are these contributions being made and how are you tracking them ten dollars at a time?"

"Steven, the donations are mailed to my Post Office Box and collected every day. Because, I've only asked for ten-dollar contributions, we receive an assortment of conveyances. Some are cash, some are checks. Every donation, regardless of conveyance, has been recorded with the name, address, and amount of the contribution. The contributions are deposited into the campaign fund account the same day they are received."

"Another question, sir. You said you don't accept anonymous contributions, but I'm sure you do receive them. What do you do when you have no address to return the contribution?"

"To date, we have had sixteen-thousand dollars contributed by anonymous persons. Those contributions are also recorded and if the bank records are checked you will find a separate account specifically set up for those contributions. You will also find charitable donations in the amount of sixteen-thousand dollars to the VFW, American Legion, DAV, Vietnam Vets, and some other smaller Veteran's organizations like 22 Kill and Wounded Warrior Project. We will continue to treat anonymous contributions in this manner, converting them to donations to Veteran organizations and other charities.

"I will not be accused of accepting donations and contributions to pad my pockets from Political Action Committees known as PACs or Super PACs. Nor will I be accused of taking contributions from organizations which Congress has banned from contributing. Banks, Corporations, and Unions were banned from making political contributions. These bans have never been lifted. Since PACs are not required to declare who has contributed to them it leaves a large hole in the system where banks, corporations and unions can violate the laws for campaign contributions and I will not be an accomplice."

"Mr. Waters, Mr. Waters."

"In the yellow coat."

"Thank you. Pam Bales, KOA7 News, Denver Colorado. Mr. Waters, what are the issues you will be addressing in your platform?"

“Pam, and the rest of you, this will be my answer and my only comment on this question at this time. We are three years from the election, two years from the primaries. There are a lot of issues now that can be addressed; however, there could be many more pressing and important issues in the coming months and years. I am not going to start a fight at this point in my campaign only to spend a lot of money and effort trying to defend a stand on an issue of non-importance in the election year.”

“One more question. Mr. Waters, it has come to our attention at KOA that you have not stated which party ticket you will run on, yet we’ve been told you have been approached by both the Republican and Democrat National Committees as well as several of the independent parties.”

“Ms. Bales, if there was a question in there, I’m assuming you are asking which party banner I’m running under. I have been approached by both the Republican and Democrat National Committees as well as the Green, Tea, Libertarian, and Socialist parties. My answer is very simple, and I made it quite clear in my opening comments. I am not a member of any party and I’m not running under any party banner. I’m an independent. That doesn’t mean Green, or Tea or any other of the several so called independent parties. I am truly the Independent candidate -- running for the people, on their support.”

Sam fields a few more questions before Terry Jacobs steps back up to the microphone.

“Last Question, Ladies and Gentlemen. Jerry Cummings, you started this conference and did the first interview, would you like to have the last question today.”

“Thanks, Terry. Sam, other than 1992, we haven't had an independent Presidential hopeful in the last century. What makes you think you have a chance of being the first?”

“Jerry, that is a very good question. Most of the Independent candidates of the past century have had limited support. They couldn’t muster the percentage numbers to satisfy the rules regarding an invitation to the presidential debates. If they did manage to get the numbers, as in 1992, there were character flaws which were brought out by the other candidates as well as the media. Their weaknesses were exploited and some of the candidates were even threatened if they didn’t drop out of the races. In 1992, I’d have to say the leading independent candidate shot himself in the foot and then tried to do a hat dance around the major mistake he had made.

"I'm not going to stand here and guarantee a win. I will tell you this and this is who Sam Waters is: I have smoked pot and I have inhaled. I have had an extra-marital affair years ago and was divorced as a result. I have had collections placed on my credit accounts and been the subject of collections, legal judgments and filed bankruptcy. I once had a drinking problem and was considered an alcoholic. I haven't had a drink in twenty years and have no intention of drinking again no matter the situation. I had a year of tragedy in 2009 and if anything would have knocked me off the wagon and back to the bottle that would have, but it didn't."

"I'm not perfect, I'm human, I've made mistakes in the past and I'm sure I will make more in the future. My past is my past, there are parts of it I am not proud of, but there is nothing I can do to change it. Nor would I want to change them if I could. These things have made me who I am and I'm proud of who I have become. A good parent, a friend to those in need, a good neighbor, and an honest and fair contractor and now, a candidate for president.

"There are very few things I am afraid of and even less that intimidate me. I'm a fighter, a survivor, a patriot and an American. I took an oath when I joined the Marines and that oath had no expiration date. I swore to support and defend this great nation and our Constitution against all enemies and I promise that I will fight for this country and the people as hard as I've fought for life to honor my oath.

"I've been known to give my all for various causes in which I have strong beliefs and feelings. Recently a good friend told me he would love to join me in this campaign, but he couldn't risk his position and the welfare of his job and family to go off playing the caped crusader with me. That may be exactly what I'm doing in trying to do what's right. I will do what's right for the people and this country, but it's what I must do.

"Thank you for your support!"

***

The next morning, headlines across the country displayed the spotlight with the bat image used to summon bat man and the caption "Caped crusader running for President!"

7
RUNNING MATES

It had been a week since the press conference and Sam had a dilemma: he needed a running mate. He wanted to have someone with similar values and convictions as himself and he needed the person to be independent of any party. He had posted an open request for applications with a complex series of questions. He had also compiled a list of possible running mates from the people he knew around Buffalo. Sam made a detailed list of all the possible candidates with notes about their qualifications.

"Kate, I need some help. Since Terry won't run with me, I'm at a loss for a vice presidential running mate. I don't want to join a party just to have the committee fill the spot. I've made a list of applicants from the internet and people I know here, but I need your view on things."

"Okay." Kate took the list and looked it over for a few minutes. "This may take some time. Did these internet people complete your questionnaire?"

"Yes. All of the ones on the list answered the questions and seem to feel like we do about this country."

"I see your notes on each, but can you show me their answers, so I can have the same point of view you do?"

"Okay, I'll go get them."

"Wait a minute Sam! Who is Michael Baker?"

"Michael is a retired Marine Corps JAG Officer. He lives in Kaycee. You met him a couple of times when I was working at Yeager's last year. Trim, high and tight haircut, square jaw, looks like he eats nails for breakfast."

"Right! That sounds like the Jarhead I married. I think I remember him and probably would if I saw him. I wouldn't count on several people on this list. I see they are all independents, but I know a few of them and there are a couple who tend to swing way left and a couple of the others sway way too far right. You'll probably find the same with the internet people. You need to keep as independently clean and middle of the road as you can. When in doubt, call a Marine. Call Baker."

"Thanks Baby, you're the best."

"And you better never forget it."

Sam made the phone call to Michael Baker.

"Michael, this is Sam Waters, I don't know if you remember me."

"Sam, there isn't anyone in this state, or for that matter, the country who doesn't know the man behind the letter. What can I do for you – legal advice?"

"No, Michael, something a lot more sinister, more like representation."

"Okay, first off, call me Mike. Michael makes me start looking for my dad. What kind of bind are you in?"

"Well, Mike, I'm in desperate need of a running mate and wondered if you would be interested in running as my Vice-President?"

"Wow, Sam. What an honor, but don't you think someone with more political moxey would do more for your campaign?"

"Mike, you are the second person I have asked and the second person who has asked me that question. So, I'll just assume you are also going to decline my request. Thank you for your time tonight."

"Sam, wait a minute. Don't be so hasty. You know what happens when you assume?"

"Yeah, yeah, you make an ass of u and me. Your point here?"

"My point is, I'm not saying no, just asking if your campaign wouldn't do better with someone more politically centered."

"I've thought about who I'd want to run with if I decided to run for the past three-months. I've thrown around a million scenarios, from joining a party to maybe just starting with a small campaign for city council or county commissioner. The road always comes back to my views on politics. I've always been an Independent and always will be, so I won't join a party. I decided that forgetting the parties and politicos was my best option. As my wife, Kate, puts it. I need to stay as independently clean as possible. As for running for a city or county position, I could run for a lesser office, but that doesn't help the people who have contributed to a presidential campaign."

"In that case, Sam, I would love to be your running mate. Of course, I will have to talk this over with my wife, but this is the opportunity of a lifetime. I saw the press conference announcing your decision to run last Friday and the Saturday headlines. You wowed the crowd and reporters. Have you decided on a platform yet?"

"Like I said Friday, it's too early to be thinking about platforms and issues. Where I've seen the other independent candidates fail is when they wait for the major campaign, that last five-hundred days to get started. That last year and a half before the election doesn't give them any time to gain the support they need. I want to get started now. We need to get a jump on the parties if we want to win."

"Agreed! I'll talk to Nancy tonight and I'll let you know what she says in the morning. When were you wanting to get together?"

"Are you able to come up to Buffalo anytime this week?

"I'm pretty free. I can be there tomorrow and give you Nancy's answer in person. I really don't think she'll say no."

"Tomorrow will be good. Hope you don't mind doing some real estate shopping."

"Not at all, Sam. What are we shopping for? Farm, ranch, bigger house, development property, what?"

"Campaign office space. I think we need a campaign headquarters where we can work without intruding on either of our households."

"Sounds good. Where and what time tomorrow?"

"How about nine, we'll start at my house? Feel free to bring Nancy. If we are going to be working together it will be nice to know everyone."

"Great. What's your address?"

"468 North Main, you can't miss it. It's the only log house on Main Street and there's a big red S on the chimney."

"Cool. When do you want to have a press conference to announce me as your running mate?"

"The press knows I'm running and they are going to be watching my every move to see what I do next. So, let's not disappoint them. I'm going to keep you a secret for as long as I can, hopefully until we start our campaign. I want to try to keep the dog and pony show to a minimum for a while, so we can work things out. Let's get together and work the computers to contact our supporters on the internet. Together with those supporters we may be able to get a commitment for many states' ballots."

"Okay boss. See you at nine in the morning."

Sam hangs up the phone and breathes a sigh of relief. He knew Mike was professional, well-educated, and passionate about the country. Sam would have preferred Terry, but felt Mike was probably a better choice.

8
SETTING THE STAGE

The next day, Mike knocked on Sam's door precisely at nine.

Mike was six feet tall with dark hair that he kept short cropped in the Marine Corps high and tight haircut. He was an infantry Sergeant who had applied for and been accepted into the Marine Corps Enlisted Commissioning and Education program or MECEP for short. The Marines had paid for his Law degree and brought him back on duty as an officer and lawyer for the Judge Advocate General (JAG). Sam was an MP assigned as a court bailiff when they first met. Mike was originally from Illinois, but called the Marines home for twenty years. Mike's dad had moved to Kaycee, Wyoming and bought a nice piece of land along the Powder River and had willed it to Mike. Mike loved the area and had settled there with his wife Nancy and son Billy when he retired.

"Morning Mike, come on in. This is my wife, Kate. Kate, Mike Baker."

"Good morning Ma'am. I believe we've already met. You came with Sam one time when he was working on my neighbor's house in Kaycee."

"Yes, I think you're right. I vaguely remember meeting you at Yeager's. Would you like a cup of coffee?"

"Yes, Ma'am, thank you. My wife should be here shortly, she had to drop our son off at school."

"That will be fabulous. What is your wife's name?"

"Nancy."

"Thanks. Now, you two go into the office and try to figure out what you are going to do." Then Kate said jokingly; "When Nancy gets here we will come in and correct your ideas."

Sam led Mike to the office, offered him a chair and took a seat at the small corner desk.

"Okay, Devil Dog, I'm all for having an independent team in the White House, so let's get started. First, we need to get you a bigger desk, so you get used to the massive Lincoln Desk in the Oval Office," Mike laughed.

Nancy had arrived just after Mike sat down and the two wives entered the office. Mike accepted the cup of coffee from Kate and introduced his wife.

Nancy and Kate could have been sisters. They were both about five foot five inches tall and slender builds. The only major difference was Kate was a redhead and Nancy was a blonde.

"Nancy, it is a pleasure to meet you. What has Mike told you about this meeting today?"

"Mike didn't say anything about a meeting, Sam. He said we were going to help you shop for some real estate. He did ask me what I would think about moving to Washington D.C. for four years or so, but I don't know why he would ask that. I've been with him long enough to know that nothing would drag him away from our Powder River ranch."

"Mike, I thought you were going to talk to your wife before you got here." Sam was somewhat perplexed since Mike obviously hadn't talked to his wife about being his running mate.

"Nancy's just messing with you, Sam. We talked last night after you called and again this morning at breakfast, didn't we, Nan?"

"Yes, we did, but it was Kate who thought you might need a shock to your system this morning and a little levity. She said you've been an absolute crab to be around since you made the announcement."

"Thanks for the kick in the pants, baby, I guess this whole thing has me a little bit wrapped around the axle."

"It's okay, you can get all involved with the campaign, but try to remember the kids and I are on your side and by your side. Now you two have work to do. I'll call Sarah Marshall to see if she can fit you in today."

"Thanks, Kate." Kate made a quick phone call to Sarah and then she and Nancy sat in the kitchen getting to know each other.

"Who's Sarah Marshall?" Mike asked Sam as the girls departed.

"Sarah has a small realty company here in town, so I'm sure she'd be willing to help us find some office space."

"Okay, so after we talk to Sarah, what's next on your agenda?"

"Hell, Mike, I just made the decision to run a week ago. This whole thing is spinning like a tornado on the plains with nothing to stop it. I really haven't had time to plan anything yet. It's like learning to swim, just jump into the deep end and try not to drown."

"That's what I love about Wyoming - all the analogies." Baker laughed.

Kate poked her head in to announce that Sarah would be able to meet with them at one o'clock.

"Mike, I think we need to put our heads together and figure out what kind of headquarters we want and how it will be manned? Me, you, and our wives will be there for now, but we should have a plan for a full-time staff when we take to the road to campaign. We also need to think about how large the space should be, not just now but over the long haul. There are forty-six-hundred people in Buffalo and more in the county who, I'm sure, will want to work to get a local boy elected President. This summer, you and I will be traveling talking to our supporters face-to-face. Kate and Nancy can run the office for a while, but we should get someone full-time to work with the girls and learn the ropes. That person should probably be hired full time and can run the office when the girls join us on the road. We will need multiple phone lines and computers. Thinking ahead, the space should be large enough to handle any growth and any number of volunteers. I don't think we need anything the size of the old Seney's department store, but we should have something moderately sized, so we don't have to keep upscaling to accommodate growth in the staff."

"I agree with everything you laid out. Do you have anyone in mind for the staff position?

"I think Mary Jacobs might be a good choice. She's smart and personable. She used to be an accountant before she and Terry started having kids. She gave up the job to be a full-time mom."

"Do you think she'll give up the mom bit to run our office?"

"We won't know until we ask her."

"Do you have any particular office space in mind?"

"I've been looking at properties as I've driven around town, but I think Sarah will have a better idea of what's available that won't break the bank."

"Cool. Sam, I know you said in the press conference 'it's too early to think about a platform and the issues' and I agree with you, but, I do think we need some sort of theme. Obama had 'Hope and Change,' Trump had 'Make America Great Again' I really think we should have a theme or slogan that sets us apart from the crowd. Something that shows we are ready for the fight with the parties."

"Yeah, I know, but I don't want to give the parties any advance notice of our plans. There's one thing, one set of rules I have lived and survived by all my life. I learned a long time ago, if you want a fight, tell people you want a fight."

"I'm afraid I missed your point."

"Mike, It's like this. If I tell you I'm going to kick your ass, I guarantee I will have a fight on my hands. You will do your best to keep me from kicking your ass and at the same time be trying very hard to kick mine. If I just keep quiet and kick your ass, fights over, done, all in. You may put up a fight and defend yourself, but your options are reactive, not proactive. Anything you do in the fight is a reaction to the first attack. Proactive almost always kicks ass over reactive and we are in this thing to kick some ass, are we not?"

"I like it! Sam that's the best election platform line I have ever heard come out of a politician."

"Please Mike, don't lump me into that group of do-nothing politicians. Just call me bat man."

"Why bat man? What's that supposed to mean?"

"Just something a friend told me the other day about causes and caped crusades."

***

Sarah met with Sam and Mike at one and helped them find the perfect office space right in the middle of downtown Buffalo and they signed a one-year lease. The next day they arranged for the utilities and phone services, then drove to Billings to buy a couple of computers. They set up the office and began the job of finding the supporters from each state among the social media and various websites and pages. Sam asked if anyone would like to be a Chairperson in their state for the Waters Campaign. The response was instant. Sam then informed the responders they would have to be volunteers for the first year, the campaign could not afford to pay wages. The number of people never faltered. Sam then told the people the Chairpersons would have to work toward getting Sam and Mike on the ballots of their respective states and they would have to fill out a questionnaire and application. Again, the numbers never changed. Sam sent the applications and within a few days he and Mike were screening hundreds of applicants to find just the people they needed.

***

Sam was right about the press and within a couple of days, the press was asking who this person was who seemed to be on Sam's right hand. Pictures with captions "Could this be robin?" Other pictures and posts appeared online asking if this man was the Independent Vice-Presidential candidate.

In March 2021, three months before they took to the road, the two men held a press conference and announced Mike as Sam's choice for running mate. Again, the conference was held at the Johnson County Courthouse and again Terry was asked to introduce Sam, which he did with pleasure.

"Ladies and Gentlemen, it is my pleasure and honor to introduce to you; the next President of the United States, Mr. Sam Waters." The crowd on the courthouse lawn cheered wildly.

"Thank you, Terry. Thank you very much, thank you," Sam said as he took the podium with his hands raised trying to quiet the crowd. "Thank You." As the noise subsided. "Ladies and Gentlemen, my good friend and the next Vice-President of the United States; Mr. Michael Baker." Mike stepped up and the two candidates took a hand and raised their arms. Again, the crowd cheered and whistled their approval. Kate, Nancy, and children took up places behind the candidates.

"Mr. Waters."

"Yes, in the blue shirt and tie."

"James Cavettis, CBS news. Have you decided yet what your Platform will be and what issues you will be looking to fix?"

"Mr. Cavettis, we are still a little more than a year from the primaries and it is still too soon to be focusing on issues which could change at any time under the current administration. I promise that you will have our answer when we launch our campaign. Right now, we are testing the waters." The crowd laughed at Sam's remark.

"Ted, glad you're here."

"Thanks Sam, Ted Woodbyne, Buffalo Bulletin, I think Jerry Cummings asked at your last conference if you felt you could win as an independent and you said yes. Do you still feel you can win the Presidency?"

"Ted, if there was any doubt about my being able to win, I wouldn't be here. Last year I felt I could win. This year with Mike as my running mate I feel even more assured. We can win, and we can make a difference." The crowd cheered at the remark. Sam saw and called on Pam Bales.

"Ms. Bales, nice to see you again."

"Thank you, Mr. Waters, Pam Bales, KOA7 News. I have a question for Mr. Baker. Do you have anything on your agenda as Vice President you would like to see on the presidential platform? And how do you feel about Sam's silence on the platform issue?

"Ms. Bales, Sam and I have talked at length about the platform we might follow to the election. We have discussed abortion, gay marriage, the war in the Middle East, Afghanistan, and the radical extremist issues. We have talked about the budget and government spending and a great many other issues currently plaguing our Nation. Throughout our talks, our main platform has remained the same. Our platform is the American people and what is best for them. Not just this group or that group but all Americans, period. I wholeheartedly support Sam Waters in his previous answers to the questions of platform. It is still far too early to address specific platform issues."

"Pam, if I may add to Mike's comment. We are America Focused so whatever our platform becomes between now and next March, you can rest assured it will be what we have researched and polled and found to be what the American want. We are for the people and what they feel is important, and not what some party committee in Washington, D.C. decided was important without talking to the people. Thank you all for coming out today. I'm sure we will see much more of each other in the months ahead." As Sam finished his comment Kate and Nancy joined their husbands at the front of the small stage. Sam turned and with Mike and their families left the podium and retired to Terry's office to avoid further questions and crowds.

"They are persistent about the issues and platforms, aren't they?"

"Yes, Mike, they are. The problem is the politicians. Since about nineteen-sixty-eight when Vietnam was a hornet's nest and people were angry over our involvement, the politicians have made a point to have an agenda -- a platform to entice people to vote for them. In the late sixties and early seventies, kids were protesting in the schools and being killed during the protests. The Vietnam horror was brought home every night in the news. Platforms became who can promise the most to end the war, change the voting age and stop the draft and these subjects became political ammunition. He who offered the best solution had the win and it hasn't changed in the last fifty years. Yes, there were other election platforms like Teddy Roosevelt's Big Stick or FDR's New Deal, but those pale in comparison to the platforms politicians break out with now."

9
A NEW BEGINNING

Sam always closed down his company in the winter because it was hard to work construction in the sub-freezing cold of Wyoming. Sometimes he would pick up some interior remodeling work, but those projects were few and far between. Most folks don't like to have their homes disrupted in the winter when they can't get away from the dust and construction clutter. He was always concerned about money in the winter and was thankful for a few extra days of Indian Summer. Those extra days allowed him to get one or two more jobs done before the seasonal closure.

Sam had set the business up to pay him a salary instead of taking money from the company's profits and he and Kate always husbanded enough money from that salary to keep the family going through the winter. Sam often worried that his crew hadn't planned for the lean winter months and might not be ready when he closed. He also worried about what his crew would do if he folded the business and took off to campaign? What would happen to them? Sam knew this Presidential campaign would be difficult at best and a different kind of task for him. He wondered how he was going to work his business and be on the campaign trail at the same time next summer? Swimming in the deep end again, and trying not to drown, he thought to himself. Sam decided to sell his company to his crew for a percentage of the profit over the next five years. Shane was a great foreman and an excellent estimator and should be able to keep the company and crew in business.

Sam wondered if he had enough savings to support him through the campaign. He knew Mike was retired from the Military and was drawing a nice pension, but Sam wondered if Mike would have the available funds to take care of his family and himself while he's out on the road campaigning. Sam really didn't want to use campaign funds to support his family. Those funds are dedicated to the campaign. He realized, however, that some of the funds would be used to pay his bills while he's out campaigning and developed a strategy for the funds. Since this campaign was now their business, Sam set up a salary for him and Mike. He set a slightly smaller salary for Kate and Nancy who would be running the campaign office. The rest of the funds would be used to provide campaign offices in the states where he has support and for hotels and meals for him and Mike while they were on the campaign trail. He talked to Ginny at the bank and set up a separate account for each family.

By June 2022, Sam and Mike had been working the computers and getting petitions together to get on the ballots in as many states as they could before the primaries begin. They had screened many of their supporters from each state to run their campaign offices and had selected over a hundred people as full-time support staff. Any other staffing would have to be volunteers.

Now it was time to develop their plan for the campaign. Sam felt that advertising was going to be a waste of money. Coast-to-coast prime-time advertising was going to be extremely expensive and Sam had a better idea. So far, the team had made a lot of progress with just their coverage in the news and on social media. Sam wanted to be in the news at least once every week prior to the primaries and three to four times a week once the real campaigning started. He and Mike agreed it was a good start, but they might want to change tactics and buy advertising later. Mike suggested they would need to have at least one city in each state with a campaign office and they added funding those offices to their plan.

Sam felt he and Mike needed to be on the ballots of all fifty states and the District of Columbia to be a viable threat to the party candidates. They had just forty weeks to get on as many ballots as they could, before the party campaigning and primaries began. If they wanted an invitation to the Presidential debates they would need to be on the ballot in at least twenty-six states and hold eighteen percent of the vote. Kate and Nancy stood looking at a large U. S. map in Sam's Campaign Headquarters Office and started the countdown.

"Kate, how are we going to keep track of where we have campaign offices and where the guys are on the ballot?"

"Sam, already thought about that and has purchased a bunch of push-pins. He made this key in the corner: we put the big clear pins on the capitals of the states where we are on the ballot. The small pins go on the cities or towns where there is a campaign office.

"We won't need to worry about states where our families live. Sam's brothers in California and Washington D.C. have already set up campaign offices." Kate puts a small pin in L.A. and D.C.

"Mike's family in Illinois is ready to set up a campaign office there. Forty-Eight states." Nancy says as she puts a pin in Peoria, Illinois.

"Wyoming is covered. Forty-seven. This is kind of fun, Nancy. For the boys' sake, I wish it were actually going to be this easy."

"That's a fact!"

The general requirement, in most states, to be nominated for a position on the ballot is one-thousand signatures on a petition. It is still up to the state election committee to accept the nomination and have a committee vote for the individual to be put on the ballot. The Republicans and Democrats are not held to these requirements. The Independent Parties and individuals have been fighting this bias for decades. The rules for acceptance for a nomination could also change, depending on who was running the committee and how they felt toward independent candidates. These things could make a big difference in how many states accept Sam and Mike for the ballot.

How many people do Sam and Mike need to talk to in order to get a thousand signatures? Sam and Mike both knew the national sales statistics -- one-hundred attempts to contact people equals ten people actually talked to and those ten people produce one sale. Those statistics won't work for Sam's campaign – they would need to have a much higher closing ratio. How much time would be needed to talk a thousand people into signing a petition to put an unknown person on the ballot for president?

"Mike, the numbers I come up with point to a need for us to be on the ballot in all the big seven states. Three of the seven historically vote Democrat, two vote Republican and two are swing states. So, let's start with those seven to build a baseline. I know it's too early to submit our petitions in some states, but we need to have them ready to rock when the primaries begin. My brother Jim was going to get the petition going in California and my other brother Mike was starting the petition in D.C. and New York and your family is going to do the petition in Illinois?"

"Yes. My brother Doug has the petition ready for Illinois and has been working on Iowa and Wisconsin. We already have the petition numbers for Wyoming, and about three-quarters of the signatures in Montana, Colorado and the Dakotas."

"Okay, let's look at the supporters in Texas and see if we can meet with them next week to start the petition."

"With only forty weeks we might want to split up to cover more ground. I could meet the group in New York, Pennsylvania, Ohio, and Indiana, while you do Texas, Arizona, Oklahoma, and New Mexico. That takes eight states off the list, but only takes four weeks off our time frame."

"That sounds good, Mike. Four weeks out up front then a week back here to regroup then three weeks each month covering the rest of the map."

"Sam, I think it's time to consider our campaign platform and what our stand on the issues will be."

"I know, Mike, but if we take on the issues we open ourselves up for a fight. I respect the media, but don't care much for their politics, so I think we should try to stay as aloof as possible. Answer direct questions with direct answers, but don't give away the farm. Our 'too early' stand has worked to keep the hounds at bay so far. Let's keep that approach until we need to change or add anything."

"Okay, by me. You're the boss and what you've been doing has been working. My dad always told me '*son, don't try to fix it, if it isn't broken.*"

"Thanks Mike. If I see a need to make a change hopefully you will know in advance. I don't intend to change the plan, but I'm on foreign soil and don't know what tomorrow will bring."

"I fully understand."

Sam and Mike have followed their plan and every week they have been somewhere in the media. They have done guest appearances on TV and radio. They have been featured in several Newspapers. Sam has tried to schedule appearances so either he or Mike had exposure in the media each week and it was working.

10
THE CAMPAIGN

June 2023. For the past year, Sam and Mike had put their plan into action. They had appointed a campaign committee chairperson in each state and have stayed in close contact. They had talked to these chair people on a weekly basis and have received reports on the progress of their petitions and their standings in the local polls. They had started circulating petitions in all fifty states. Their supporters had been willing to volunteer their time to get the signatures and other requirements for the candidates to be added to the ballots for the 2024 election. When time permitted in states where they could do so, Sam and Mike had personally spoken with state election committees and presented them with petitions.

Sam had formulated a plan to be in the headlines of the news every day, either the local news where they were, or in the National media -- they were going to make the news daily. Sam and Mike had seen the effectiveness of Sam's plan with the media and how much coverage they had been getting without paying for expensive advertising. They had also invited the media to attend every donation to charity.

Although, the invitations kept them in the media spotlights, both men were very caring and aware of the issues facing America and believed the visits were more than just a campaign stunt. Kate had nested away three-hundred-thousand dollars in anonymous funds and they were receiving more anonymous contributions daily. It was prearranged that Sam and Mike would draw on these funds for the benefit of the various charities they visited. The plan worked well and it was far less expensive to make news by giving their anonymous funds to charitable organizations than to buy advertising. They decided to continue their plan of staying in the news to save money on advertising until they need it. Randolph Hearst once said, "There is no greater weapon than the news" and Sam and Mike were taking full advantage of that weapon.

Sam sold his company to Shane Nelson, his foreman, on contract terms that would keep them both in fair financial status for the run of the campaign.

Kate and Nancy polled the social media sites and Internet supporters for issues that were important to the people and have given the results to Sam and Mike. It seemed that every month and every diverse demographic would change the priorities of the people. There were some items that would hold a high position in every poll. It would be those items that built the campaign platform.

Sam and Mike had been preparing for the launch of their main campaign for nearly two years. The election was nineteen months away and they had a major jump ahead of the parties since the party candidates would first have to campaign for and win their party's nomination -- then campaign for the election. Because they were not subject to the caucuses and primaries, Sam and Mike could focus directly on the election giving them a one-year head start over whoever would run against them.

Sam and Mike were technically ahead of the parties in another arena. They had been out to the states and had set up many of their campaign offices. Although the National Party offices were always open they wouldn't know who they were working for until six-months prior to the election. Sam's supporters and volunteers weren't working for the Party, they were working for the candidates. They were working for Sam and Mike.

Sam and Mike had met with supporters, and influential and prominent people who could help with the campaign. They had shaken hands and kissed babies all over the country, but most importantly -- they had been in the news. Sam and Mike made headlines somewhere in the media every week and had reaped the benefits of that media coverage. They were becoming well-known and popular and they were ready for the year ahead.

***

"Well, Sam, it's D-Day. Good Luck! Let's hope our strategy works."

"Thanks Mike and good luck to you too. I hope this schedule of ours works as well. Hopefully, we can pull off a big enough percentage to be invited to the debates. We have just over a year to make eighteen percent or more of the vote."

"We look pretty good in the initial polls, Sam."

"Yes, but we can't really go by those polls at this point. There are eleven Democratic hopefuls and nine Republicans, as well as the slew of Green, Tea, Libertarian, Socialist and other independent party candidates. We can only hope the debate committee doesn't change the rules like they have in the past to prevent independent candidates from participating. We need to stick to our guns, and stay true to our platform without deviation and we should at least put a scare into the parties. We have planned a conference call with each other and our chair-people every Friday, but I think we should do two a week with each other. The second call would be a brief call to make changes in our itinerary. Maybe Tuesday and Friday."

"You're the boss, Sam. I'm just along for the ride and what a ride this is going to be."

"You've got that straight! Let's ride! See you in four weeks."

On that note, the two candidates said goodbye to each other and their families, and headed for their airports. Buffalo and Sheridan, thirty miles away, have small airports, but flights out of either of the small communities were usually expensive. Most travelers chose to fly out of Casper, Wyoming, one-hundred-thirteen miles to the south or Billings, Montana, one-hundred-sixty-five miles to the north to save money. It often cost less to drive to one of the other airports to catch a flight, than to fly out from home.

Sam headed for Casper for his flight to Denver where he planned to rent a car and whistle stop the cities and towns in Colorado. After a week in Colorado, he would spend a week in New Mexico, Arizona, and Nevada, then return to Buffalo. Sam and Mike had success with that itinerary for the past year and between them, they had visited all fifty states and the six territories.

Mike headed to Billings for his flight to Atlanta. He would cover Georgia, Alabama, Arkansas, and Missouri, before heading home.

The two men had decided they were going to try to visit at least one major city and two smaller communities per day. They needed to talk to as many supporters and people as they could before they moved on to the next stop.

Kate and Nancy were coordinating with supporters to arrange events which would keep Sam and Mike in the press almost every day. A hospital visit, serving at a soup kitchen, visiting a homeless shelter or children's hospital and Veteran's facilities and hospitals making sure all the local media were informed so the event would receive the greatest media exposure.

***

As Sam exited the concourses in Denver, the media was already there to meet him.

"Mr. Waters! Now that we are only eighteen months from the election have you and Mr. Baker decided on a platform for your campaign?"

"I'm sorry, what is your name?"

"John Brooks, CNN, News."

"Well, John Brooks from CNN, News. This Campaign is about respect, which you haven't shown to me or your fellow correspondents. I will give you the chance to ask that question again after you wait for me to call on you for questions. Now, you in the purple jacket."

"Yes, sir. David Williams, KOB TV. Sir do you still think that running as an unattached, unsponsored independent candidate was wise?"

"Well, David, wise probably wouldn't be my first choice of words; but yes. I feel it was and still is the best and right choice."

"Mr. Waters, if I may. What do you think your chances are of becoming the next president?"

"David, you are asking that question and are probably more up to date and in tune with the poll numbers than I am. Your TV newsroom is probably giving you constant updates through the earbud you're wearing. Let me ask you, David, what do the polls tell you my chances are?"

"Mr. Waters, Mr. Waters." The reporters vie for the next question.

"Just a minute everyone, I'm waiting for David's answer."

"Mr. Waters, the KOB news room informs me that you are currently running at nine percent of the vote with just over a year and a half to go before the election. If you stay on pace you are projected to have twenty-eight percent of the vote before the debates."

"Thank you, David. That's pretty good news, wouldn't you say folks?" A small crowd had gathered, and they cheered loudly at the news. "Now let me say this. I have every bit as much chance of winning this Presidential race as any one of the party candidates. Maybe a better chance, since I don't have to beat all the other party members to be nominated before I can concentrate on the election. Green shirt, your question."

"Mr. Waters, Chris Newly, Denver Post. Since you apparently upset Brooks from CNN and he left with his crew, may I ask you the question Brooks was so rude with."

"Of course, Chris. Mr. Brooks epitomized what my platform is about. I am about respect. Respect for the Flag. Respect for America, Our Country. Respect for each other, not only as Americans, but as Humans. This Presidential race isn't about being Republican, Democrat, Green, Tea, or any other Independent Parties, it's about the American belief that together we can accomplish anything. We have led the world financially, led in technology, led in the space program, and in the development of human rights. Somewhere along the line we have forgotten how to be human, forgotten how to be world leaders. There are people in our Government who have called us sheep. I say we aren't sheep, but slaves. Slaves to the industrial machines of corporations and banking who dictate to our Government representatives through expensive lobbying how the rest of us must live our lives.

"I'll say this again, we aren't sheep. When a wolf grabs a member of a flock of sheep, the flock will follow the wolf for a distance. However, the flock will, after a short time, stop following the wolf and return to their lives. We are not sheep; for we continue to follow the wolves. We continue to live under the laws and rules of the wolves while they do not live by those same rules. They are the masters and we are the slaves who do their bidding.

"I say, No More! It's time for real change -- not hopeless promised change built on the promises of politicians.

"Stand UP, stand with me and Restore America."

"Mr. Waters, another question if I may. Restoring America is a strong statement. What is your plan to restore America?"

"Well, Chris keep your head up and your mind and ears open and you will get the answer to that question. Blue dress." He points to the lady in the blue dress.

“Thank you, Teri Reid, Clear Channel Radio News. Mr. Waters, you and Mr. Baker have been very low profile on the issues. Now that you are beginning your campaign can you shed some light on the issues which make up your platform?”

“Teri, Mr. Baker and I have been traveling around this country for the past year. Every day, we have talked to the citizens of the numerous towns and cities we have visited. In those conversations, we have asked what issues are important to this country. We have heard every possible answer imaginable; but, there has always been one issue which remained constant throughout all fifty states and the thousands of people we have talked with. That one issue is how our Government, our Representatives, show no respect for the people who put them in office. Once in office, all the campaign promises are forgotten and swept away like dust in the wind. This lack of respect ends now. The American people want their voices heard. They want to know they are being represented, that their representatives aren’t in the pockets of big corporations, big banks or the hundreds of other special interest groups that roam the Capitol halls. America is the issue. The American People are the issue. Therefore, this is our stand on the issues. These are the only issues which matter and the greatest issues we will fight to reform.”

“Mr. Waters, please, another question. Haven’t the people told you about their concern over Climate Change, Abortion laws or any of the numerous issues being brought forward by the candidates in the party campaigns?”

“Teri, yes, we have heard some comments on those issues, however, most people don’t care either way. Oh, they might have an opinion, but those issues really aren’t critical. Politicians create issues which make people think there is an issue. Then the politicians make those issues seem like they are something very important and something that everyone should be aware of. Politicians make the issues seem like the most important things on the minds of the American people. This is the politician’s way of making everyone think they are doing something to work for the greater good, while performing a magic show of smoke and mirrors to hide their personal or party agenda. Let me ask all of you a couple of questions:

"Abortion and Climate Change have been issues in every election for the past forty plus years. Why hasn't anyone in Congress solved these issues?

"How many times have you listened to some candidate for office talk about some issue you didn't care about?

"How many of you have ever said to yourself – there must be a lot of people who feel strongly about this for it to be an issue in the election?

"Or how many of you have asked yourself why this issue is important?

"The News networks are very good at conducting polls for this or that opinion. When was the last time anyone did a poll to identify what's important to Americans? When was the last Poll taken to see if people really care about the issues politicians bring to the campaign every election? Take those two questions back to your newsrooms and see how Clear Channel, or MSNBC, or CNN or any other agency feel about running those polls. My bet would be they would be very uncomfortable with that suggestion. Those questions don't sell news.

"Mr. Baker and I have asked those questions, we have polled the people and we are prepared to answer those questions for the people.

Now ladies and gentlemen, I have to get to my hotel and prepare for the rest of the year."

***

Mike was on the plane to Atlanta when the stewardess turned on the news at the request of another passenger. Mike watched as Sam was interviewed in Denver. Mike knew he would likely have the same reception in another hour when he landed. He was glad to have some time to prepare for his press coverage.

As he landed and started toward the baggage claim area, he could see the concourse exit ahead and the swarm of reporters just outside. He was prepared for the barrage of questions.

"Mr. Baker."

"Yes, in the pink hat."

"Thank you, Judy Collins, Atlanta Journal-Constitution. Can you tell us in more detail how you plan to Restore America?"

"Yes, Judy, we plan to restore the time-honored traditions based in this country's history. A history of respect for our elders. A history of defending our great nation against foreign and domestic invaders. A history of compassion for our fellow man. A history of freedom from slavery. Sam Waters hit the nail squarely on the head when he said the people of this country aren't sheep, but slaves to the industrial complex and to the big banks. It's time to break the chains and there is only one candidate who is willing and ready to do that. Sam Waters. Next question, in the gray jacket."

"Yes Sir, Barry Waters, no relation, CBS News. Mr. Waters was asked in Denver about your low profile on the issues. Do you share his feelings on the issues?"

"Barry, Mr. Waters and I have talked to a lot of people around the country and he expressed exactly what we have heard from almost everyone we talked with from small towns to large cities, the sentiment was the same. The biggest issue of concern for the people of this country is feeling like our elected representatives are doing the job they were hired to do, and that is to represent the people. As Sam said in Denver, this is the only issue that matters and the issue we will fight to reform."

"Mr. Baker, please, another question. Aren't you at all concerned about climate change and global warming?"

"Barry, let me ask you and the rest of the media the same question only rephrased. Are you concerned with global climate change? Do you spend restless nights and hopeless days wondering if your face was going to melt off because we are destroying the ozone?" The news group is uncomfortably silent. "I know at least one of you should be willing to break with the rules set up by your networks and answer my questions. Tan Coat."

"Tony Reynolds. WSB-TV. Sir, although Global warming is a concern, I do not have sleepless nights or troubled days and I rarely think about it except when it comes up in the news. About the only time it does come up is around election time every two years. I know the climate issue is out there and people are working on both sides of the issue, but it is virtually silent except in election years."

"Thank you, Tony for giving an honest answer and that is how Sam Waters and I feel on the subject. That is basically how the people we talked with feel about the subject. It is a concern but not so great a concern as to be an issue. So, Tony, do you have some questions for me?"

"Yes Sir, thank you. How do you feel when the news media refers to you as bat man's robin?"

"The same as I feel about comments calling Sam, the caped crusader or bat man. That's what we are, a Dynamic duo, fighting for real change in Government, fighting to curb the corruption, to end the greed and stop the deals which exempt Congress from the laws they press upon the people. Demanding respect, not just for the people in Gotham City, but Nationally. It is a great pleasure to be considered in that spotlight. Now ladies and gentlemen, I have busy days ahead and would like to get some rest."

Both Sam and Mike called their wives as soon as they arrived in their hotel rooms and were briefed on the agenda for the next day and the daily media event. The wives couldn't always get a daily event for both men, but they did manage to keep one or the other in the media daily. The calls home to family would have been a normal evening routine anyway, but they also helped Sam and Mike by passing messages to each other through their wives. This additional method of communication helped them to be prepared for whatever the media would throw at them for the next few months.

11
CHANGE OF PLANS

Sam and Mike had been on the road for three months and each had covered ten states. Two candidates had withdrawn from the Democratic race and another representative has added his name to the list of Republican candidates. Early polls indicated that Senator Dwayne Johnson led the Democrats and Congressman Neil Grainger led the Republicans; but, the first primaries were still five months away. Regardless of the polls, anyone could step in and take the Party Nomination. The Independent parties had their usual two or three candidates who will remain virtually tied until June, then one will pull ahead by a couple of percentage points.

Sam and Mike contracted for several more campaign offices in the states where they had strong support. They visited those offices and hired full-time people to run them. In many cities, Sam's campaign offices were directly across the street or even next door to the Republican, Democrat, or other party campaign offices. It may have been paranoia, but since Sam's offices were the first in these communities, it appeared that the other parties were trying to keep tabs on him. Some of Sam's office managers had even reported visits by competitor candidates.

Campaign expenses kept climbing. With the office rents, utilities and full-time staff, Sam's campaign expenses were running at one-hundred-seventy-thousand dollars per week. Luckily, most of the personnel staffing the offices were volunteers, but there were still those on the payroll who coordinated the activities of the volunteers. Sam was beginning to worry about the campaign funds and costs. He looked at the expense statements in the emails he was getting from Kate and wondered about his finances and whether they would hold out until the election in sixteen months. He and Mike had been staying in the cheapest, non-fleabag motels they could find, limiting their meals, and using compact economy rental cars, but the bills kept adding up.

"Kate, what's the status of the campaign bank account?"

"You don't need to worry yourself about that Sam. You just stay focused on what you're doing and let Ginny and I worry about the finances. Do you want Mary to start sending a bank printout to show where your funds are?"

"You're a doll and I miss you. I'm sure you girls can handle the budget, but you know I will still worry. I know what this is costing, and I would hate to get down to the wire and run out of money. You mentioned Mary. Did she decide to come to work for us? She was hesitant when I asked her."

"Yes, Mary did come to work for us, but I think it was more at Terry's bidding rather than choice, but she has picked up the routine quickly. Although she won't admit it, I think she's having fun. Now, don't worry about the money. Your campaign contributions are still coming in at about the same pace they were before you guys went on the road. The list of total supporters who have sent contributions is twenty-one million, give or take a couple of thousand, so you are just about halfway to the goal of fifty-eight million you set in the beginning."

"Cool. I don't know why I always worry about money. You have kept my business and the family finances running smoothly for years. Do you have any statistics on how many states have us on the ballot so far?"

"As far as I can tell, it looks like about fifteen and a couple of those are swing states. I'll send you a text with the whole list so far."

"What swings do we have?"

"You are very strong in Colorado, Nevada, and New Mexico. Mike made a good showing in the south east. Florida, North Carolina, and Virginia all have you on the ballot. Your brothers have been campaigning for you in D.C. and California; but haven't gotten a commitment for the ballot yet. Mike's family is campaigning in Iowa and Wisconsin and you are on those ballots. Illinois polls show you being very strong, but you aren't on the ballot there either, but Mike's family is generating a lot of support for you."

"Damn, we really need to be on the ballot in the big seven. If we can't win at least a couple of those then we don't have a chance and, if we aren't on the ballot, we can't win the state. We weren't scheduled to hit Texas, New York, California, or Illinois until later in the campaign; but I think we need to concentrate on them until we can get a ballot commitment one way or the other.

Since I'm not scheduled to talk to Mike for a couple of days, can you tell Nancy we are changing the itinerary and to have Mike head for New York, Pennsylvania, Indiana, and Illinois. Promoting the Hometown boy sentiment in Illinois. I'm headed to Texas then across the Southwest and out to the coast."

"Are you going to be home for the holidays?" Kate asked.

"No, unfortunately, but I know how the people in this country feel about holidays and family. So, tell Nancy to meet Mike in Illinois to be with him and his family on Thanksgiving. You and the kids join me in Los Angeles. We will spend Thanksgiving with Jim."

"Sounds good, the kids will love seeing their cousins. Should I tell Mike what we're doing."

"I thought I just said to tell Nancy the plan, so she can tell Mike."

"No, Dear, your brother, Mike. We need to find a code name for him, so we don't get them mixed up in conversations."

"Since he chooses to live in the political chaos known as D.C., how about Muddy? Muddy Waters." Sam laughed at his comment.

"How about just MW? I don't think he would appreciate being muddy all the time." Then Kate and Sam both laughed at her comment.

"I'd better get busy if I have to book a flight to Dallas for tomorrow. Give the kids a hug and kiss for me. And don't forget to text me that list of states. Love you baby. Talk to you tomorrow night."

"Love you too. Rest well."

Sam hung up the phone and wished he were back in Wyoming sitting in front of his fireplace with Kate beside him on the couch. He missed her and the kids. He wondered how Toby was doing with his math. He always seemed to have trouble with math, but Sam thought it was just a way to get closer to his dad. Sam didn't mind and enjoyed the time with his son. He liked the time with his little muffin, Lauren too, and missed her as well. He was thinking about Kate and the kids when the cell phone beeped bringing him back to the small hotel room in McAlester, Oklahoma. He picked up the phone and read Kate's text.

On the ballot in Colorado, New Mexico, Utah, Oklahoma, Florida, Georgia, Alabama, North and South Carolina, Virginia, Arizona, Missouri, Mississippi, Montana, both Dakotas, Wisconsin, Iowa, and of course, Wyoming. Several states are on the fence. Kids say hello and they love and miss their dad.

Sam smiled at the message and turned to his computer to book the flight to Dallas, Texas.

12
EMBEDDED PRESS

There was a knock on the door and Sam looked at the clock. Midnight! What moron is banging on my door at this hour. Sam opened the door ready to voice some explicit words when he saw it was Jerry Cummings.

"Jerry, what are you doing here?"

"Hi Sam, NBC and my station have been watching you and Mike make news all over the country and want to be part of it. So, I'm the embedded reporter for your campaign until the election."

"Really, are you going to be jumping back and forth between me and Mike? How can you be the imbedded reporter for the campaign if you aren't covering both of us?"

"No, I'm not jumping back and forth, I'm your dedicated reporter. The Station recognized you and Mike aren't campaigning together, so they assigned two of us. You know Bill Kerr, from our staff. He usually covers stories in Sheridan and Gillette. He's going to be Mike's shadow and should be knocking on his door about" Jerry looked at his watch "now!"

"That's great, where are you staying?"

"With you of course, got a spare bed?"

"Sure, but I can't pay your way on my campaign. Not only would it be out of budget, but it would look like I was trying to taint the news."

"Seriously, Sam, it's just for the night because there aren't any vacancies in town. NBC is paying our way and wouldn't want to cloud your campaign."

"Thanks Jerry, you had me worried for a moment. I'm glad you're here, I can use someone besides the walls to talk to and in these small towns there isn't much on TV. Kind of like Buffalo."

"You've been making quite a name for yourself. bat man would be proud of you and Terry Jacobs is kicking himself for not taking you up on the running mate position."

"How did you know about that?"

"After you left, I went up to Buffalo and interviewed practically the whole town. I was just looking for some background from some of your closest friends. About everyone said they were a close friend, but everyone said Terry was your best friend basically since birth."

"That's true. Our mothers were best friends and Terry and I were born just an hour apart. We've been friends a long time. We were in the same sports and clubs in school. Joined the Marines on the buddy program out of High School. I guess you could say we've been together through thick and thin."

"That's a remarkable story. With all that background between you, why did he turn you down?"

"You remember the line about the caped crusader that got everyone calling me bat man?"

"Sure, you answered my question at your announcement press conference with the comment."

"Terry was the first to call me that, when he turned me down, he said he couldn't risk his family or his position to go play caped crusader with me."

"Sometimes we have to consider our personal responsibilities. I've talked to Kate and your kids and they are holding up just fine. Toby said he misses his dad's help with his math and Lauren misses your bedtime stories."

"Thanks, Jerry. Now I'm home sick and just want to forget this whole thing."

"You can't do that! Toby and Lauren are really anxious to pick out a bedroom in the White House."

"I don't doubt that. Toby started talking about being the first kid right after your interview."

"Sam, do you know where you stand right now?"

"Yeah. Kate just texted me a list of the nineteen states where I'm on the ballot. If you've been following me in the news you know that I ask at least one reporter per media rave what my status is. I've been told anywhere between fourteen and seventeen percent. I think the numbers may be skewed a bit. I don't think the polls account for where votes are going after the primaries when only one candidate per party emerges."

"Well, yes, the numbers are skewed, but not like you would think. You are ahead of the numbers. Let me see what Kate sent you." Sam hands Jerry his phone and Jerry says as he reads the message "Yes, yes, yes. She missed a couple. Washington state,

Alaska, Idaho, Kansas, and Nebraska all have you on the ballot also. Looks like you and Mike are going to the debates."

"Not quite Jerry. The debates are still twelve months away. We may be on the ballots, but we need to be eighteen percent of the vote in the polls and from what I've been told we aren't near there yet."

"Well, I hate to be the one to burst your bubble my friend, but your current poll numbers nationwide are at nineteen percent with twelve months until the debates. You will easily withstand the results of the primaries. How are your funds holding out?"

"Kate says we're fine, we have over twenty-one million donations."

"Twenty-one million donations? Are you still asking for just ten dollars per supporter?"

"Yes. I don't see any reason to beat the people up every five minutes for more money. There are some of our supporters who have contributed more so that balances out the anonymous contributions. We are still turning those into donations to charity."

"That's incredible. Two-hundred-ten million dollars for your campaign, ten dollars at a time without anonymous or PAC contributions. I've seen the news where you have given almost ten-million dollars to charities along the way just in the last three months. Remarkable. According to the agenda Kate gave me to find you, your next stop is Little Rock, Arkansas?"

"No, Jerry, we had a slight change of plans tonight. We need to pick up as many of the big seven as we can. I hope you weren't pre-booked on a flight to Arkansas."

"I'll just have to change it. Where are we going?"

"Dallas, Texas"

"Dallas? Okay. What do you mean you have to pick up the big seven?"

"The Big Seven electoral states. Texas, California, New York, Florida, Pennsylvania, Illinois, and Ohio. If we can win those seven states, we hold two-hundred-nine electoral votes. That would leave only sixty-one votes to reach the two-hundred-seventy needed to win the election. Five of the remaining higher electoral states or a mix of ten states with lower and mid-range electoral votes. If we have the seven and can win Michigan, Georgia, North Carolina, New Jersey, and Virginia, we win the election. There are other high electoral states and we may need those if we don't capture any of these twelve."

"So, where to after Texas?"

"New Mexico, Arizona and California for the holidays. My family and I are going to spend Thanksgiving with my brother in LA. Will you be going home for Thanksgiving?"

"I would like to be with my wife and kids, but I'm supposed to stick with you until the election. Guess I'll be having dinner by myself at a Denny's somewhere in LA."

"Bull! Call your wife and have her fly out to LA. You're going to be part of the campaign family, so you're going to be part of the Waters family for the holidays. See if NBC will cover the cost, if not, I will. I will even treat everyone to a trip to some of the attractions of the west coast."

"Are you sure your brother won't mind you bringing your whole entourage with you?"

"Jim and MW got me into this mess, so they can live with me inviting a new friend and your family."

"MW?"

"My other brother Mike, MW for short, to keep from getting confused with Baker." As Sam finished the explanation, his cell phone beeped a text notification.

MW will be at Jim's for Thanksgiving.

"Well, Jerry, it looks like you'll get to meet the whole fam damily. Both of my brothers will be at T-day dinner in L.A."

***

A throng of reporters unexpectedly greeted Sam as he cleared the baggage claim in Dallas.

"Mr. Waters, why have you changed your travel plans?"

"Good morning, Mr. Brooks, CNN. Nice to see you again even if you haven't learned anything about respect since our last meeting three months ago. Steven, in the yellow blazer, I'll take your question."

"Thank you, Mr. Waters, Steven Booker, MSNBC. Sir, many of us have the same question as Mr. Brooks and are anxiously awaiting that answer. Could you please take a minute to answer him?"

The other reporters nodded their agreement, so Sam obliged them.

"Mr. Baker and I changed our plans, so we would be visiting states in an order that will bring us closer to our families for the upcoming Thanksgiving holiday. I will be traveling across the southwest to California to be with my brothers in L.A. and Mr. Baker will be traveling across the north central to be with his family in Illinois. Mr. Brooks, since the rest of the press corps has offered you the floor, do you have another question."

"Yes, Sir. Isn't there another reason for the change -- a real reason -- a more political reason? And isn't the real reason that you want to insure your acceptance on the ballot of the largest electoral states?"

Sam glanced questionably at Jerry who shook his head that he hadn't leaked the big seven electoral state conversations.

"Mr. Brooks, does CNN purposely look for the rudest reporters on the planet and then train them to create yellow journalism? In case you aren't familiar with that term, yellow journalism is that reporting which has no requirement for being based on research or facts. It is very comparable to the spittle which spews from an infant's mouth. However, I will address the question.

"The unfortunate fact about presidential elections in this country is that they are determined, not by the popular vote, but by an electoral system which is out of date and in desperate need of refining to bring it consistent with the needs of the country today. Mr. Baker and I felt it necessary to change our plans for the real reason I originally stated, which is to be with our families for the approaching holiday. If you had done any research or had even a modicum knowledge of geography, you would have seen how our original itineraries took us in the opposite direction, away from our families. Yes, it is true, we did choose a path to our families which contained states with larger electoral votes. Once again if you look at a map and trace a path from where we were to our destination, it is very hard to travel from one to the other without passing through at least a few of those higher electoral states. However, that was not the reason for the change as Mr. Brooks suggested. Even if we were chasing electoral states, how would that make us any different than any Democrat, Republican or independent candidate who concentrates millions of dollars and campaign time to the largest of the electoral states while ignoring those states with only three or four electoral votes. Steven?"

"Thank you. Mr. Waters, how do you feel about being so popular in the polls? Do you think it has anything to do with your Caped crusader theme?"

"Steven, I can't say that I don't get slightly excited when I see the poll numbers; however, I have seen many times where the polls show one outcome, and another happens. I won't start counting on the polls until they close on the second Tuesday of November next year. As for your question about my poll numbers being a result of the Caped crusader comments – I feel that if the press assumes that their comments and constantly referring to me as bat man have any affect the on-poll statistics, then they must think the people of the United States are weak and extremely shallow. I believe the general population of this country is much stronger and quite a bit deeper than that.

"Pam, you're a long way from home, but it's good to see you."

"Thank you, Pam Bales, KOA7 news, Denver, Colorado. Mr. Waters, you have said repeatedly, you are not in this campaign to lose. If you do win the election, what will you try to accomplish first?"

"Well, Pam. I'm emphatic when I reiterate that I'm not in this campaign to lose. I think my first order of business will be to get moved into the White House without my children killing each other over which bedroom they will have." The press gallery laughed at the comment and began vying for position for the next question, but Sam cut them short.

"Ms. Bales do you have another question?"

"Yes Sir, on a more serious note. What will you do first."

"Seriously. On my first day in office after the inaugural, I will call a joint session of the houses of Congress and tell them what they've been missing for the past hundred years. Ladies and Gentlemen, thank you, but now I have to go secure my name on the ballot of the great state of Texas and it's thirty-eight electoral votes."

The press corps laughed -- immediately picking up on Sam's final comment as a chide to Brooks.

13

IN THE HUNT!

The Friday before Thanksgiving, Sam made his scheduled conference call to Mike and his campaign office chair-people for a first-hand progress report from his running mate and supporters.

"How's it going Mike?"

"It's going, but slowly. Wisconsin went okay, and we are on the ballot there and in Minnesota. I can't tell if New York is just sitting on the fence or if they are going to refuse. So, flipping arrogant in everything else they do, but so wishy-washy politically. On the ballot in Indiana, heading into Illinois tomorrow and meeting Nancy and the kids for Thanksgiving on Thursday. How about your end?"

"On the ballot in Texas, New Mexico and Arizona. California won't add us unless we manage a fifty percent share in the polls or get on one of the party tickets. I told them, if we're at a fifty percent share we don't need California anyway. That statement didn't make me very popular with the election committee. Okay, let's get the roll call. Mike would you stay on the line when we're done? I need to talk to you for a minute."

Sam called off the states and the campaign chair-people gave him the status of their state. Each chair reported whether the candidates were on the ballot, local poll percentage, what activity they were doing to promote Sam and Mike and what the parties were doing.

Sam and Mike gave them constructive suggestions, advice and kudos for a job well done.

"Does anyone have a handle on who's leading in the party races?"

"Sam, this is Joan and Felix Martin from Pennsylvania, I was just watching the news and the polls show, Johnson and Grainger leading in the debutante party ball, but there wasn't any information on the Libertarian Green Tea Social."

"Thanks Joan, I like that Libertarian Green Tea Social and debutant party ball. Where did you come up with those?"

"Well, Sam. We looked at it from the point of view that the four largest independent parties are the Libertarian, Green, Tea and the Socialist party of America. Hence, Libertarian Green Tea Social. Everyone knows that most of the Dems and Reps are poor little rich kids who have spent more time at debutant events than they have learning about the people of this country. So, Debutant party ball."

"I like it. There ought to be somewhere I can use that before the election. Mike do you have anything to add?"

"It would seem from the number of states with us on the ballot and the poll numbers as far as they are correct that we are just a little bit away from being invited to the Presidential debates. Thank you all for your support, your dedication to our candidacy, and for all of the hard work you and your volunteers have done."

"Mike is absolutely correct. You all have done a wonderful job, but we are a long way from finished. After Christmas is when we must really get down and dirty in this campaign. I don't mean dirty like the parties do. I mean roll up our sleeves and go for the win. January starts the caucuses and primaries for the debutants. Right now, regardless of who is leading in the polls, it is still anyone's game. The Republicans and Democrats have nine candidates each in the primaries. Granger and Johnson may be leading now, but January first they are all dead even. That's when the iron is hottest, and we need to strike and gain as much support as we can. We need to be watching as the party candidates drop out and try to contact as many of their supporters as we can to shift them to our side.

"That was the business. Now, I want to take this opportunity to thank you all and wish you a very happy Thanksgiving. I know Mike and I have something to be thankful for this holiday season and it is all of you and the volunteers and all of your hard work. Our next chat will be the first Friday in December. Have a safe and pleasant holiday."

***

"What's up Sam? We normally talk after the roll call. This is the first time you've asked me to stay. Your request sounded ominous and worried. What's going on?"

"It's not like that, Mike, I just have a lot on my mind with the holiday. Kate and I are very excited to be spending

Thanksgiving here in LA with my brothers and I know you are spending the holiday with your family in Illinois. I want to wish you all the best for Thanksgiving. Like I told the troops, you and I have a lot to be thankful for. Jerry's wife, Meg, and his son joined us this week and the kids have been having a blast going to Disneyland, Magic Mountain, and Knotts Berry Farm. What is your reporter doing for the holiday?"

"Nancy, told me that you had invited Jerry and his family before I saw the story on the news, so I jumped on the band wagon and invited Bill and his family to have Thanksgiving with us in Illinois."

"Cool. Let's plan on being back home for Christmas. We have a good jump on things and I think we need to start planning our presence at the debates."

"Debates? Aren't we putting the cart before the horse? I know we are gaining in the polls and we are definitely in the hunt, but we have some major hurdles left to overcome."

"No, Mike, I don't think I have the cart before the horse at all. Jerry and the NBC polls show us at twenty-two percent and we are on the ballot in thirty states. If we can keep up our momentum, the debate committee will have to include us. I would like to be at twenty-five percent by the first of the year, but I think that's pushing it a little. We will just have to knuckle down the week between Christmas and New Year."

"Cool, I guess I need to be asking Bill and NBC for more input. Just didn't want any appearance of trying to influence the press. Where are you off to after Thanksgiving?"

"Not sure Mike. I was going to head up to Oregon, Washington, Utah, Idaho, Montana, and the Dakotas. Cover all the Northwest, but we have a lot of big electors around the great lakes as well as Indiana, Kentucky, and Tennessee. We still have the northeastern sea board to visit too."

"Let's play it this way, Sam. You do the Oregon to Dakotas trip. We have good response through the central and south-central states, so we can be in contact with them between working the twenty we need on the ballot. I'll do the Northeast sea board and New England states and head for home. After Christmas, we can jump into Kentucky, Tennessee, West Virginia, and the rest of the south east and south. We can also spot check some of the swing states while we are in the vicinity. Someone is going to have to go to Hawaii and Alaska too."

"Sounds like a plan, Mike. We need a good working plan for after the first, but we can work that out over the Christmas break. Have a great holiday with your family and I'll see you at home in three and a half weeks."

"You, too. See you soon."

14
WHAT FACE TO WEAR TO A DEBATE?

Christmas season in Buffalo, Wyoming was eight inches of fresh snow and temperatures in the very low teens. Christmas was always chaotic for the Waters and Baker families. Both families always had a family reunion at Christmas and rotated the location around the country. Because they had spent Thanksgiving in California and Illinois with their brothers and sisters, they decided a quiet family Christmas at home would be nice.

Quiet would have been nice, but wasn't to be the case. Sam and Mike had planned to get together at Sam's house to discuss the debates. The news team of Jerry and Bill and their families had come down from Billings to help Sam and Mike with the issues and the four families had a great holiday in Buffalo.

"This has been an absolute blast, Sam. Even if we lose, I can't thank you enough for allowing me the opportunity to be on this ride with you."

"Thank you, Mike, for making the stand with me, but we aren't through yet and when has "lose" been in the Marine Corps dictionary?

"We've made a good run so far on our respect and restore platform, but the debates are going to ask for our perspective on specific issues. We aren't going to be able to dodge the questions with the standard answers that have marked our campaign so far. It's time to break out the big guns. It's time for that fight I told you about two years ago when I made the announcement."

"I remember. So, the debates are where we tell the other parties we're going to kick their ass?"

"No, Mike. The debates are where we just come out and kick their ass. Remember, if you tell someone what you are going to do, it's a fight. If you just do it, it's over, done, all in, you win. We must keep the parties reacting to our campaign. If they get the upper hand and start being proactive, our fight will become a lot harder."

"Cool, Sam! I have always liked that thinking."

"Jerry and Bill, why don't you and our wives be the panel, audience or moderator. Give us your questions and we will work out the answers right now, so we can rehearse them in order to be ready in September and October."

"Sounds good Sam, but I'm going to throw in a twist. I want you and Mike to oppose each other. Play the devil's advocate and don't let your opponent off the hook until the bell rings. You guys are going to have to be ready for anything the Republicans and Democrats can throw at you. We don't have to worry about the Libertarian Green Tea Social, because they have nowhere near the percentages needed for an invitation to the debates. The debutante ball is bringing the same garbage they bring every election and it has been rehearsed the same way for decades, so we need to be fresh and new on those issues.

"This year, like 2016, the moderator is responsible for deciding the questions for the first and last presidential debate and the vice-presidential debate. The second debate is internet, phone, and live audience questions. The rules never change. There are six segments which the candidates rarely get through. When the issue is presented, each candidate will have two minutes to respond, then there will be a general discussion. The discussion is where you will gain or drop in the polls. This is where you need to be on top of your game."

"Kate, why don't you fire the first question."

"Okay. Mr. Waters, what is your opinion on the issue of abortion?"

"Getting right to the meat of the matter aren't you, Kate?"

"Sam, you know the debutantes will be right on top of issues like this and you better have your ducks in a row and come out with your guns blazing or you can just come home after it's over. Now as the Irishman says, 'answer the farking question'."

"Okay. It is my opinion that Government gives too much attention to several questions which should not be addressed by any candidate for any office.

"We have separated church and state to ensure one doesn't have influence over the other. The separation was further defined so schools could not make children pray.

"We cannot demand a separation of state on some religious issues then demand the state get involved in others. You can't have it both ways. We either have a division of church and state or we don't.

"Abortion and gay marriages are Church issues, moral issues, not State issues. I do not believe that a government that is of, by and for its people has the right to tell those people how to live with their moral convictions. That is why the founders of this country demanded religious freedom. It is in our history that we cannot force religious convictions on others. These issues are between the people and their God. They should be able to deal with their religious and moral conscience without the interference of the government."

"Wow, Sam, you just lost the entire bible belt." Bill says trying to decide whether Sam's answer will be suicide or revelation.

"Maybe a few Bill, but most will agree that you can't have it both ways and the church really doesn't want Government interference with their religion because that could lead to a whole slew of Governmental intervention into the affairs of the church. Next Question."

"Mr. Baker, Same Question."

"I agree with what Sam Waters said in the debate last week. We cannot have it both ways. We cannot demand separation of church and state on one hand and make government responsible for religious rulings on the other."

"Good approach. It shows unity in the two of you and is in keeping with the respect and restore platform, but I have to wonder how much damage that stand will cause. Meg, your turn." Jerry commented.

"Sam, you are a Veteran. What do you think of the twenty-five-year-old conflict in the middle east?"

"Most of the conflicts throughout history have been about money, control of land mass or power. This threat and conflict in the middle east is about none of the above. It is about hatred and the genocide of a population.

"There are factions, pieces, and people in every religion who believe theirs to be the only true religion. There are religions which believe every soul must be baptized to enter heaven. There are others which believe only a certain number of people will be allowed into heaven and others will live in some type of purgatory. In this day and age, most of the Christian based religions don't attempt to drive out, destroy or kill off everyone who does not believe as they do. However, there have been times in history where they have done just that. The crusades and inquisitions are proof of that.

"The Middle East is full of people who believe theirs to be the only true religion and all who believe otherwise must be destroyed. The genocide or enslavement of the infidels. The only way that belief can be changed is to destroy those who follow that doctrine. The genocide of the radical extremists. There is no right or wrong here, there is only survival. It is purely a matter of preservation of life and I will defend America's right to exist on this planet at all costs."

"Wow. Mr. Baker, same question, I think, but I'm not sure I'm going to like the answer."

"Meg, Sam isn't a monster who will continue to run the country headlong into a war of attrition with the extremists. He's a realist who has been in the Middle East and has seen first-hand how these people think and what they think of us. Although, the Quran is not very different from our Bible in its principles, it, like all religious doctrine, has been subject to interpretation, which was the primary reason King James had the Bible translated. Anyone, can twist the scriptures into a document to serve their needs. It is all in the interpretation -- an interpretation which can make the Quran or the Bible very different from their original doctrine; thus, making their religion and world entirely different from what others believe. The radical factions and extremists have translated their beliefs into terrorism and hate and are even further removed from their religion and are very dangerous to us and our beliefs and customs. We have seen the news for the past nineteen years showing the rise of the extremists and the total disregard for life these people have. We have no choice if we are to survive."

"Eye for an eye and the world is blind." Meg quoted an old adage.

"We aren't talking equal retaliation, eye for an eye." Sam interjected. "The destruction of evil must be swift, and it must be complete. I'm tired of seeing our young men and women come home in flag draped aluminum cans. I'm for taking off the gloves and letting our military do what needs to be done to end this thing once and for all."

"It seems we have broached a very emotion packed subject, so I have a suggestion. Why don't we call it a day? Let's write down some of the pressing issues of the day and what we've seen online and in our conversations with people. We need also to take a very close look at what issues the other candidates are standing on. We can get back together tomorrow about noon and try this again."

"Good idea, Jerry. I guess I touched a pretty sensitive nerve asking that question of two Marines."

"Sorry, Meg, we do get going a bit when that subject comes up. See you all tomorrow."

Sam apologized, and everyone said their goodnights and headed for their homes. Bill and Jerry were spending a couple of days in Buffalo rather than drive home to Billings every night. As Kate closed the door she turned to face Sam.

"You know, Sam, you were pretty hard on Megan and she was just doing what you asked and was asking questions about issues you are likely to encounter at the debate."

"Maybe, Kate, but this is also the issue everyone has pussy footed and danced around in every debate and election since 9/11/2001 when those factions of the Al Qaeda destroyed the twin towers. There are people in this country who are willing to give up everything to protect the good ones and I agree we should, but we cannot continue to let the bad ones run free and rampant destroying our culture. Let's put it behind us for the night and get something to eat."

"Well, Sam, I just don't think that would be a good face to wear into the debates."

15

TRAINING FOR THE FIGHT

Sam, Mike, Bill, and Jerry met the next day at noon as agreed, but the wives decided to pass. Instead they took a day of spa treatments and shopping in Billings.

Jerry and Bill fired questions at Sam and Mike for the better part of six hours and gave suggestions to improve their answers. By six o'clock they had debated every issue ranging from a rehashing of abortion and gay marriage and the conflicts in the Middle East to Government spending and the deficit. They had reviewed and revised six pages of questions on every conceivable issue which might arise during the debate. Sam and Mike were now prepared to train for the fight. All they needed now was the invitation to debate. Sam and Mike have played devil's advocate until they are mentally exhausted.

On the way home from Billings, Kate and the other wives talked about what a great day it was and how much they enjoyed the companionship of new friends.

"Before we call this a day, how would you all feel about a Christmas cookout at my house? Sam is a great cook on the grill and I have fresh cut prime rib steaks from the butcher in Billings."

"Kate, that sounds wonderful. Do you have enough steak for all the adults and kids?"

"Sue, there's plenty for everyone. Didn't you see the butcher load half a cow in the back of the truck?" The girls all laughed at Kate's comment.

"Kate, I don't know if a cookout is such a good idea. I'm not sure I'd be very welcome after last night with Sam and Mike and the middle east thing. I got them pretty riled up."

"Oh Meg, don't be silly. Mike can get pretty stormy and intense about military stuff and I'm sure Sam gets the same way, but the storm blows over quickly and there aren't any hard feelings. Am I right, Kate?" Nancy said encouragingly.

"Yes, indeed. Sam was worried that you would be mad at him last night after you left. They are mean, lean Marines but they have a soft side very few ever see. Meg, I'm not letting you off the hook for dinner. I will tie Jerry to the table if that's what it takes to make you stay."

"As much as I'd like to see that, I don't think Jerry would like it much." They all laughed and continued conversing on a variety of subjects for the remainder of the trip to Kate's house. Once there, Kate lit the grill just outside the back door and went in. Inside, she handed Sam enough steak to feed a small army, then turned and invited Mike, Bill, and Jerry to dinner.

"What am I supposed to do with these?" Sam asked.

"Cook them of course, silly boy. The grill is already lit and should be ready in a minute or two. I'll put on some corn and mashed taters."

The group ate and had some great conversation that didn't center around the campaign. They talked about kids, family, what they wanted for Christmas and New Year's Resolutions, but not the campaign. As everyone was getting ready to depart for their homes. Sam approached Jerry.

"Jerry, I have something to ask you."

"Sure, Sam what is it?"

"If I manage to win this thing I would like you to be my White House Press manager."

"Gee Sam, I'll have to think about that and talk it over with Meg."

"I know, and I wouldn't expect an answer tonight, but think about it. Bill, I would like you to be there with me too. We've made a great team so far in this campaign and I think with your help we could have a great presidency."

They all say their goodnights and head for home. Even Meg had a great time.

***

Although Sam had said he wanted to be at twenty-eight percent of the polls by the first of the year, he decided to take the week off and be with his family. The four men get together daily and rehearsed the questions and issues for the debates until the responses became second nature. No matter which order the questions were asked or how they were phrased, Sam and Mike were on top of them. They were ready.

16

A RUN FOR THE MONEY

After bringing in the New Year, Sam and Mike were back on the campaign trail. This time they were traveling together to show a unified front. Grainger and Johnson were still leading the polls, but Sam was gaining ground and had twenty-four percent of the polls and was on the ballot in thirty-seven states by the end of January.

Jerry and Bill, advised Sam to hire a Campaign Manager to help with their campaign. Bill suggested Joe Thorson would be a good manager for the team. Joe was an independent Manager, who had worked on several different independent campaigns over the years. Although, Joe's track record for success was lack-luster, he was the only truly independent Manager available.

Sam agreed to talk to Joe to see what he had to offer.

Sam found Joe to be an amiable, good natured gentleman who believed in backing an independent party candidate but not necessarily a total independent – the first strike against him.

"What changes would you make to our current campaign?" Sam asked as he continued the interview.

"You need to call a press conference and address your position on the issues. You won't keep the interest and support of the people if you don't open up as to where you stand on the issues. You also need to advertise. Radio and television reach more people than just staying in the news. You have had good success so far, but you can't keep it up. People lose interest if you don't stay in front of the crowd and simple news coverage doesn't saturate the market share you need to win the election." Thorson responded.

Strike two. Sam and Mike had managed to gain the poll percentages needed for an invitation to the debates and were on the ballots on over a third of the states. Many of those states had big electoral numbers and even though being on the ballot didn't guarantee a win, it still improved the odds.

"Joe, what will it cost my campaign to hire you as my Campaign Manager?"

"My usual fee is sixty-five-thousand dollars per year with an initial three-year contract."

“Okay, what do I get for one-hundred-ninety-five-thousand-dollars?”

“I will manage your campaign for the remainder of this run for President as well as any run for a Congressional office should you attempt one for the next two years.”

“Why would I be using your services after I win this election?”

“Sam, let’s be realistic. You are putting up a good fight, but you are a longshot, at best, for the win. You haven’t held an office before, you are not a party member, and you are a virtual unknown. After you lose this election, if you want to stay in politics you will have to be elected to a Congressional or Senatorial position to gain the savvy to cast yourself into the Presidential limelight for another election run.”

Strike three, Thorson had insulted Sam by insinuating he had no chance of winning this election which made Sam commit even further to sticking with his own plan. Sam remained adamant about not letting the media know anything until it was too late to make an issue of it. The debates were going to be the place they would announce and defend their position on issues, not before. Just six weeks before the election, the media would have to work extra hard to come up with any dirt to counter Sam’s statements. The Platform had worked so far, so why not let it finish the ride.

Sam thanks Thorson for his time and thanks Bill for the recommendation; but, continues to let Kate and Nancy manage the campaign.

Sam and Mike watched the news about the Iowa Caucus on February first. Grainger won for the Republicans and Johnson won the Democrat side. Republican Sandy Bishop withdrew from the race even though she was ranked fairly high in the polls. The Republican party asked her to step down to reduce Grainger’s opposition. They offered her the Vice-Presidency for her cooperation.

During the next week, Sam and Mike added another state to the list of ballots, bringing the ballot count to thirty-eight, but the state commitments were becoming harder to get. The remaining states wanted to see a higher poll percentage, or a greater number of names on the petitions or any number of other requirements. The campaign staffs and volunteers were working over-time to meet the state deadlines.

Sam and Mike were again in front of the TV on February ninth watching as the New Hampshire primary unfolded. Grainger won again, but Johnson lost to Steven Wilton. New Hampshire was Wilton's home state, so the result really wasn't a surprise.

March, April, and May were favorable for all the candidates. As expected Johnson won the Democratic nomination and Grainger won the Republican. The Green Party's leading candidate was John Smith, and the Tea Party's Candidate was John Jones. Naturally, the two were jokingly referred to as alias Smith and Jones within the Waters camp. Carol Dushannon got the nod from the Socialist party and Wilbur Justus was the Libertarian candidate. The final stage was set, let the campaigns begin

The debates were four months away and Sam and Mike had been talking to each other daily going over and over the issues, rehearsing their answers to the questions. They had been hounded by the press for answers to their position on the issues, but had held their ground and stuck to their campaign platform of respect and reform. Although the press corps had continually asked for a stand on the issues, they had not asked a direct question. Sam and Mike were very happy to give indirect elusive answers. They had set an example and their platform has become a very powerful message. As they traveled around the country they had seen a growing number of people, including the press, showing more respect to one another. If nothing else, they had given the country a little unity in caring how they treat each other.

Sam and Mike have been concentrating their efforts in the swing states and those with vast industrial and farming communities. Even though they haven't been officially invited to the debate, they have arranged their schedules, so their nights are spent practicing and rehearsing the issues.

Kate and Nancy decided to join their husbands on the campaign trail as soon as the kids were out of school in June. Mary Jacobs had been working in the Buffalo campaign headquarters office and was very familiar with Kate's routine and eagerly took over, so Kate could campaign with Sam. Mary collected and sorted the contributions and Terry recorded them and took them to the bank for Ginny to deposit.

One day, Terry asked, "Ginny, I know this campaign has to be costing a fortune and each week I bring thousands, hundreds of thousands of dollars to deposit. Just out of curiosity, how are the funds holding up?"

"Terry, you know I can't disclose or discuss customer accounts."

"I know, I was just wondering."

"I will say this, they aren't going to run out of money unless they go brain dead and get stupid."

"That's good to know. I'm glad Kate is with him now. I've known him long enough to know that the closer to the finish line something gets, sometimes he gets stupid and does things that really don't help his cause."

"Kate will keep him in line, sure enough. Let's just hope she's enough."

Sam and Mike had ballot commitments from forty-seven states. The states which would not allow the independent candidates without a party were New York, California, and Hawaii. Sam's brothers were continuously applying what pressure they could to the campaign committees to recognize the independent candidate. Sam and Mike had met all the requisites set forth by the state to add their names to the ballot, but the committees wouldn't budge. Sam's brothers, James and MW, had petitioned the Governors of New York and California to intervene and force the election committees to add Sam to the ballot. Each petition had over forty thousand signatures –James and MW were impatiently waiting for the answer.

Sam and Mike had also been gaining in the polls by a couple of percentage points per month, without disclosing anything more than the Respect and Reform America platform of the campaign. By August they were showing twenty-eight percent of the vote. They had enough of the vote and were on the ballots in enough states to be invited to the Presidential debates. They were looking forward to letting the people know they were in this fight for them. They were anxious to tell America what they wanted to do for the people and were excited about telling the people how they planned to restore America. They were ready to kick some ass.

Sam had researched the independent candidates who ran in previous election years like a coach reviewing game films before meeting the other team. Now, Sam and Mike together reviewed the game films so to speak of the past independents. They looked for anything and everything that would indicate what the candidates did or didn't do which could help in this campaign. Most have done well in the early days of the campaign, but as the road and financial stress started to take their toll, the candidates started doing or saying foolish things that damaged their positions and ultimately led to their losing their percentage of the voter population.

Sam was the first independent candidate to be invited to the debates since Ross Perot in 1992. Perot had achieved a thirty-seven percent share of the vote in many states, but was only on the ballot in twenty-four. During the months leading up to the debates, Perot was criticized for being vague on his platform, for changing his stand on issues and sometimes for his use of wording which caused his poll position to drop to just over twenty percent. Sam and Mike had to be careful not to repeat history.

***

The problem with the voting population is the fact that the majority are either Republican or Democrat. Most voters, in the beginning of the campaigns, will follow their party believing one of their candidates to be the best for the position. After a few months, candidates drop out of the race or are defeated in the primaries. Those people whose candidates are no longer running find a new candidate whose views closely reflect their own. Occasionally, they turn to the independent candidates, but usually not in the numbers needed to secure a place in the debates let alone win the election.

Sam, had twenty-eight percent of the vote in the polls and was on the ballot in forty-seven states; the best showing of any independent candidate. He had the greatest chance of being a threat to the major parties than any third-party candidate since 1912 when Teddy Roosevelt's Progressive Party had more electoral votes than the Republican Party, Eighty-eight to eight. Roosevelt had a good showing, but he still lost the election to Democrat Woodrow Wilson who won an astounding four-hundred-thirty-five electoral votes.

Sam and Mike had not only been reviewing the game films of the past independents, but also the game films on their present competition. Johnson was a career Senator from Alabama and a Southern Democrat, very liberal and very opinionated. Grainger was also a career politician in the Congress. A staunch Republican, and extremely right wing, from Wisconsin. Smith and Jones were typical Green and Tea party candidates, business owners who were tired of the bureaucracy of the Federal Government. Dushannon was the socialist answer to everything, when in doubt nominate a woman. Maybe they thought: if they could pull the women's support vote they would pull their husbands and have a chance of winning. It hadn't worked in twenty years, but you had to hand it to them -- they were persistent. Last, but not least was Justus, the libertarian. Wilbur had run for just about every office with an elected official in North Carolina. He did manage to win a seat on a city council once, another persistent candidate. Smith, Jones, Dushannon and Justus held about eight percent of the vote total.

One thing about it, Sam was in a position to give the parties a run for their money.

"Well Mike, here we are. To tell you the truth, three years ago when I stood in the rotunda of the Johnson County Courthouse and made the declaration to run, I honestly never thought we'd get this far. I figured we'd run out of money, support or energy long before today."

"I hear that, Sam. When you asked me to run with you and you didn't have any ideas for a platform, I thought we'd be done in that first year. Then you dropped that bomb on the press at the airport in Denver and I knew America had a President. I prayed every day that the American people would see what I saw that day. I think that accounts for about twenty-eight percent of the polls."

"Thanks Mike, I really appreciate that, and I am sincerely thankful you said yes to be my running mate. Let's go pull a trigger."

17
PULLING THE TRIGGER

As the time for the debate approached, MSNBC's Tony Cross and Stan Blackwell were in the announcer's booth at Ames Hall on George Washington University's Mount Vernon Campus.

"Tony, what a great place to be tonight."

"Right Stan, for the first time in over thirty years there will be three candidates on the stage. Republican Congressman Neil Granger, Democrat Senator Dwayne Johnson and the surprise candidate, the Independent, Sam Waters."

"According to the current polls Congressman Grainger is leading with thirty-six percent. And would you look at this -- Sam Waters is in a virtual tie with Senator Johnson at twenty-eight percent. Apparently, the voters, who would normally align with and be spread throughout the independent parties, are leaning toward the true independent Waters."

"Tony, it will be very interesting to see if bat man will come out from under his mask and cape tonight. So far, his campaign has been a mystery. Running on a platform of respect and reform without saying much at all about his views on the issues makes me wonder if he even knows what the issues are."

"Stan, Waters has shown he is as cool as a cucumber and I'm sure he not only knows the issues, but is well prepared to debate them here tonight. Waters is smart and has played his cards quite well so far. Running his entire campaign on just a little over forty-six million dollars, and that includes the nineteen million he has given to the numerous charities, making the actual budget for his campaign just twenty-seven million dollars so far."

"Smart like a fox, Tony. He has only asked his supporters for a mere ten-dollar donation. He has taken every anonymous donation and given them to charity. He has refused every Pac and super Pac that has offered him campaign contributions. Yet, here he is tonight, the third candidate in the debates, and well seated to possibly be the next President of the United States."

"This first of three debates will either bring out the best or the worst of Sam Waters. As we saw in 1992, it is so easy to be a forerunner, but a few misspoken words and phrases can completely crush a candidate and destroy any hope of a win. Waters is facing two men who are seasoned politicians and they will be looking to trip the newcomer up any way they can. If they can find the weakness in his armor, you can bet they will exploit it on every issue. Waters must remain calm and collected and not let the others ruffle his feathers or he will lose. This debate will bring out the true Sam Waters and next week's Vice-Presidential debate will tell the tale of the former JAG Marine Mike Baker.

"Stan, this has to be the most watched debate in history. Sam Waters has roughly forty million followers and many more globally. If he wins the election, it could easily send shock waves around the world.

"That is so true. Countries which have been historically run by a couple of groups may now find an independent group coming forward to challenge the norm. Now, let's go down to the floor and Bridgette Collins."

"Thank you, Stan. Good evening America and welcome to the first Presidential Debate of 2024. I'm Bridgette Collins and I will be your moderator this evening. The Presidential debates are drafted by the Commission on Presidential Debates, a non-profit and nonpartisan organization. The candidates have been advised of and have agreed on the rules. I have chosen the questions and those questions have been sealed. No party or person has been allowed access to the questions. The debate is in six segments, I will read the question and each candidate will have two minutes to respond after which we will enter general discussion on the issue of the question.

We ask that you hold your applause throughout the debate to be respectful of those wishing to hear from the all of the candidates.

Ladies and Gentlemen, our candidates for President of the United States. Senator Dwayne Johnson, Congressman Neil Grainger, and Mister Sam Waters."

The three men walk onto the stage amid cheers from the audience. They shake hands and Johnson and Grainger proceed directly to their podiums. Sam approaches Bridgette and thanks her for the introduction then turns to his podium.

"Thank you, Mister Waters. Gentlemen, your first question -- what is your feeling on the issue of abortion?"

Sam's whole entourage of family and friends visibly cringed as Bridgette finished the question.

"Mister Waters, you won the coin toss, so you get to answer first."

"Thank you, Bridgette. Ladies and Gentlemen, I am going to answer this question as well as another which may come up tonight or might come up at some other point in these debates or the debate of my running mate Mister Baker.

"It is my opinion that Government gives too much attention to several questions which should not be addressed by any candidate for any public office.

"We have separated church and state to ensure that one entity doesn't have influence over the other. The separation has been further defined, so schools could not make our children pray.

"We cannot demand a separation of state on some religious issues then demand the State get involved in others. You can't have it both ways. We either have a division of church and state or we don't.

"Abortions and gay marriages are Church Issues, Moral Issues, not State Issues. I do not believe that a government, of, by and for its people has the right to tell those people how to live with their moral convictions. The founders of this country demanded religious freedom. It is in our history and our constitution that we cannot force religious convictions on others. These issues are between the people and their God, they should be able to deal with their religious and moral conscience without the interference of the government.

"If the Government and the Church fail to maintain the separation of church and state, the first place Government will cross the lines of separation will be to make any reference to God politically incorrect because it might offend someone. We have already seen this first step. Government has removed the word God from many monuments, doctrines, and documents because it has become offensive to someone. The next step will be to remove the church's non-profit status and the third will be to tax the church. The taxation of the church has already been circling in social media, and it is only a matter of time before we see more Government intervention in Church affairs."

You could have heard a pin drop in the auditorium. Sam reached for the bottle of water on the podium and looked to gage the reaction of the other candidates. Johnson had a strange smirk on his face like the cat who just ate the canary. Maybe he thought he would finally be able to bury the new comer. Grainger was aghast, staring at Sam with his mouth half open as if wanting to say something, but too shocked to find the words. Bridgette was speechless as well until Tony cued her from the booth.

"Uh, yes. Senator Johnson, your answer"

"Ladies and Gentlemen, I have to disagree with Mr. Waters. I believe the Government has a responsibility to the people of this country to help them in those moral crises. There are those who would be stricken from the house of God without intervention. Abortion is killing a human being and thus should be abolished at all costs. Mr. Waters seems to think God is dead in America, he is not. Enough said. If elected I will fight every day to serve God against the Godless. Thank you."

"Congressman Grainger, your answer please."

"Ladies and gentlemen, both of my fellow candidates make good points. Unfortunately, I cannot agree with either of them. I can't agree with the good and righteous Senator who stands here tonight and preaches faith and God and abortion being the killing of a human being, when just last year the Senator voted fourteen times in favor of extending the funding for planned parenthood and supported abortion legislation.

"I also cannot agree with Mr. Waters, who believes government shouldn't govern. I cannot agree with Mr. Waters' statement about the separation of church and state. We must intertwine the two on occasion to keep good order. He believes we should let the people decide what is right and wrong, but we should tax the churches. When elected I will support anti-abortion legislation and insure this country's moral values are held to the highest standards."

"Senator, Mr. Waters it seems the congressman has thrown down a gauntlet. Would either of you care to respond." Sam motioned for the floor. "Mr. Waters."

"Thank you, Bridgette, ladies and gentlemen. I have never said or believed that our government should not govern, I stated that our Government should not interfere with the moral convictions of the individuals. The question was, what was my stand on abortion? I answered that question. I did not cast stones on the water as Senator Johnson has, claiming that the Government has the right to judge and dictate human religious and moral values. Neither, have I attempted to bypass the question by casting suspicion on my fellow candidates. If you want my opinion, ask. I have no problems answering."

"Mr. Waters if you are so open, why did you not answer the questions on the subject prior to tonight?

"Congressman Grainger. Until tonight I was never asked this question. In fact, until tonight I have not been asked any specific questions on the issues politicians believe are pressing on the public. You, on the other hand have been elected to represent the people. In your twenty some years in the House, what have you done to resolve this issue and keep it from being a primary issue in every election?"

Grainger bypassed Sam's question with another assault. "You say you have not been asked for your stand on the issues. Were you honest when you wouldn't answer the questions of one John Brooks from CNN. Or were you being open when you told Chris Newly from the Denver Post to keep your head up and your mind and ears open and you will get the answer to that question."

"Congressman, John Brooks was rude and disrespectful of me and the press corps. Your own campaign Secret Service Security Detail kept Mr. Brooks from gaining any access to your press briefings. At both of my media raves where Mr. Brooks was present, I answered his questions. The first had to be asked by another correspondent, because Mr. Brooks had packed up and left the conference. The second, I answered at the request of the press corps.

"As for Chris Newly, he didn't ask a question that I did not answer. He asked how my platform of reform was going to work to reform America? Yes, I answered the question by telling him to pay attention and wait for the answer. I talked with him in Denver again last month and asked him if he had the answer to his question. His reply was, and I quote 'ten-fold.'

"Now, sir, if you are finished trying to destroy my character and the character of Senator Johnson, I have some questions for you on the issues. You dodged the question I asked just a minute ago, so, I will ask it again. Can you answer why we see the very same issues in these debates every election? Why, in the twenty some years you, Senator Johnson, and the rest of the career politicians, have failed to resolve these issues? What has Congress done to resolve them? While you are searching for a good politically correct answer, I will answer these questions for you. You have done absolutely nothing! You preach what you will do for the audience which will give you the most votes and secure your office. Then you do nothing.

"So, if we are finished mudslinging, I believe Bridgette has more questions on actual issues for us to debate." Grainger has no response and is again staring at Waters with his mouth half open.

"Thank you, Mr. Waters. Senator Johnson, do you have any further comment on this issue? Is there any further debate on this question?" Neither Grainger or Johnson responded.

"No. We will move on to the next issue. We have been involved in a series of conflicts in the Middle East continuously for the past twenty-three years. What is your view of this conflict and what can we do to resolve the issues in the Middle East? Senator Johnson?" Even though Johnson and Grainger will answer first, the Waters team again visibly cringe at the question, knowing how Sam is likely to respond.

"I believe we have to be fair to our allies in this conflict. The Russians have been aiding the Governments of the Middle East in trying to defeat the radical extremists and we must continue to afford them the opportunity for success. We need to shelter the refugees of this war and provide them safety, comfort, and sanctuary. It is our humanitarian duty to do so. Then we must assist our allies in other countries to defeat the terrorists and their enemies who are hiding in the indigenous population."

Johnson appeared to be totally unprepared to debate the Middle East issue and although he answered the question his answer was very brief and mechanical. He engages in the discussions; however, his points are more personal opinion and innuendo rather that debatable responses. Johnson would keep up this pattern of short apparently unprepared and unrehearsed answers for the entire debate. The earlier smirk on Johnson's face when Sam answered on the abortion issue has turned into a solid scowl and he is showing outward disdain for both Sam and Grainger.

"Congressman Grainger, your remarks."

"We have been dragging our feet on this thing in the Middle East for far too long. We need to bring our servicemen and women home and let the Middle East do what it has done for thousands of years and take care of itself. All those different Arab tribes have been fighting among themselves since the beginning of time. Nothing we do will bring peace to the region, so I say let the chips fall where they may. May the best Arab win. If elected, I pledge to have all our Soldiers, Sailors, Airmen, and Marines out of the Middle East within six months of my taking office. Mr. Waters, I'm really anxious to hear your response to this one."

"Thank you, Congressman. I can appreciate your choice on this issue and would love to see our young men and women safely home, but leaving the extremists unbridled in the Middle East is not the answer. It is true that the Arab nations have been fighting with one another for centuries, however, if we leave them to deal with the extremists we will be telling our Middle Eastern allies that we don't care about them. We can't afford to let the chips as you say fall into the hands of the extremists. Senator Johnson's approach of leaving it to our allies isn't the answer either and I surely do not condone being a sanctuary for the refugees. The European Nations who have been sanctuary for the refugees have opened their doors to terrorists and extremists. That is not an option for the United States.

"Historically, wars have been fought over money, land and power. Radical Extremists do not care about these things. They believe they are the mercenaries and emissaries of their God and dying for their God against their enemies is the greatest of honors. Any organization which believes death is the ultimate sacrifice to be accepted and gain a seat beside God cannot be reasonably dealt with. We have seen this time and time again in the conflicts of this country. The Philippines suicide attacks only ended after a third of the male population was destroyed. The Japanese Kamikaze and Bonsai attacks in World War Two, only ended after the first atomic bombs were dropped killing nearly half a million Japanese. The Korean and Vietnamese soldiers who believed they would find grace and be smiled upon in the afterlife if they died in mortal combat against the American intruders only changed that belief after American forces were evacuated to the sounds of the propaganda machines saying we were defeated and in disgrace. The radical extremists in the Middle East are no different. They believe they must kill the infidels or die trying to be accepted by their god. The difference is that no withdrawal of troops will ensure the cessation of hostilities. No mass destruction of a core element to dissolve the extremist infrastructure will stay their belief that infidels must be cleansed from the earth. Their belief is that we are lesser people and a scourge upon the earth that they must destroy or enslave every one of us.

"There are two ways this conflict can end. They win, with their doctrine and belief that all infidels must become slaves or die: basically, meaning the genocide of the Christian people and all other non-Muslims. Or we, win! Since slavery is not an option for us, in order for us to win we must destroy the evil: meaning the genocide of the radical extremists. This conflict isn't about who has the most money, or the most land or even the most power. It's about survival."

Sam's answer brings the smirk back to Johnson's face and once again leaves the Congressman and Bridgette speechless.

"Ahem," Bridgette clears her throat, "has anyone a comment for discussion?" Johnson motions for the floor. "Senator."

"Mr. Waters do you seriously think genocide is the solution in the Middle East? Do you have no conscious objection to wiping an entire civilization from the face of the earth? What kind of sadist warmonger would want to engage in a war with such a drastic outcome? I have traveled to the Middle East and spoken with our allies who are resolved to put an end to the hostilities just as we are. We must give them the aid and support to continue in routing this evil and bringing peace to the Arab Nations. I almost have to agree with Congressman Grainger to bring our boys and girls home, but believe we must stay to support our allies."

"Senator it isn't sadism, it is realism! It isn't warmongering, and we have been engaged in a war with that drastic outcome for the past twenty-three years. We have been fighting a war of attrition for the past two and a half decades. This has become the longest continuous conflict in our history and we are no closer to resolving the situation than we were twenty-three years ago. The only thing we are able to show for our time in the Middle East is the arrest of Hussain, the killing of Bin Laden and the tragic loss of thousands of American lives both on and off the battlefield. The radical extremists in the Middle East are still a threat and their numbers are growing. They have no problem building a following because Congress and the Senate place restrictions which bind the hands of our military and which embolden our enemies. The bolder our enemies become, the more aggressive they become, and the more lives are lost. As I stated, extremists do not value anything – not money, not land, not power nor human life. They value only one thing and that is the honor of dying in the name of their God against their enemies. You cannot negotiate with them, because there are no bargaining chips. No matter what you offer, it has no value in comparison to being able to sit next to god. There is nothing they want other than the genocide or slavery of the infidels and any others who oppose their belief. The only way to survive is to act – swiftly, ferociously and permanently."

"Mr. Waters, you obviously do not have the tact or political savvy to have viable international relations. You say we cannot negotiate with the extremists yet we have managed through negotiations to keep them contained for the last sixteen years."

"Congressman, if the negotiations you refer to – is negotiating with threats of retaliation, or the belief that there is strength through superior fire power – then, yes, your negotiations are working. If keeping seventy-thousand U.S. Troops on the ground in the Middle East to contain the extremist's expansion is the negotiations that you consider managing to keep the extremists contained. Then you have a very twisted definition of negotiations and management. We have yet to contain the Extremists. What you refuse to see is the infiltration of extremists into all of the countries who accept refugees including the United States. What you refuse to see is the aggression and destruction those infiltrating extremists are bringing with them. It's time to wake up and smell the coffee rather than the crap you're shoveling on top of the American people."

After a long pause Bridgette proceeds to the next item on the agenda.

"Okay, is there any further debate on this issue?" No one answers.

"Next question. We have had some good years of recovery, but the national debt and deficit are still in the trillions. How do you propose to resolve this issue? Congressman Grainger."

“Thank you, Bridgette. I am going to defer my first answer option to Mr. Waters and I will follow the good Senator.”

“Very well, Mr. Waters, same question.”

“Thank you, Bridgette, and thank you Congressman. This country is upside down in its debts because of its deficit. That sounds like a stupid answer, but that has been our Government’s answer for years -- of course the debts are upside down because of the deficit. So, what has been the solution so far? According to Congress, it’s easy to fix! We cut funding for this program or that program and order the mints to produce more money. We stop paying for aid to other countries until they start to pay their fair share. We drop out of international programs where the United States is paying the lion’s share while the other member nations sit back and get fat on our money.

“Those all work to reduce the deficit, which is a shortfall in the amount of money available in relationship to the amount of money paid out. So, if we aren’t paying out vast sums of money into these programs it reduces the deficit. This is a good thing, but it doesn’t solve the problem of how we pay off the nation’s debts. Our debts, or what we owe to other countries is different than the deficit although the deficit creates many debts. Apparently, the definitions confuse some of the people in the House of Representatives who are responsible for monitoring and deciding where money should be disbursed. The deficit is, as I stated, a shortage in the amount of money available to the money paid out. We are offering payment of more money than we have. We are, in essence, borrowing the difference thereby creating a debt.

“Here’s an example, we buy a thousand dollars of some commodity from say Japan, but we only have five-hundred dollars in the treasury. This is the deficit. Japan agrees to let us have a line of credit for the other five-hundred dollars. Now, we have a debt.

“We have shipped most of our industry and business out of the country until we no longer have a gross national product. We no longer produce anything in America that we can sell overseas. Many of the larger corporations, <u>our companies</u>, make their products in some other country and then import them back into the U.S.

“We have to start making money from something other than taxation of the people, because there aren’t enough working-class people to pay off our debt by themselves. Government can only tax us so far to pay the debts before we have nothing of value left to tax.

"What must happen in order to pay our debt and get the country back on its feet? What does our Government need to do to in order to pay off its debts and rebuild the country? If our Government can continually bailout banks, insurance companies and corporations when they have financial problems, why doesn't it bailout the innovative small companies with financial problems? Why doesn't it support new companies with fresh ideas? Instead, we offer bailouts and support to major corporations which send their production overseas and then make deals with Congress to avoid paying the import taxes when they bring those products back into the U.S. Yes, we continue to support and bailout big business while the small fresh and innovative businesses are forced to close their doors. Why is it, the only time these small businesses get the help they need is when they pay, or promise to pay their representative either directly or through campaign contributions?

"We need to bring money back into this country. We need to stop bailing out corporations, banks and insurance companies and bring industry and the industrial corporations back to this country."

Senator Johnson passes his turn and Bridgette directs the discussion back to Congressman Grainger.

"That's a pretty strong statement, Mr. Waters. Just how do you plan to accomplish bringing industry and corporations back to this country. We have tried several different tariff tax approaches to force companies back into the country. However, when labor is so cheap in the countries they moved to, they can pay the taxation from what they save on labor. We tried to give them tax breaks and other incentives and they still prefer the foreign countries. What magic wand do you have which will change corporate thinking? What idealistic incentive do you propose, which will get industry to change their corporate spots, to stop focusing on profit over the good of the country or the people in the United States?"

"Presently, we don't charge any import or export taxes to companies which have headquarters in the United States. I'm not going to suggest imposing an export tax on our companies. Here's what I do propose. I propose a tax on imports for any product which comes into this country from any foreign country. Even if it is manufactured for a U.S. based company, an import tax of ten percent of the products' retail value will be applied. In addition, every company with a net income of over one million will pay a revenue tax of ten percent of their gross profit each year. Ten percent of the import tax and the income tax payments will be distributed to those small businesses with a gross income less than one million to help them grow and build our economy. We will help them grow into larger corporations and businesses who eventually pay their share to help the next generation of businesses. The other ninety percent will be used to pay off our debts and only after the debts are paid and we are solvent as a country again will we consider the use of corporate taxes for other programs. There are no loopholes if the big corporations can't live with that, then move your headquarters to one of the countries that manufacture your products and we will impose an import tax of twenty-five percent of the products' retail value on the products you import into the United States."

Again, the silence on the stage and in the auditorium, was deafening. Now, both Johnson and Grainger have Cheshire Cat grins, thinking Sam has just destroyed his chances of winning industrial and corporate America.

"Gentlemen, our time is up. I want to thank the candidates for this evening's Presidential debate. Although we did not finish the entire six segments we did focus on Abortion, the Middle East Conflict and the National debt with some very different ideas being voiced by the Independent Mr. Waters. Again, I thank the candidates for an interesting evening. I'm Bridgette Collins, MSNBC news. Now to Tony and Stan for closing comments."

"Stan, I really can't begin to explain what just happened here. Waters opened the debate with a statement which can only be defined as suicidal with the religious groups and their convictions about abortion and gay marriage. I must agree with his statement, but I can't believe that we just heard a candidate for President actually come out and dismiss those issues as not keeping with the separation of church and state. Waters has some intestinal fortitude."

"Right, Tony, then he follows that dismissal by shutting down Grainger's assault on Johnson and himself by asking the million-dollar question – what have the career politicians in the House and Senate done in the past twenty years to resolve this issue?

"He blows the doors off of the debate and left both the Republican and Democrat candidates flat-footed and speechless when he came out on the Middle East issue talking about genocide and survival in relationship to radical extremists and terrorists. I'm not sure what to think about his answer to this one but he made some very positive assertions about how to handle the extremists."

"That's very true, Stan. I don't know if Waters was trying to end his campaign right here or if he is really as smart and tough on the issues as he appeared.

"Waters nailed the coffin shut on both Grainger and Johnson when he completely shut down both candidates with his plan to bring money and industry back to this country, which I must say was absolutely brilliant."

"Tony, Grainger has to be seriously beating himself up for allowing Waters to make his statement out of turn and Johnson even more so for passing on the subject completely.

"There was no way any other candidate in this election could have been prepared for Waters. He has given absolutely no ammunition, made no earlier statements of his views on the issues and, as he stated tonight, he has not been directly asked a single question by any reporter on the issues presented tonight. Overall, I would put him ahead, simply because he completely controlled the debate."

"Stan, I have to agree. I've never seen a candidate with the poise and directness of Waters. He was absolutely flawless. He masterfully executed his answers like an artist painting a detailed picture completely dominating the canvas of his opponents. Early polls indicate the viewers agree Waters took this one. It will be very interesting to see how Baker handles next week's Vice-Presidential debate. I'm sure the candidates will be much better prepared for Baker than they were for Waters here tonight. For MSNBC, this is Tony Cross and Stan Blackwell, at Ames Hall on George Washington University's Mount Vernon Campus, good night."

***

During the next week, the news media had varying reports on increases in Sam's ranking in the polls. CNN gave him a three percent increase, Fox showed seven percent and NBC showed ten percent.

Although, Sam's opening comment on abortion during the debate had very little effect, one way or the other, on his poll percentage through the Bible Belt, it gained him several points among the alternative LGBT lifestyle community. He had established himself with the military prior to the debate and strengthened that position with his statements on the Middle East. Big business joined in his support looking at the savings of almost twenty percent in their taxes. Small business also jumped on the Waters band wagon seeing the possibility of new government money for growth.

Sam had pulled the trigger and in a big way. The night before the Vice-Presidential debate, Sam had gained ten percent and was standing at thirty-eight percent across the board in the polls.

18
TURNING UP THE HEAT

On Tuesday, the third of October, the Vice-Presidential Debate was getting ready to start and Mike Baker was ready. He was in the greenroom making slightly sarcastic comments about his opponents.

"Mike, these guys are going to be a lot readier for you than they were for me last week. Stay on your game and keep the pressure on them. If they spout BS call them on it. Acknowledge the facts they get right and respect those, but don't give them the benefit of the doubt where they aren't crystal clear. We should continue to show the American public who these politicians really are and who they really represent. Go kick some ass Devil Dog.

"You got it, Sam. I'll just do what I've been doing and following your lead."

"Good luck, Mike."

"Thanks."

Sam finished his pep talk as the reporters began to give their opening comments for the debate.

"Good Evening, Ladies and Gentlemen. I'm John Thomas and I'm here with Tan Nguyen in the Moby Arena of Colorado State University, where tonight, Fox News has the pleasure of moderating the Vice-Presidential debate. Once again, there will be three candidates on stage. Democrat James Hurly, Republican Sandy Bishop and, of course, the Independent candidate Michael Baker.

"Tan, this has been an unbelievable campaign for Waters and Baker, the dynamic duo from Buffalo, Wyoming. They have beat the odds and are on the ballot in forty-seven states. Waters, came out strong and kept the pressure on Johnson and Grainger totally dominating the first of the debates last week. What do you think Baker will do tonight to keep up the momentum that Waters generated?"

"John, these guys have been a complete mystery and a continual string of surprises; from Waters writing his letter to the editor of the Buffalo newspaper four years ago, to the total domination of last week's debate. Waters and Baker have been on top of their game and on top of this campaign. Waters has a playbook no one has been able to copy and has become a household word, a legend virtually over-night since he announced his candidacy. I would really hate to try and predict what Baker may do tonight. There have been times in this campaign where I seriously thought Baker was doubling as the campaign manager. At others, it was clear that Waters held the reins. I don't think I've ever seen two running mates who were so connected."

"Tan, I can't agree with you more. Not only have they been full of mystery and surprises, but Waters has run what could be the least expensive candidacy since the days of Kennedy and Nixon, spending less than one-tenth the amount spent by any other candidate in this race including the independent party candidates. He has challenged a system which has never favored a third party let alone a lone independent candidate with absolutely no party ties. Tonight, with only five weeks left until the election, Waters is leading in the polls with thirty-eight percent of the vote. A two percent lead over Congressman Grainger, who last week was ten percent above Waters and Johnson."

"Grainger isn't out of the chase yet, John. Although, Waters jumped ten percent this week, Grainger didn't really lose anything and is still sitting at thirty-six percent -- just two points behind and close enough to eliminate Waters in the electoral vote. Senator Johnson, with only twenty percent of the polls, is pretty much out of the race; but, unlike the Green and Tea parties, the DNC won't admit defeat until the last vote is counted and possibly recounted several times."

"Very true. Most of the jump in Waters' poll numbers came in the form of another surprising turn in this campaign. Both the Green and Tea parties have withdrawn from the race and pledged their support to Waters. The Libertarian and Socialist parties have congratulated Waters on the debate last week and it seems possible they will also withdraw and pledge to support Waters. That could possibly give Waters another six percent. An eight-point gap would certainly be a little more difficult for Grainger to overcome with a little over five weeks left until the election. With Johnson's refusal to drop out and Grainger's popularity, we could very easily see a split in the electoral vote which would cause the election to be decided by the House of Representatives. That may be what

Grainger is hoping for, knowing he would be able to sweep a House vote.

"It will be interesting to see what happens in the next five weeks and extremely interesting to see the continuing saga of Waters and Baker, tonight. Let's go down to the stage where Sherman Knight is ready to kick off tonight's debate. Sherman!"

"Thank you, John, Good Evening, America, and welcome to the Vice-Presidential Debate of 2024. I'm Sherman Knight and I will be your moderator this evening. The Presidential and Vice-Presidential debates are drafted by the Commission on Presidential Debates, a nonprofit and nonpartisan organization. The candidates have been advised of and have agreed on the rules for this debate. I have chosen the questions and those questions have been sealed. No party or person has been allowed access to the questions. The debate will be in six segments. I will read the question and each candidate will have two minutes to respond after which they will enter into a general discussion on the issues of the question. We ask that you hold your applause throughout the debate to be respectful of those wishing to hear from all candidates.

Ladies and Gentlemen, our candidates for Vice-President of the United States: Governor James Hurly, Congresswoman Sandy Bishop and the Independent candidate Mr. Michael Baker."

The three candidates walked onto the stage and shook hands. All three candidates approached and shook hands with Knight and thanked him for the introductions. They then took their respective seats around the large table.

"Congresswoman Bishop, you won the coin toss backstage, so you will answer first on this question. For over forty years climate and global warming have been major issues for the candidates. We have been in and out of international commissions and treaties and are no closer to solving this issue today than we were so many years ago. What is your position on the climate issue and where do you intend to take the United States."

This is the only issue Sam and Mike had been asked about directly and Mike had answered the question with a question and put the issue to rest. Sam's entourage wondered how much ammunition they had given up in Mike's statement and how it would affect them tonight.

"Thank you, Sherman. Good Evening, fellow Americans. Global warming and climate issues have plagued us for far too long. There are scientists on both sides of the issue who will agree with whoever is paying the most for their opinion. The lobbyists and special interest groups would have us believe all the gloom and doom hype and have made predictions time and again which have never come to fruition nor been backed by scientific evidence. Each year the climate control groups lobby Congress for more money for research while petitioning for regulations and stricter guidelines for American industry. America cannot afford to keep throwing good money after bad to support a global warming posture which takes jobs from the people and starves families in favor of clean air and renewable energy. Congressman Grainger and I agree that the issue of global warming and climate control isn't an issue we need to be concerned about. We need to re-evaluate the regulations which restrict fossil fuels and get America working again."

"Thank you, Ms. Bishop. Governor Hurly same question."

"Thank you, Sherman. Good Evening Ladies and Gentlemen. The truth about global warming and our climate issues is the fact that too many people take the warnings for granted. We must protect our planet. We must do what we can to eliminate fossil fuels by creating an environment safe from dangerous emissions from industry and automobiles and increase our renewable energy resources. The gloom and doom, as Ms. Bishop stated, are not hype but a real threat. Mr. Baker has brushed aside the warnings and made light of it in a media rave several months age, where he asked the press if climate issues were of any major concern to them. Of course, the reporters said no – they only want news. Senator Johnson and I have spent many hours discussing the best ways to approach this issue and propose to eliminate all fossil fuel use by 2026 and increase our usage of renewable water, wind, and solar resources by two-hundred percent by that date. Thank you."

"Mr. Baker, same question"

"Thank you, Sherman. Good Evening, Ladies and Gentlemen. As Sherman stated when he opened this question, the issue of global warming and climate change has been going back and forth for more than four decades and we are no closer to an answer today than we were forty years ago. For every scientist who tells us there is a problem, there is one who tells us there isn't. As

Congresswoman Bishop pointed out, on the issue of climate change, science is for sale to the highest bidder.

"Mr. Waters and I have not discussed this issue as often as our esteemed opponents; however, the one time we did discuss this issue we decided to put an end to it. Until science can come together and give us definitive proof that there is an issue, we will no longer play the game and will no longer use the taxpayer's money to financially support any further research or debate on this issue. Mr. Waters and I are not saying there isn't an issue or that we don't need to protect our planet for future generations; what we are saying is give us something more than the divided and conflicting science of the past forty years. We need to further the development of our renewable energy resources if for no other reason than it makes good sense.

"To put a moratorium on fossil fuels as Governor Hurly suggests is ludicrous. Government has been trying to eliminate fossil fuel use for longer than the climate debate has been going on and the world is still reliant on those fuels. Why? Because we haven't yet developed a viable alternative. Until we have a viable replacement, until we can light and heat our homes, run our automobiles and trucks, and cook our food without using sources of energy which come from fossil fuels, we cannot eliminate the use of those fuels. Thank you."

Sherman opens the subject for discussion.

"Ms. Bishop, would you like to respond to either of your opponents?"

"Yes, thank you, Sherman. Mr. Hurly, do you truly believe the world can simply eliminate fossil fuel use in only two years? We haven't been able to reduce its use even significantly in decades. We've been developing wind power and have wasted hundreds of thousands of dollars and acres producing massive wind farms which are only capable of producing thirty to forty percent of our electricity. Even more valuable farmland acreage has been wasted with large solar collector arrays. Those acres cannot be farmed, and the solar farms only produce fifteen percent of our electricity. If we continue to expand these vast wastes of farmland, we will eventually have no place to grow the food required to feed the people. At least Waters and Baker understand this is a waste of time and money."

Mike signaled for the floor and Sherman acknowledged

"Ms. Bishop, I neither said or implied renewable energy is a waste of time and money. If elected Mr. Waters and I will continue to fund research into renewable energy. If science can unite in a single position on climate change, we will also consider funding research. We need to continue to achieve a higher standard of product – one which will not use or destroy large acreages which could and should be reserved for food production."

"Ms. Bishop and Mr. Baker, you are both very misguided." Hurly pipes in. "Mr. Baker if you would read the paper or watch TV you would find the proof you are in search of. Science has united and made a computer enhanced model of how much damage we have done to the planet and how that damage is going to affect us in the very near future. Ms. Bishop, you and Congressman Grainger see the statistical evidence of science as hype. You can't see that the writing is on the wall. We need to make changes, or we won't have a country or world to change. We must act now, which is why Senator Johnson and I are adamant about ceasing our reliance on fossil fuels once and for all within two years. It can be done, we just have to force industries' hand and make it happen. You gave statistics about the percentage of energy being produced by the wind farms. The Senator and I have seen many of those farms in our travels around the country. I have several in my own home State of Iowa. We have counted in the immense number of wind turbines and the relative few which are actually turning. If we turn them all on and open them up, we would have a greater source of energy than any other imaginable."

Mike again takes the floor

"Mr. Hurly, it is you who appears blind and misguided. The media: TV, radio, newspapers, and criers on the street are in the business of making money from the news. They will support whichever side of an argument produces the biggest gain in profits for the company. We need a unified scientific front of all the world's scientists. We won't ask the media, we won't search the web, we want to hear one of these comments from the horse's mouth: Yes, there is or No, there isn't a problem.

"When you and the Senator were traveling through those wind farms, did you happen to stop and ask any of the project engineers, why they weren't spinning? My guess is the answer to that question is no. Mr. Waters and I did stop and ask. There are several reasons those turbines aren't running. Some are down for maintenance, others are stopped for safety reasons due to wind conditions. But the biggest reason is that there is no place for the electricity to go. No one is using the excess energy.

"Here's where you fail in your promise to cease the use of fossil fuels. You and Senator Johnson will spend the next two years trying to get Congress and the Senate to agree on the wording of a bill to cease the usage of fossil fuels. You will not have support from any state which relies on oil production for a large percentage of their revenue. You are left with approximately twenty states and those forty Senators won't carry the vote on your bill. You lose the ability to carry out your promise of no fossil fuel use. You won't get your bill passed in the House for the same reason. There isn't a state west of the Mississippi, including California, which doesn't rely on the production of fossil fuels for a large portion of its revenue. There are many states east of the Mississippi as well who rely on those fossil fuel dollars. You are finished before you begin.

"Ms. Bishop, you and Congressman Grainger are also blind to the facts. You cannot ignore the issue and hope it will go away. It hasn't faded away in the past forty years and it won't in the next four. We need to develop renewable energy in order to sustain life as we know it. Our natural resources in the fossil fuel arena are limited and we've been sucking them dry for well over one-hundred-fifty years. They will eventually run out though, probably not in any of our life-times. We need a good renewable energy alternative, but we haven't found one yet. There are plenty of young innovative companies that have brilliant ideas and could use a little bit of the Government's support, but won't find that support from a government which swings like a pendulum on the issues."

"Thank you for your responses, however, it is time to move on to the next question. Mr. Hurly, there has been a lot of discussion lately about Social Security and welfare reform. What is your opinion on this topic? What do you think can be done to improve Social Security?"

"Thank you, Sherman. Social Security is just fine the way it is. It has helped the aged for the last ninety years and it will continue to do so for the next hundred years. We do need to reform Welfare. This program has needed reform for a long time. We need to do more for our indigent people, better subsidies to take the burden of utilities and rent off those who can't afford them. We need to improve the impoverished housing and provide food and daycare for children before and after school and free public transportation. We need to take care of those children as they grow by providing free public education until they graduate college. If elected, Senator Johnson and I will work to ensure this reform happens in welfare."

"Mr. Baker, your statement."

"Mr. Hurly is absolutely correct in his opening statement that welfare needs reform. However, that is the only part of his statement that bears anything closely resembling reality.

"Social Security and welfare have been broken since the conception of the act in 1935. The plan for the Social Security Act was to have a mandatory retirement investment so the retired persons would have some type of income in their elder years. That was a good idea and it does benefit a lot of people as they achieve that elusive goal of reaching retirement age.

"However, to get approval of the Act by the House and Senate, it had to have certain stipulations. Certain allowances for those who found themselves temporarily unemployed, and I will stress - temporarily unemployed. A welfare fund for those who were looking for work during the great depression was another good idea since most of the welfare would go to people who had or would pay into FICA at some point. It was intended as a temporary benefit, NOT a lifestyle."

"Come on now, Mr. Baker. Social Security isn't broke. There's money there for the elderly. The public continues to pay into FICA and Medicare, so the account will continue to grow."

"Mr. Hurly, I respected you in your opening statement. I did not interrupt you as you told the audience how you plan to take even more money from those who work to support those who don't. Please, do not interrupt me again!

"I didn't say Social Security was broke, I said it was broken. The first recipients of Social Security began collecting benefits without ever having contributed to the plan. This put a burden on the act for money that had not yet been collected. The first Social Security retiree, we will call him Mr. Jones, retired one day after Social Security started collecting FICA and had contributed a total of five cents. His lump sum check from Social Security was seventeen cents, a difference of twelve cents. This wasn't a huge amount until you calculate how many other Mr. Jones' there might be. Who paid the other twelve cents? Where did that money come from? Three years later, a woman, Mrs. Jones, retired at age sixty and opted to draw the monthly benefit. During her three years of working and contributing to FICA, her total contribution was twenty-four dollars and seventy-five cents. Her monthly benefit amount was twenty-two dollars and fifty-five cents. She lived to be one-hundred years old and collected over twenty-two-thousand-eight-hundred-eighty-eight dollars in Social Security benefits. Again, I ask, where did that money come from? How many more Mr. and Mrs. Jones' were there?

"The Social Security Act was further hindered by the fact that it was passed and signed into law in the middle of the Great Depression when most of the country was out of work and many people used the new Social Security/Welfare Act to support their families. Since there had been limited contributions to FICA the whole Social Security/Welfare program started in deficit with Congress using the Federal Budget Omnibus to borrow money from other agencies to keep Social Security and welfare working until the people could get through the depression and back to work.

"Congress still uses the budget to keep Social Security funded in addition to raising the age of retirement when it looks like they might have to take money out of the Congressional pay coffers. When I was growing up my father gave me a definition of retirement. He said when people live to be sixty years old they could stop working and live off the pension they received from working and the Social Security fund they paid into. Of course, since the program was broken, Congress had to break down the benefit, so it would be less if you retired at sixty but more if you kept working until sixty-two. The elderly became slaves to the system -- having to work increasingly longer to receive the benefit of all those years paying into FICA. Then the goal of retirement moved even further away. A person had to work until age sixty-five to reap their full benefit. Then sixty-six. It is high time Social Security became its own act without welfare or any other encumbrances. With its own account, untouchable by members of Congress or the Senate, and closely monitored by any number of the support groups for the elderly – it could grow enough to support many generations. It is also high time elderly citizens were freed from the chains of a government which cares little about them.

"Welfare, should fall under the labor laws for unemployment and Workman's Compensation and be held to the same standards and limitations that we put on unemployment. Entitlements are only for eighteen months and you must be looking for work. No Exceptions! No Extensions."

"Ms. Bishop your comments"

"Thank you. I cannot agree with either of my opponents. Mr. Hurly clearly holds the belief that Social Security is fine, and Welfare needs to be enhanced, while Mr. Baker sounds like he and Mr. Waters want to scrap the whole system and start over.

"My closest support would be for Mr. Baker, however his eighteen-month limitation plan, with no exceptions does not allow for those who find work with meager wages who need support while they look for a better opportunity. The plan Congressman Grainger and I have for Social Security is simply this - we balance Social Security by raising the contribution by two and a half percent per pay period, give those who are already drawing Social Security a five percent raise. It will be the largest raise in benefits in the last two decades.

"For welfare, we will raise welfare entitlements by two and a half percent for those single persons on welfare and five percent for those with children."

"The question is now open for discussion. Mr. Hurly, would you care to start?"

"Thank you, Sherman. It seems both of my opponents are unaware that we, as a nation, take very good care of our seniors, but our inner cities need a dedicated effort on the part of the Government to help support those who cannot work. Thank you."

"Cannot work is the whole point Mr. Hurly. How do you plan to differentiate between those who cannot work and those who simply refuse to work?" Baker asked as he saw an opportunity to jump into the discussion.

"Mr. Baker, in the inner cities, there is no need for that distinction. Those poor people have no jobs and there are no businesses or industries coming into those communities to help them out."

"Why are businesses and industries, or even government, needed to help in the inner cities? Government has helped the inner cities for the past ninety years since the creation of welfare and they are worse off today than ever before.

"I used to have a bird feeder in my backyard. Every day, I would go out and fill the feeder with fresh millet. The birds loved me and that feeder because they no longer had to look for food or do the work required to feed themselves and their young. Pretty soon I noticed there was bird crap everywhere. I noticed the birds would get extremely agitated and noisy when the feeders started to get low, even though there was still a lot of food in the feeder. The birds even began attacking me and my family. One day, I removed the feeder, cleaned up all the bird droppings and went about my life. The birds went back to looking and working for the food they needed.

"In the guise of helping our indigent, we have crippled them and their communities. Like the bird feeder, we have given these indigent free food, utilities, rent and money, taking away the willingness to work and provide for themselves. Why should they work when the government gives them anything they want? If they make enough noise the Government gives them more. Government has created a society, a subculture, of slaves. The sad part is the people don't even know they're slaves. They are pawns on a chessboard awaiting their turn to be sacrificed. They are the cannon fodder for the next great war or civil war. Whole communities of people are so dependent on government welfare they won't stand up against the very thing that is keeping them from a better life. It is time to break the chains and give the inner cities some real help to start feeling some pride in themselves and getting them back on their feet. It's time to take away the bird feeder."

Congresswoman Bishop took the floor.

"The only way we can help is to increase the FICA and Medicare and boost retirement and welfare. We still need to help the inner cities, but the only way to do that is through the Grainger Plan."

Mike addresses Bishop's comment.

"Ms. Bishop, the Grainger plan has some serious flaws that anyone with a basic understanding of math can point out. You plan a two and a half percent increase in FICA and Medicare taxes on those individuals who are still working, so you can give a six percent increase to those who aren't. How does this fix the problem? Your plan puts the whole system further in the hole than it already is while adding more taxes to the already burdened working people."

"Mr. Baker, I don't know where you got those numbers. Congressman Grainger's plan has been tested in the best computer scenarios and will work to bring Social Security and Welfare into a very effective system."

"Ms. Bishop, I got my numbers from you. Did you not state in your opening remarks that your plan would increase FICA and Medicare taxes by two and a half percent?"

"Yes, that's true two and a half percent per pay period."

"Excuse me, you are raising FICA and Medicare five percent per month. Does that figure include the employer contribution?"

"No, it doesn't. It is a two and a half percent per pay period increase to both contributors."

"Okay, I stand corrected. How much will your plan increase Social Security and welfare?"

"Five percent to Social Security and two and a half percent to single welfare recipients and five percent to those with children."

"I rest my case. You are increasing FICA and Medicare taxes by ten percent per month on the people and businesses who are working. You are giving five percent to those on Social Security, so you have five percent left. Then you are giving five percent to welfare recipients with children and two and a half percent to single persons. You have just given away twelve and a half percent while only collecting ten percent. Where are you going to get the other two and a half percent? You want to increase taxes to not only keep a broken program broken, but break it even further. Thank you, Ms. Bishop and Congressman Grainger, it really isn't any wonder the country is in the state it's in with Congress people like you in control of government finance and spending."

Sherman took control of the floor and thanked the candidates and the audience. He then summarized the debates' points and transferred control to John and Tan in the booth for closing comments.

"Tan, Baker kept up the pressure that Waters put on the candidates last week and continued to turn up the heat on the Party Candidates as he, like Waters, once again took command of the debate and successfully shut down the other two candidates. He found the flaws in their programs and shot holes in them for everyone to see. Truly amazing."

"Yes, John. It's hard to believe these two unknown candidates from the least populated state in the United States can come into the debates against seasoned politicians and totally dominate them. Baker, like Waters, came into this debate with guns blazing. From the first question on global warming, Baker had Hurly and Bishop on the ropes. Then on the Social Security issue, Baker very pointedly told Hurly to 'not interrupt' him again. He completely shut Hurly down and Hurly was apprehensive for the rest of the debate. I don't think the Governor from Iowa was expecting to be admonished for being rude on national television."

"Tan, the look in Baker's eyes and tone of his voice when he told Hurly not to interrupt him, had me frightened up here in the booth. I can only imagine what Hurly was thinking. But then with a whole softer side Baker tells that story about the bird feeder. Where did that come from?"

"I have no idea John, but it was quite the analogy of the welfare system we have today. Between the bird feeder story and the point that the elderly are slaves to a Social Security system that changes the rules at the whims of Government -- Baker made some very clear points. Then he followed that up by shooting holes in the Grainger and Bishop plan for Social Security. I have to give Waters and Baker another win."

"I have to agree, Tan. Two down and two to go for the Waters camp. Can the duo gain enough to carry the electoral college in five weeks?"

"They're definitely putting on a show, but they must win the electoral vote. If the Electoral vote is split, it will be up to the House of Representatives to choose the president. Even if Waters has the popular vote, I can't imagine the House going with the independents. From Fox News, I'm Tan Nguyen."

"and I'm John Thomas, from Moby Arena of Colorado State University. Good night."

***

Sam succeeded in dominating the next debate even though Johnson and Grainger had come far better prepared than they had been in the first debate. Johnson continued the attempt to make Waters look like a sadistic warmonger with no religious morals and Grainger attacked him on every issue attempting to poke holes in Sam's platform and stand on the issues. Both Johnson and Grainger found themselves on the defensive within minutes and regardless of how they tried to make a comeback, they were unable to break the calm surface of Sam Waters.

The final debate was decidedly very close. Johnson and Grainger stuck to the issues and were well prepared. It seemed the candidates took their cue from Sam and were attempting to be more respectful of each other. The commentators again gave the debate to Sam, but admitted it could have gone to any of the three candidates.

Sam and Mike, with the aid of Jerry, Bill and all their wives, had prepared well for the debates and the poll numbers showed the approval across the country. Sam was at fifty-four percent in the polls after the last debate. Sam's brothers, Jim and Mike, walked into the California and New York election commissions and demanded that Sam be put on the ballot since he had not only met the petition requirements long before the deadline, but now had his fifty percent share in the polls. California capitulated. New York and Hawaii followed the next day. Sam was on the ballot in all fifty states two weeks before the election.

19
ELECTION NIGHT

It was the big night for Sam and Mike. Their campaign had gone much better than anyone expected, culminating with a very successful series of debates. They are at fifty-eight percent in the polls, but would they have enough support to carry the electoral? They would have the answer to that question in about six hours.

Sam and Mike with their families and Jerry with Megan and the rest of the campaign entourage were sitting in the greenroom of the Denver Convention center watching the election results come in. Sam had chosen to rent the Denver location for the election night rally for many reasons, the least of which was having enough room to accommodate the vast number of supporters and followers who have traveled from all over the country. There were even some international travelers, who joined the crowd to cheer Sam and Mike to victory.

Jerry and Bill were assigned to cover the candidates from the beginning of the campaign and were completing that assignment tonight. Bill was on the convention center floor interviewing supporters and some of the more notable guests. Jerry was in the greenroom with Sam, Mike, and their families.

"Sam, I'm not sure who is more nervous about tonight. Mike and I are about to jump out of our skin while you look like a duck on water just as calm as can be. Just tell me you are paddling like the devil to stay afloat in all of this activity."

"Heck, Jerry who wouldn't be a ball of nerves on a night like this? We have been chasing the brass ring on this merry-go-round for over three years and it looks like we might catch it tonight." Kate took up Sam's defense.

"Right now, I'm not nervous at all," Sam counters. "We have come a long way and made some huge strides for future independent candidates along the way. We have proven to the people that they don't need to be slaves to the system if they make their voices heard and they can have a voice in the election process.

"If the polls are accurate no one will have the two-hundred-seventy electoral votes needed to win the electoral. Even if we have the popular vote, the House of Representatives will be responsible for deciding a winner. The House will pick Representative Grainger, one of their own and one of the 'Good Ole Boys,' to be the President. The House can't or won't oppose the parties or the moneymen who keep them in office.

"I will sit here and watch as the numbers stay even until the votes are in from Hawaii. I will give my sorry, I tried and failed speeches. Everyone will be sad when they leave tomorrow to return home. In six months, I will be just another also ran that no one will remember in a year. And maybe, in another forty years, another independent will research what we did and could have done better. Then maybe they will win."

"Wow, Sam, where did that come from? Aren't you the one who told me that lose is not in the Marine vocabulary? We win, and we will win this thing. There certainly were doubts about a person running independent of any party, but you did it. Everyone had doubts about us making it to the debates, but we did, and we kicked ass! Now here we are on the second Tuesday of November, waiting to hear every press reporter in the world say Sam Waters has won! Sam Waters is the new President of the United States of America!"

"Okay, okay. Thanks for the shot of optimism, Mike. Yes, we have had a great couple of years and lose, still isn't in my vocabulary. We have won many battles in this campaign and have set the bar higher than any candidate in the last century, but we aren't the ones who will select the winner here. If people truly want change, then the American people must continue to walk the walk and vote. So far, a good many people have given up the party line and shown us their support, but tonight, will tell the tale of how far they will go. Are they really willing to dump the party lines and actually vote or will they simply step into the booth and hit the button that votes 'ALL' for whichever party they choose."

"Gentlemen, NBC is telling me that the numbers are starting to come in from the East coast precincts." Sam, Mike, and Jerry turn to the television monitors, scattered around the greenroom, as the technical staff turns them on.

"Good Evening America. I'm Tony Cross and I'm here with Stan Blackwell to host the 2024 election night coverage. Stan, what a rollercoaster ride, this campaign has been. The two top party candidates, Johnson and Grainger, vying for position early on. Clearly winning their party's nomination and virtually tied in the polling at the forty-five percent mark. Then the Independent, Sam Waters, comes from out of nowhere to chip and chisel away at the Democrat and Republican parties. Who would have imagined these two guys from Northern Wyoming would emerge as major contenders in tonight's Presidential election?"

"That's right Tony, and what a surprise it was when all of the Independent parties gave up and pledged their support to Waters and Baker. When Waters announced he was running, he made a comment about being the caped crusader and the press dubbed him bat man. I'll tell you, Waters and Baker <u>are</u> a dynamic duo -- climbing the polls like a ladder and completely dominating the debates. I wouldn't be surprised at all if there is an upset in the making. Tonight, anything is possible. Johnson has made a comeback in the polls and is currently at twenty-five percent. Grainger, too, has come up in the polls since the last debate two weeks ago and is currently at forty-two percent. Waters has lost a bit with his silence since the debates. People are wondering if he has the endurance for the long game dealing with the Senate and House of Representatives daily. He may have taken the debates by storm against one member of each house, but how will he fare against the five-hundred-thirty-five members of Congress?"

"Stan, I think Waters has the long game in mind. I think his silence isn't a sign of weakness, but a change of gears. He is putting the campaign behind him and focusing on the White House and putting his respect and reform platform into effect.

"We have some early numbers coming in from precincts in the Northeast. Maine is showing Waters leading with eighteen percent of the vote in. Connecticut, also shows Waters leading with seven percent of the vote. Look at this. In New York Waters is leading by a two to one margin with twenty percent of the vote in. It's remarkable that New York, Grainger's home state, would have Waters this far ahead so early. Pennsylvania, New Hampshire, Massachusetts, New Jersey, Rhode Island, and Vermont all show Waters leading. I know the night is young and we have a long way to go, but if Waters can hang on in New York, Pennsylvania and New Hampshire it will be a big step in the electoral vote."

"Hang onto your hats boys and girls, it is definitely going to be a wild ride tonight."

"Okay, now I'm nervous." Everyone in the greenroom laughed at Sam's comment and they start joking about having a paramedic handy when Sam's victory is announced.

***

"Stan, I hate to say I told you so, but with the East coast polls closed and ninety percent of the vote counted - Waters has made a great showing winning in Maryland, Pennsylvania, North Carolina, Massachusetts, Maine, New Hampshire and so far, he's doing well in the central states."

"Yes, Tony, but he is going to have to work some magic to make up the electoral votes lost to Grainger. Grainger was declared the winner in New York, Florida, New Jersey, Connecticut, Delaware, District of Columbia, Rhode Island and Vermont giving him ninety-two electoral votes to Waters sixty-four."

"We can't dismiss Johnson yet either. He won in Virginia, South Carolina, Tennessee, West Virginia for thirty-eight votes. As I said earlier, Tony, tonight is going to be a wild ride."

***

"With the polls closed in the central and mountain states, Waters has virtually swept the West, winning Texas, Illinois, Ohio, Arizona, Indiana, Colorado, Wyoming, Montana, Nebraska, both Dakotas, New Mexico, Kansas, and Michigan. That gives Waters two-hundred-fifteen electoral votes, he is only fifty-five electoral votes from being the next President."

"Right, Tony, but with only eighty-one electoral votes left. It may be hard for Waters to pull off the win. Even if the candidates receive an equal split, no one can reach the two-seventy mark. California has always been predominantly Democrat and those are the votes Waters will need to win the electoral vote. Congressman Grainger and Senator Johnson are too far away to gain the two-hundred-seventy electoral votes, but if Grainger wins any of the states and Johnson draws California's fifty-five votes, Waters will have to face the vote of the House of Representatives. What a cliffhanger this election has been."

"There is no way you could have said that better, Stan. We have been on the edge of our seats for the last twelve months and tonight we are hanging on with our fingernails. With mere minutes until the polls close in California the race is too close to call. All three candidates are virtually in a tie. Waters must win California to have the electoral win. With eight percent of the vote counted all three candidates are within hundredths of a percentage point. There is only a three hundred vote margin between the leading candidate Johnson and the trailing Grainger and Waters is comfortably right in the middle. All three camps are completely quiet. We have been monitoring the three election headquarters all night and they are more like a morgue than campaign headquarters. Everyone is focused on the television monitors watching the numbers. There have been minor surges of excitement as the candidates win a contested state. Whenever Waters wins a state he and Baker walk out into the convention center and yell to the crowd "We got another one" and the crowd cheers and whistles, but we haven't seen the boisterous activity of the previous election headquarters. Grainger and Johnson are both hoping for a California win which will shut down Waters. Waters needs a California win to keep the House from burning him by choosing Johnson or Grainger. Waters leads the popular vote overall, but if he can't win the electors he will have to sell the House."

"Tony the polls just closed on the coast. The next couple of hours, while we wait for the ballot count, will be the nail biters."

20
WINNERS AND LOSERS

The clock was working, but the hands seemed to barely move as the hours slowly ticked by awaiting the vote count from California, the West Coast, Alaska, and Hawaii. The candidates are each passing the time in their own fashion.

Grainger was in the greenroom of his convention hall in Green Bay, Wisconsin. He had his feet up on the counter and a Cheshire cat smile as he watched Oregon cast their electoral vote for him. His supporters had cheered every time he had won a state and they were confident he would be the next President even if the election went to a House vote. Grainger, himself was confident he would win the House and was equally confident Waters wouldn't win California and the electoral votes needed to win the election.

Johnson was in the greenroom at his headquarters in Birmingham, Alabama. He was pacing the floor, nervous as a long-tailed cat in a room full of rocking chairs, hoping to hang on to enough of the electoral vote to be considered in the House vote. He was confident he would win Hawaii, but that count was still hours away.

Sam was Sam -- cool and confident. He had already conceded the fact that he was going to have to face the House of Representatives in December. He was prepared to fight the House regardless of the outcome tonight. The House had a Republican majority and Sam could easily see Grainger getting the nod from the House. Johnson wasn't any threat at all. He had been out of the race for some time, but, hadn't rolled over and given up.

Toby and Lauren came over to their father. Lauren sat on Sam's leg and looked at him with her big brown questioning eyes.

"Hi, guys, what do you think of all this?"

"It's all pretty cool Dad, but we were wondering," Toby paused long enough for Lauren to echo.

"Yeah, Dad, we were wondering where we are going to go to school? Are they going to have an arena at the White House, so I can practice barrel racing?"

"Dad, Lauren and I both have a lot of questions concerning the move to Washington, but we know you have a lot on your mind tonight, so we can wait to ask, but we would like to know if you are going to have time for us when you're the President.

"Lauren, I will have to find out about the barrel racing and let you know. Guys, I will always have time for you. I know these past two years have been hard on you with me being out on the road doing this campaign, but I promise that whatever happens in the next few days I will be there for you. Deal!"

"Deal!" The kids said in unison as they left Sam to sit with their mom.

Sam was thinking about his kids and how much he had missed over the last two years and thinking about his speech to the House next month. Sam said to himself "Maybe if I don't win the electoral I should just pull the plug and go home with Kate and the kids.

Suddenly the greenroom speakers blared the news.

"**WATERS WINS! WATERS HAS WON THE ELECTION!"**

"Tony, for the first time since George Washington, we have an Independent in the White House."

Right, Stan. California, in a complete flip from normal, has voted for an independent. They were the last holdout to have Waters on the Ballot, adding him just a few weeks before tonight's election. Independent Sam Waters has two-hundred-seventy electoral votes, Grainger has one-sixty-seven and Johnson finished with ninety-nine. What a truly remarkable story Waters has been."

"Tony, I wonder which States' ballots are going to be challenged this election? Seems one or the other of parties has called for a recount of various state ballots in every election since 2000 with the Bush versus Gore Florida fiasco."

"This race was very close over all, but Waters unexpectedly won some very key states and several battleground states and managed to win the two-hundred-seventy electoral votes to become the 46th President of the United States. Waters has been amazing in the race for the White House, I wonder what he's going to pull out of his utility belt when he takes office in January. Let's go now to Jerry Cummings and Bill Kerr who are at the Denver Convention Center with Sam Waters. Bill are you there?"

"Yes, Stan, but it's a little hard to hear you. As I'm sure you can hear, the Waters headquarters is in absolute pandemonium. The instant California cast their votes for Waters this crowd went crazy. The Champaign is flowing here tonight. Jerry, how are things in the greenroom?

"The atmosphere here which has been mostly watch and see all night has lit up like a Christmas tree with the announcement that Waters had won. All the independent parties called within seconds of the announcement congratulating Waters on the win and pledging their support during his term in office. Sam is currently on the phone with Senator Johnson, we are waiting to hear the report on that call. Grainger hasn't called yet, but I'm sure it's simply timing on his part.

"Sam, what did Senator Johnson have to say?

"Senator Johnson, conceded the election, congratulated me on both my campaign and this evening's victory. We spoke for a few minutes about the future of the country and we both expressed our desire for a unified Congress working for the good of the people." One of Sam's campaign assistants tells Sam he has a phone call. "Excuse me, I have Congressman Grainger on the phone."

"There it is Stan, Johnson, conceding the victory to Waters and expressing a desire for a unified Congress. I see Sam coming back. Sam, that was a brief phone call from Grainger, what did he have to say?"

"Jerry, the Congressman very simply conceded the election, congratulated me on the win and said my biggest fight is still ahead in the next four years. The fight to get either the House or Senate to listen to an independent. He may be right, but, I'm geared up for that fight. Now I have to talk to the people out front."

"Thank you, Sam and congratulations. Bill, we're back to you."

The crowd is cheering and howling. Terry Jacobs is on the stage trying to get everyone to settle down.

"Ladies and gentlemen, if I can have your attention please! It is my very immense pleasure to introduce to you, my best friend, a great contractor, who now gets to fix the paneling in the Lincoln bedroom, remodel the Oval Office. The forty-sixth President of the United States, Sam Waters, and Vice-President, Mike Baker."

The crowd goes crazy, as Sam and Mike take the stage. The scene is utter chaos. There are photo flashes and people yelling, screaming, and chanting, "WE WON!" It is a full ten minutes before

Sam can speak and be heard above the crowd even with the public-address system.

"Thank You. Thank You very much. Thank you. Thank you, my friends and thank you America.

"When you win an award, you are expected to give an acceptance speech. A speech in which you share how grateful you are for the award. Well, I can't tell you that I'm grateful to be your president, but I am truly grateful for all of your hard work, perseverance, dedication, and support. You prompted me to act against my personal judgment and run for office and we won.

"This was not a campaign I would have voluntarily put myself into. It was your show of support, you, walking the walk that made me decide to run. It was your dedication which kept me going when there were times I just wanted to go home to Kate and my kids." Sam signals Kate, Nancy and the children forward on the stage.

"I am not going to make promises about how the next four years are going to turn out, but what I can tell you is this – I will work as hard every day of the next four years as I have during this campaign to ensure that you do not regret the decision you made tonight.

"I want to thank those who made this possible. My friends, and family, the folks from Buffalo, Wyoming, who I think are all present here tonight, and the people of the United States. Thank you for your support. Thank you for standing with me. I have said since the beginning, it is easy to "Talk the Talk," but extremely difficult to "Walk the Walk." Tonight, I want to thank all those people, who for the past three years have walked the walk. To those who spent countless hours running my campaign offices, thank you. To the volunteers who walked the walk literally for mile upon mile to find the supporters to sign the petitions which put me on the ballots. There are so many people who have worked to make this night, this dream, a reality.

"When I began this campaign, I had doubts and concerns whether the people of the United States could be brought together by a single, simple person doing the right thing. The country has always pulled together in times of crisis. The Day of Infamy, when Pearl Harbor was bombed, the 9/11 World Trade Center disaster, but you have also come together in times other than war. You came together for the victims of Hurricanes Katrina and Andrew and several other disasters, too numerous to name. You have come together for the victims of tsunamis in the Pacific rim. Earthquake victims in countless countries around the globe. And tonight, you came together to put an Independent candidate in the White House and I won't let you down."

The crowd's cheers are deafening.

"I have received phone calls from both Senator Johnson and Congressman Grainger, conceding the election and congratulating us on a well-run and admirable campaign and for the victory. I told them both, that I hoped we could work united for the good of the American people. They agreed that we should work together, however, they confided that our hardest fight is still ahead. The fight of bringing together the parties for the common cause of the American People. WE WILL CONTINUE THE FIGHT."

Again, the crowd cheers. Mike, who has been standing beside Sam during his speech, turns and motions the rest of their families and friends to the front of the stage where they all join hands and raise them in the air. Sam and Mike walk into the throng of people shaking hands with the many people who helped them and the varied guests.

Unlike the elections of the past decade, there were no demonstrators, no hecklers, no protestors -- just people who supported the newly elected President. Sam said to himself 'the protests will probably start tomorrow.'

21
TRANSITION TO OFFICE

Sam and Mike were excited to the point of almost being giddy over their victory. No one was protesting about their election and the support being shown was awe-inspiring. Now it was time for them to start developing a plan to take office. Sam and Mike spent the next week deciding who they wanted to appoint to their cabinet. Over the years Sam had followed the careers of various legislators, judges, department heads and Governors and was aware of those who actually "served" their country and the people. Sam wanted to keep the independent framework, so they chose people they knew and trusted to do the job for the American people. Sam asked Terry Jacobs to consider the position of Attorney General. This time Terry didn't hesitate and accepted the position. Sam traveled to Washington, D.C. to meet with the outgoing President and make transition arrangements for the White House and the office. After that was done, Sam went to the Pentagon to meet with the Secretary of Defense, a Marine he had served with several times and knew he was a man of integrity.

"Mr. Secretary, I'm not sure you are aware, but we served together several times while I was in the Marines. I have profound respect and admiration for you and your accomplishments."

"Thank you, I didn't know we served together; but now that you mention it your name does ring a bell. You were an MP, right."

"Yes Sir, that is correct. Please call me Sam."

"If we are going to be on first names, please call me Jim."

"Okay, Jim. I know you have mentioned retiring after the inauguration. I'm hoping your decision doesn't have anything to do with me or my views on various issues."

"No, Sam. I believe you are a committed patriot and that you truly believe in this country and our military. I'm behind you one-hundred percent and would be very pleased to remain in my position in your administration, but, I have served this great nation for nearly sixty years. I feel it's time for someone else to handle the reins. There are plenty of people out there who will stand up and serve you well in this position."

"I appreciate your support and honesty, Jim. I have a request for your last duty as Secretary."

"Yes, Sir?"

"I want you to recommend your replacement. I would prefer an independent, someone who is not party bound, but I know how hard that may be in the higher ranks of the Military where politicians play. I would like someone who believes like we do in a strong military and American pride: who feels an obligation as a veteran and patriot to serve the people. Do you think you can do this for me?"

"Sir, it would be an honor."

"Thank you, Jim, it has been my honor to finally meet you in person and I look forward to seeing your recommendations. Have an Oorah day, Sir. Semper Fi!"

"Do or Die" Jim replies.

The Semper Fi greeting of the Marines may be answered with either: "Do or Die" depicting the dedication of the Marines to accomplish any mission regardless of the risk to life, or "Till we Die" following the "Once a Marine, Always a Marine" motto of the Marines.

Sam made a stop at the Supreme Court to speak with the Justice of the United States, the Chief Justice of the Supreme Court. He noted the vast volumes of documents she was sorting through for the next session's agenda and wondered how many cases could be overlooked in the sea of paper.

Sam made a couple more stops in Washington before heading home.

There was a slight chill in the air, but the temperature was mild for Washington, D.C. in November. Sam took a walk around Memorial Park and stopped for a minute at each of the War Memorials to say a short prayer for the Service Men and Women who served in those conflicts. He stopped at the Washington Monument and muttered softly to himself, "It's just you and I, George."

"What was that, Sir?" Sam's Secret Service agent, Peter, asked.

"Nothing, Peter. Just thinking aloud about George Washington being the only other truly independent President of the United States."

"Yes, Sir, and the two of you are in very good company."

"The two of us, with the other forty-four Presidents?"

"No, Sir. Just you and Washington. You are already a better President than many who have served in the Oval Office."

"I appreciate the sentiment, Peter, but the proof will be in the pudding. We will see at the end of the next four years if I measure up.

Did you know that Washington's years as President began with corruption in the Congress? In 1776, the Continental Congress had amassed a debt to the Continental Army. They had promised the men who joined the Army, a sizeable salary for serving in the revolt against the English. After the war, the Army came to Philadelphia beseeching Congress to pay the wages they were owed. Congress and the Army, debated the debt amount for several days and in the dead of the night, the Continental Congress crept out of Philly and for the next twenty-four years whenever the men of the Continental Army located the Congress they would attempt to collect on the wages and Congress would change the location of the Capitol. Finally, in 1800, Congress bought a town called Funkstown and all the area around it. They renamed the town Washington after the first President and dubbed the surrounding county, the District of Columbia, and the new Capitol of the young United States. The first order of Senate business was to pass a law making it illegal to try to collect a debt from the Congress. Those who tried were arrested and sent to prison."

"I never knew that. Thank you, Sir for sharing it."

Sam turned to face Peter and smiled. "Next stop is Arlington National Cemetery."

Sam and Peter and the rest of the Security detail walked through the Arlington National Cemetery, stopping briefly to say a prayer at the Tomb of the Unknown Soldier, and ending up in front of the Marine Corps Memorial in time for the evening parade of the Marine Corps Band and the Silent Drill Team. Sam stayed to watch the parade and told the Commanding Officer, he would like to meet with the Marines. After the ceremony, Sam walked behind the Memorial and shook the hands of the Marines assigned to the two Marine units and congratulated them on a magnificent performance. He stepped back in front of the formation and yelled Semper Fi, and the Marines reply in the traditional "Till we Die."

"Sir, I have served on several Presidential Details over the past twenty years and you are the first who has walked the Memorial Park and Arlington and paid homage to those who served to make and keep us free. You are going to be a very special kind of President. One George Washington would be proud of, even if his congress was criminal."

The next day Sam boarded a plane for Wyoming.

***

The two weeks in Washington were fast paced and productive. Sam had talked to Mike every day to discuss various recommendations for the cabinet. Mike, even though he had his own schedule of transition duties, had managed to come up with some key recommendations. Sam looked over the list and noticed most were veterans. Sam was aware the military had vast resources and had asked Mike to push those resources to the limit. If there was a military equivalent to a cabinet position, Mike had found it and found a person to fill the slot. Jim had called and recommended the current Commandant of the Marine Corps, General Robert Chaffey, as his replacement for Secretary of Defense. Sam agreed and thanked him for the referral and his service and invited him to visit the White House any time. Terry Jacobs was also a veteran who served with Sam in the MP's. When they had finished their enlistment with the Marine Corps, Terry went to College and became a lawyer, while Sam went to college for business.

Terry was scheduled for the grueling requirements of Senate confirmation the first of December.

Sam and Mike spent Thanksgiving at home and then left again for three more weeks in Washington to complete another phase of their transition and turn the rest of their cabinet list over to the Senate, returning home in time for Christmas. It just happened this year's Christmas reunion was in Wyoming. Only this year wasn't going to be simply family – it was to be family and the extra forty Secret Service agents assigned to each family. Sam and Mike both believed Christmas was a holiday which should be spent in the company of family. Since the Security Detail agents couldn't be at home with their families, Sam and Mike invited them to join in a Wyoming Christmas. The agents accepted the invitation and agreed they would pay their family's travel to Buffalo and Kaycee. It was a wonderful time for all at both homes. Later that evening Peter approached Sam.

"You know, Sir, you have added another first to my list of things I have never encountered with any previous president. In all my years on the Presidential Security Detail, I have never had my family invited to a dinner of any kind including Christmas. I imagine the same holds true for the other agents. Thank you, Sir. You are going to be a great President."

"Thanks Peter. When I was in the Marines and had to assign holiday duties, I would always try to assign duty on Thanksgiving to the married men and women, most of which are thankful all year for the blessings of their families. I would assign duty to the single Marines on Christmas, because I have always felt that Christmas was to be shared with families and have done my best to make sure my families were always together at this time of year. Let's go get some leftover turkey and make a couple of sandwiches. Oh, and another thing whenever it's just you and me, please just call me Sam."

"Okay, Sir, Sam it is, but only when it's just you and me."

Over the next few days all the Security Detail agents thanked Sam and Kate for a great Christmas.

***

The Security Detail agents and their families enjoyed the serenity of Wyoming until the twenty-ninth of December then the families headed to their homes and everyone went back to work.

Sam and Mike spent another four days working on the plan for the first hundred days in office and left for Washington on January second for the last phase of transition before the inauguration. Their families would join them on the twentieth for the ceremony. Sam had talked to Toby and Lauren about staying in Buffalo until the end of the school year, but they said they wanted to be with their dad. Sam wasn't sure if it was really to be with dad or to be in the White House. Either way their comments made him feel good. Mike had the same reaction with his family. He explained to Billy that the Vice-President doesn't live in the White House and he was a little unhappy.

“Dad, if we don’t live in the White House, where do we live?” Billy asked

“Well, there’s a house not far from the White House for the Vice-President. It is by the National Observatory and sits on a hill with a great big yard and lots of trees.”

“Oh, brother!”

“What? Son.”

“Big yard and lots of trees, I suppose I will have to mow the grass and rake the leaves like at home.”

Mike laughed at his son’s comment. “No, son, I think they have grounds keepers for that.” and they both laughed.

Mike, had shadowed the departing Vice-President for three days getting familiar with the Senatorial routine. He met the Majority and Minority party leaders and met the Whips. The Whips are the assistant party leadership, basically the second in command of the party. They also act as the Senate Leader in the absence of the Vice-President. Mike watched as the Vice-President left the Senate Whips in charge of the Senate as he went to play racquetball or entertain one or more lobbyists. Mike wasn’t impressed and decided during those three days there would be a new Sheriff in town after the inauguration and the Senate Whips would only be used when Mike was not in D.C.

Mike had also met with several Senators who seemed truly glad to see someone with fresh ideas in the White House. Mike wasn’t sure if they were sincere or blowing smoke up his tail feathers. He also met with some of the older group of Senators, the good ole boys as some would call them – career politicians who had in Mike’s opinion worn out their welcome many years ago. They were not as happy to see the independent duo in the White House and weren’t ashamed to vocalize their feelings. Mike was anxious to go to work.

***

On inauguration day, Sam and Mike were sworn in and they enjoyed the parade and the festivities associated with the changing of the Presidents with their family and friends. Sam had about two-hundred guests in the portable bulletproof viewing box and several hundred more in the bleachers along Pennsylvania Avenue. Many of these guests had been invited to the inaugural dinner and ball in the evening.

Sam called a joint session of the House, Senate, and Supreme Court for the next day and let everyone know there would be consequences for those not in attendance. He also invited the press and all of the lobbyists to attend.

The Congressmen and women and Senators weren't impressed by the threat of consequences and expressed their disdain at being treated like servants openly and in Sam's and Mike's presence. The pages accompanying the representatives openly laughed at the remarks offered by their employers.

Mike looked at Sam.

"This is going to be a long four years, Sam."

"That's why we will change it within two years."

22
FIRST THINGS FIRST

Everyone in attendance at the joint session of Congress stood as Mike introduced Sam. "Ladies and Gentlemen -- The President of the United States, the Honorable Sam Waters." There was some applause, but not the fanfare of election night or the previous day's inaugural as Sam moved to the podium.

"Please be seated. Mr. Vice- President, will you please take the roll." Mike stood and began the roll call of representatives. He pronounced each name alphabetically and received an "Aye" from the representative before advancing to the next name.

"Mr. Clarkson," there was no response. "Representative Jeffrey Clarkson, from Illinois?"

Sam and Mike had agreed that if a name was called twice with no response the floor would return to the President.

"Mr. President it appears Mr. Clarkson is not in the chamber or will not answer."

"Thank you, Mr. Baker. Mr. Clarkson apparently either did not receive the message for this joint session or chose to ignore it. I told the American people the platform for my campaign was respect and reform. If Mr. Clarkson did not receive the message to be here today, then we will reform our method of delivering our messages. If Mr. Clarkson has chosen not to attend, he has disrespected his constituents in Illinois, the members of Congress present, me, and the Oath of the office he represents."

One of the Senators asked to speak.

"Mr. President, Senator Jason Reynolds, Florida. Are you aware of the amount of business we do every day? We had only sixteen hours' notice of this session. Sir, that was hardly enough time to clear our schedules for this meeting. Mr. Clarkson may have had appointments."

"Yes, Senator Reynolds, I do understand the amount of business you do every day, and yes, I did call this session only sixteen hours ago. However, you have had nearly two years notice of this session."

"Sir, how could we have two years notice of a session, when you were only elected three months ago? The Chamber floor hoohawed and chuckled at Reynolds' statement knowing he was expressing a fact and making this new President look like an idiot.

"Mr. Reynolds, I was asked by Pam Bales of KOAT News in Denver, at the beginning of my campaign for this office, what I would do on my first day as president. I answered; I would hold a joint session of Congress. I realize, all of you doubted I would be here today and it would be business as usual. The election settled those doubts and you all had three months to clear your schedules for today.

"I realized that many of you may have had appointments which you could not reschedule. I called this session in the late afternoon to allow you time to conduct your urgent business and clear the rest of your schedules.

"It seems odd to me Mr. Reynolds, why you would be standing up for the absent Mr. Clarkson, when you and the majority of representatives obviously managed to clear your very busy schedules to be in attendance. I ask each of you who may see Mr. Clarkson this evening or early tomorrow to give him a message -- I ask you to pass on to Mr. Clarkson to please come see me. In case he is unsure of where he needs to go – the address is sixteen hundred Pennsylvania Avenue. Thank you. Mr. Vice-President please continue the roll." Mike continued the reading of the names. When he is finished, he had passed the floor back to Sam thirty-two times for absent representatives; Eight Senators, twenty-three Congressmen and one Supreme Court Justice who were not in attendance.

"Ladies and Gentlemen, I realize thirty-two of your colleagues being absent is a very small number in comparison to the five-hundred-thirty-five of you. However, can anyone tell me what that number of absences represent to the people of this nation? Anyone? Since you all seem to be unaware of how your absence relates to the people you represent, let me enlighten you. Eight Senators. If each of those Senators was from a different State, then one-half the population of eight states had no Senate representation here today. If they happen to be from the same states, that would mean the total population of four states were not represented by Senators here, today. Depending on which four states, it could mean that a total of one-hundred-eight million Americans were not represented today. One third of our total population can count on not being represented with concern to laws passed by the Senate on any given day, on any given issue. The twenty-three Congressmen and Women absent represent approximately sixteen-million, of their constituents. One Supreme Court Justice represents the law for three-hundred-million Americans. That is unacceptable, and we are going to work to reform this problem and we are going to start right here, right now. Will the Senior Justice of the Supreme Court please come to the podium?" Justice Michelle Weaver approached.

"Mr. President, may I ask a question before we proceed further?"

"Chief Justice, you just asked a question. Do you have another?"

"Yes, Sorry Sir. I understand your math on the missing representation of millions of Americans when Congressmen and Women and Senators are absent, but how do you figure, one Supreme Court Justice being absent denies law to the entire population of the country?"

"Let me ask you a few questions and we will see if our math coincides. Does the Chief Justice vote on every issue before the Supreme Court?"

"Yes, Sir."

"What happens if a justice is absent and the decision is a draw. Four in favor, four against."

"The Court will issue a Pur Curiam, basically, upholding the lower court decision."

"So, although, somewhere along the road to the highest court in the country someone felt the case had merit to be heard, because the decision is split, it refers back to the decision of the lower court. Then on the appellate review, at least four Justices agreed with appeal, but because the Supreme Court, the highest court in the land had a draw the case is sent back to the lower court. Because a justice is absent or recuses themselves on the issue the arguments fall on deaf ears and no justice is served. What happens when the issue before the court is a Judicial Review of a Senate or Congressional Bill, which the people have to live by? Or a constitutional amendment? How is the review affected by an absence?"

"A Constitutional or Judicial Review will be stalled on a tied vote. The law will have to wait until all justices are present before proceeding."

"At times when there is a delay in the review, do the documents ever become overlooked in the great piles of paperwork the court receives every day?"

"Yes, Sir, and our math is tracking now, sir."

"I thought it might be. So, does everyone now see why one missing justice affects the lives of the entire population? Do you also see why one missing representative affects the population of their district or state?" There is agreement from the floor. "There are not simply five-hundred-thirty-five people in this chamber, for here sits the entire population of this country through your representation. Justice Weaver, did you administer the Oath of Office for the President of the United States, to me yesterday?"

"Yes, Sir."

"Did you also give the honorable Mr. Baker the Oath of Office for the position of Vice-President?"

"Yes, Sir"

"Then would you say Mr. Baker and I have the right, the duty and the power to confirm your oath of office?"

"Yes, Sir. I would believe so."

"Please, raise your right hand and repeat after me. I, state your name, do solemnly swear (or affirm) that I will administer justice without respect to persons, and do equal right to the poor and to the rich, and that I will faithfully and impartially discharge and perform all the duties incumbent upon me as Supreme Court Justice under the Constitution and laws of the United States; and that I will support and defend the Constitution of the United States against all enemies, foreign and domestic; that I will bear true faith and allegiance to the same; that I take this obligation freely, without any mental reservation or purpose of evasion; and that I will well and faithfully discharge the duties of the office on which I am about to enter. So, help me God.

"Thank you, Justice Weaver by the power vested in me by the people of the United States of America I confer upon you the title of Chief Justice of the Supreme Court and Justice of the United States.

"Justice Weaver will you and the Vice-President, now administer the oath of office to your Supreme Court Justices?"

Justice Weaver calls forward the Justices and has three of them stand before Mike. Mike and Michelle administer the oath for the Justices and they confer the appointment to the Supreme Court and turn toward the President.

"Mr. President the oaths have been affirmed and appointments conferred to the Justices."

"Thank you. Now, I would like the Senators who are present to make your way to the front of the chamber. Justices, please administer the oath of office to the Senators present."

The Justices turn to the Senators.

"Please raise your right hand and repeat after me. I, state your name, do solemnly swear (or affirm) that I will support and defend the Constitution of the United States against all enemies, foreign and domestic; that I will bear true faith and allegiance to the same; that I take this obligation freely, without any mental reservation or purpose of evasion; and that I will well and faithfully discharge the duties of the office on which I am about to enter. So, help me God. Thank you, ladies and gentlemen. By the power vested in me by the people of the United States I confer on you the Title of United States Senator. Mr. President the Oath of office and title have been given conferred to the Senators present."

"Thank you, Justices. Senators return to your seats please. Would the members of the House of Representatives please stand? Justices, will you now administer the oath of office to the House."

The Justices administer the Representatives of the Congress, their oath of office and confer their title of Congressman and Sam thanks them and asks everyone to return to their seats.

"Every person in a Federal position regardless of how great or small must take an oath for the position they are assuming. You take the oath voluntarily. Yes, it is a requirement of the job, but you can always say 'I'm sorry I just can't abide by the oath and not take the office. It's your choice and if you noticed the oath you took has no expiration date. There is no place in the oath which states 'this oath is restricted to that period you are in office.'

"So, let's look at what you just committed the rest of your life to.

"I do solemnly swear (or affirm) that I will support and defend the Constitution of the United States against all enemies, foreign and domestic. I take this first sentence very seriously. There are people everywhere who would like nothing better than to dismantle our constitution and our way of life. Some of those people are right here in this room. Every two years the people in this room propose over two-hundred amendments to the Constitution. Ladies and Gentlemen those are not the actions of someone who supports and defends the constitution. I do believe there are small parts of the Constitution which need some fine tuning to make them fit with the United States of today in relationship to the size of the country at the time our forefathers drafted it. I do not agree that the entire document should be rewritten as some of you propose.

"Next sentence of the oath -- That I will bear true faith and allegiance to the same. Senator Reynolds what does that sentence mean to you?"

"Mr. President, this isn't pre-school where you just call out someone's name and ask for an answer. There are protocols."

"Yes, Senator Reynolds there are protocols and one of those protocols is when your President asks you a question, you give him an answer. If you don't have an answer, you say politely, I'm sorry, I don't have a satisfactory answer to your question. You don't whine like a preschool child and try to cast a diversion from having to answer the question. With the B.S. out of the way, Mr. Reynolds What does the sentence mean to you?"

"Mr. President, I'm sorry, I don't have a satisfactory answer."

"See! It really isn't hard to be polite and respectful to one another. Thank you, Mr. Reynolds. Which Congressman or Woman can tell me what the sentence means to them? Where are the Congressmen from Arizona?"

"Here, Mr. President. Sonny Smith, Arizona's first district. The sentence means, we as representatives of the people, must always be faithful to the people and to the constitution and pledge our allegiance to keeping its fundamental purpose safe from those who would destroy it."

"Did everyone hear what Mr. Smith said? We, as elected representatives of the people, must always be faithful to those people. We must be faithful to the Constitution which was drafted to give us guidance and protect basic human rights. We must protect the fundamentals of the Constitution from those who would seek to destroy it.

"Well said, Mr. Smith. There is a reason the first and second sentences are combined, and the reason is they both address the protection of the people and the Constitution.

"The last part -- I take this obligation freely, without any mental reservation or purpose of evasion; and that I will well and faithfully discharge the duties of the office on which I am about to enter.

"This is clear. You are volunteers. You chose to campaign for the office. You chose to take the oath of office. You chose to accept the duties of the office you serve. Now, you are here and must faithfully discharge the duties of your office, which is, as has been pointed out, to protect and serve the people who elected you and protect the Constitution of the United States.

"Ladies and Gentlemen, we work for the people of this country. They do not work for us. They pay our salaries, put a roof over our head and food on our tables and provide for our transportation. What do they ask for in return? They ask that we honor our oath, that we ensure their inalienable rights. That doesn't mean we give them everything they ask for. It means we don't stand in the way of them being able to earn and achieve those things they want. The pursuit of happiness" There was broken applause from the floor.

"Ladies and Gentlemen, it is time to rebuild respect in this country. It is time to respect each other. Respect our families. Respect our teachers. Respect our law enforcement. We need to rebuild trust in the Government and rebuild the respect our government had prior to Korea, when we were the most prosperous and powerful nation in the world." Again, broken applause from the floor.

"Let's get to work! Would the Senate and House junior representatives please come to the podium? If you are the most junior person in your house, please come forward." Senator Albright and Congresswoman Dontae approached the podium.

Senator Ben Albright was thirty-two years old, six feet tall, married with a young son and another baby on the way. He was a republican businessman who had just won the election from Utah's first district. Ben's father had always educated him that there were two kinds of representative in Washington – those who work for their money – and those who don't. Ben was looking forward to finding out which side of that fence Sam sat on and working with him.

"Senator Albright, currently, you are the junior and newest member of the Senate. After the next election, you may be the Majority or Minority Leader of the Senate. I am tasking you with this list of items I would like to accomplish this year."

Congresswoman Cheryl Dontae was a firecracker lawyer from Missouri's second district. She had proven herself as the Branson assistant DA, under her father, and had run for congress to try to undo the 'good ole boys' control of the state. Although, she was a Democrat, her father was a Green party independent who had served a term in the State Senate. He had reinforced in her the knowledge that the party line didn't mean a damned thing if it didn't serve the people. She too was looking forward to working with Sam.

"Congresswoman Dontae, you are the junior representative in the House and in two years you could be Speaker of the House. I am tasking you with this list of items I would like to see from the House this year.

"Ladies and Gentlemen, the lists I just handed to these two junior members of this Congress require you to work together. You may not like the person across the aisle and you may not like me, but here we are. We are sworn to the same oath to represent the same people. If we don't work together, banks, corporations and unions won't suffer. Special interest groups won't suffer. The ones who will suffer are the ones who put you in office with their votes. The ones who helped fund your campaigns and worked their tails off in your campaign offices as volunteers. The American Taxpayer suffers. They won't suffer anymore; at least not on my watch.

"Ladies and Gentlemen, we will meet again in a joint session at two o'clock on the Twenty-eighth of February and the thirtieth day of each month thereafter. Make sure your schedules are clear and you are in attendance. Thank you."

The members of Congress stood and applauded as Sam folded his notes and walked through the crowd, shaking hands, and taking a moment to talk to some of the representatives. Mike hit his gavel calling the session back to order as Sam exited. About an hour later, Mike joined Sam in the west wing of the White House.

"Well, Mike. What did we accomplish today?"

"You made Reynolds look like an ass."

"Thanks. That will go a long way in the approval polls in thirty days."

"At least it was something constructive on your first actual working day in office. I think you may have made some of those men and women think about their positions and who they work for. Especially the speech about what an absent representative really means in relationship to population represented."

"Maybe. What's on the agenda for tomorrow?"

"You wanted to put together the Executive Orders on elections funds. Time to go to work."

Sam kept his word and talked to every Representative who had been absent from the joint session. He had them reaffirm their oath of office and reminded them what the oath meant. Sam also reminded them of the number of people they represent and emphasized that those people are not being represented when their representatives are absent from a session of congress.

23
THE BAG OF WORMS

On Sam's second day in office he invited the press to the oval office.

"Ladies and Gentlemen, for me to reform our Government, we must reform your representatives, so they work for you. To make that reformation, we must start at the beginning. The first step in procuring a Government position is the election. So, that's where I chose to start. Yesterday, as many of you may have seen in the news, I reaffirmed the Oath of Office for all our Representatives, Justices, and Department Heads.

"Today, I signed five Executive orders.

"The first concerns three campaign laws which were signed into law between the beginning of World War I and the end of World War II. The Campaign Contributions Act of 1907 established a Federal ban on campaign contributions from banks and corporations. The Act was amended in 1943 to contributions from unions. The Corrupt Practices Act of 1925, limited Campaign expenditures.

"My first Executive Order concerns these Acts and is in four parts:

One, it issues a continuation of the Campaign Contributions Act banning campaign contributions from banks, corporations and Unions and reinstates the Corrupt Practices Act limiting campaign expenditures to fifty million dollars.

Two, it establishes reporting criteria for all contributions on all levels of Government. All campaign contributions must be reported, and the report must be detailed with Name, address, and contact information for any contribution of ten dollars or more. This includes Political Action Committee contributions. PAC contributions are required to identify the contributors who make up the PAC and the exact amount of any contribution. These must also have the name, address, and contact information of any contributor donating ten dollars or more. Currently the candidates must report any contributions received for their campaign but simply list a PAC without an accounting of who contributes to the PAC. PACs are now required to report their details as well. No exceptions.

Three, it establishes criteria for administering sanctions against those who would attempt to circumvent the law. If a PAC accepts contribution from any of the three banned entities the contribution will be struck from the candidate's account and deposited in a special treasury account for use in paying the national debt. All involved will forfeit the amount of the contribution. In addition, the PAC will be barred from any contributions to any candidate on any level for five years. If a candidate accepts an illegal PAC contribution, they will be charged with accepting a bribe and punished accordingly, the least of which will be banned for life from running for any public office on any level of Government. Our Government is no longer the game board of banks, corporations, unions, or any other special interest groups.

Four, it establishes a law for Federal Government campaign candidates, in which campaign contributors must submit all contributions to the U.S. Treasury in the name of the candidate being supported. The Treasury will set up a special account for each candidate's contributions and with the assistance of the Government Accounting Office, GAO, will ensure that Banks, Corporations, and Unions are not contributors.

Likewise, I have recommended that State and Local Governments establish laws which mirror this order. State or Local Candidates, like the Governor or Mayor, would have their political contributions go to the State or Local Treasury in their name.

No contribution for any political campaign will be given directly to the candidate. The Treasury will issue the candidate a debit card with a limit of the funds available in their contributions account for use during the campaign, not to exceed the fifty-million-dollar limit set by the Corrupt Practices Act.

If the candidate is defeated, any residual funds in the account will be transferred to the general fund and used toward paying the National Debt.

If a candidate is elected, the funds will remain in their account and be added to any contributions for future election or reelection campaigns. Any interest gained by these accounts will also be channeled to the general fund for payment on the National Debt.

If a candidate chooses not to campaign for further office or has reached their maximum term of office, the funds will be transferred to the general fund for payment on the National Debt.

All anonymous contributions regardless of candidate will be used to support and update the Veterans Administration and programs for Veterans and other charities.

Any politician found accepting personal contributions in a manner other than as described above will be prosecuted for accepting bribes and the contributor will be prosecuted for bribery.

Each candidate for political office must file a financial declaration showing all personal and family assets prior to announcing their candidacy. A candidate may use personal and family monetary funds without restriction, but must account for any gains, of any amount, to personal or family wealth.

Since some of our representatives have questionable ethics and may be tempted to accept bribes, we must establish criteria to ensure their contributions are used for pursuing the political office -- not for lining their pockets or working against the interest of the people. We can attempt to prevent our representatives from accepting bribes from special interest groups by making it more difficult to do so, but, unfortunately, there will still be those who will try.

"Before yesterday's joint session of Congress, I spoke with the Treasury to make sure this action could be managed. I was told by both the Treasury and GAO that they could handle the new accounts and approximately how many new civil service personnel would need to be hired. For the current year there will be no new personnel requirements. I asked them to set up the first account, this will be my account. The account was confirmed this morning and I deposited six-hundred-forty million dollars, the residual of my campaign contributions, into it. Those funds will be made available to me should I decide to run for reelection in four years, or will be made available to the general fund if I don't run."

The phone lines in the outer office immediately light up and it is all the staff can do to answer them. Sam knew his action would send Congress into a frenzy and had briefed the staff before he met with the press. Sam's staff responded simply and politely that the

President will address the issues at the joint session on February twenty-eighth.

"My second Order, might offend some; however, I refuse to change history because it offends you. History is in the past. It happened. We may not be proud of some of it, but we cannot return to those dates and change it: therefore, we will correct all instances where someone prior to my term attempted to change history. The words 'So Help Us God' will be added to the World War II Memorial at the end of President Roosevelt's Day of Infamy Speech. President Roosevelt said those words on December 7th, 1941 after the Japanese attack on Pearl Harbor. We will not continue to change history to be politically correct. We will restore as many of our historical monuments and public places as possible to their original appearance. If the monument or artifact has been destroyed, we will replicate it as near to the original as possible. This order also makes it a class three felony to deface, mar, damage or destroy any historical monument, marker, memorial or park. We, as well as many other countries around the world, have placed historical sites and various National Treasures under the protection of the United Nations. The United Nations Educational, Scientific and Cultural Organization (UNESCO) has failed in their duty to protect these monuments; therefore, we must step in and take charge of these historical items.

"My third Executive Order calls for a suspension and investigation of all laws, Acts, Bills and Mandates passed in the last hundred years. These suspensions will be in effect until the governing body, whether House or Senate can make the appropriate changes. This order is also in five parts.

One, this order suspends many current regulations, laws any regulation containing riders which do not support or concern the regulation. If it couldn't pass without the riders, it should not have been passed.

Two, it suspends any regulation containing more than three-hundred-fifty pages, about the average size of a novel. If it is longer than a best-selling novel, no one in Congress read it before the vote and I will ask any of our senior representatives to explain to me what the bill says. If it is too long for the public to read, it is too long to be effective. The omnibus bills would be the exception because it details the budget for all Governmental departments and agencies and that record is minimized to ten-thousand words and five-hundred pages.

Three, it suspends any regulation containing verbiage which contradicts itself or which the public or an attorney can't understand. If the lawyers can't understand it, how can the public?

Four, it suspends any regulations which were passed on a deal to exempt Congress from the regulations they imposed on the public. We are all Americans. Our representatives in Congress are not above the law and must follow the same laws required of the people.

Five, it suspends those laws and regulations which no longer apply to the current size and scope of the country. If the law cannot be amended, it will be revoked or rescinded.

"My fourth Executive order, removes the Uniformed Division or UD of the Secret Service. Effective eight months from today the U.S. Marines who have protected the President since 1776 will again assume their role and duties. The UD currently guard the White House acreage buildings and grounds. In eighteen months, a new Marine Barracks will be built on the White House grounds and a Marine Military Police Company will be permanently stationed at that barracks. The personnel of the UD will be further assigned by the Treasury Department which oversees the Secret Service. There are thirteen-hundred officers in the Uniformed Division which costs the American taxpayer over eighty million dollars per year. The cost for thirteen-hundred Marines trained to do the duties of the UD is approximately forty million dollars per year. A savings of forty million dollars. For what it costs now for the UD, we could double the number of Marines if necessary.

"Although, on the surface, these actions may appear insignificant to most of you, they will be helpful in reforming our Government into a government for the people and aid in decreasing the deficit and paying some of our debts.

"My last Executive Order, I'm sure will aggravate a few Congressmen and Women and more than a few of you who receive welfare and government aid. This Order will also stir up a lot more commotion in my outer office. I have ordered the Internal Revenue Service to revise the tax forms for this year to reflect a ten percent tax across the board for all taxpayers. If your employer withheld more than ten percent of your wages, you will be refunded the overpayment. If they did not withhold ten percent, you will owe the difference. There are no deductions. No earned income credits. No charitable deductions. You pay ten percent. Government employees who draw their salaries from the taxpayers, pay taxes on those wages. Government in the past five decades has chosen to tax military wages which come from the taxpayers. Then they decided to tax Social Security which was contributed to Social Security by tax payer. We seem to tax every person who works and earns a salary from the taxes paid into our Government except the one group who draws those wages for not working or contributing anything to the system which supports them. This year everyone who has drawn a welfare check will pay ten percent of their income into the IRS. The constitution states, we cannot tax a single person unless we tax every person equally. This year every person will be taxed equally." The phones had not stopped ringing since the initial statement on the Orders, now every line was lit.

***

The next day the protests began. Those on welfare took to the streets to protest the fact they were being treated like everyone else and having to pay tax on their income. Sam had opened a bag of worms.

Sam's first thirty days in office was a series of Executive Orders which renewed regulations and laws which were still very much valid and needed. Some were written long enough ago they have been forgotten and are not enforced as they should be. Other Orders suspended outdated laws which no longer applied. Still other orders fixed holes in regulations which provided for certain groups to be exempt. One such law is bribery and Sam saved it for the joint session.

24
AN ATTITUDE OF INDIFFERENCE

Sam wanted to visit with Senator O'Mahoney from Wyoming to congratulate him on his election as an independent. Peter walked Sam through the underground tunnels from the White House to the Senate building. They climbed the stairs and entered the elevator on the first floor. The young uniformed operator was talking to another young person in more casual attire.

"Third floor, please." Peter told the operator as they entered the elevator.

"Yes, Sir." The operator acknowledged Peter's request and turned back to his friend. With their backs to Sam and Peter, the operator asked his friend.

"How in the world did that hick, Waters, ever manage to win the election?" Peter started to say something to the pair, but Sam stopped him.

"I have no idea, but he won't last long. The people in this building won't work with him and he will run back to his mommy in wywywyoming."

"Where is Wyoming anyway?"

"I think it's out in the Pacific Ocean somewhere around Hawaii."

The pair continued to make comments about Sam and he took in the conversation until the elevator reached the third floor.

"Excuse me, gentlemen. Who do you work for?" Sam asked.

"Man, we work for the Senate." The two answered in unison and give each other a high five.

"Let me give you an easier question." Sam stated. "Who's your boss?"

"I'm an aide to Senator McBain from Delaware," stated the casually dressed male.

"My boss is Mr. Duffy, in the general services office downstairs." said the elevator operator.

"Thank you. I want you to go tell the Senator and to Mr. Duffy to report to Special Agent Peter Martin in Senator O'Mahoney's Office as soon as possible." Sam ordered as he started to exit the elevator.

“Hey Man, who do you think you are? You can’t just order us around.” Declared the operator as the aide noticed Sam and Peter didn’t have the normal visitor's pass.

“Where’s your pass? You need a pass. How did you get in the building without a pass? We’re going to have to call security. You wait right there.”

The operator at the aide’s cue, picked up the elevator phone and pressed the button for the Capitol Police Dispatch for the building. Peter again wanted to stop the operator, but Sam stopped him. “Sir, we have intruders without a pass on the third floor at elevator one.”

“Son, before you hang up, will you please ask the dispatcher to bring Senator McBain and Mr. Duffy with them?” requested Sam.

“What? I’m not going to tell him that.”

“Then will you allow me the use of the phone?” Sam asked.

“Why do you want the phone?”

“I need to talk to the Police Dispatcher and ask him to bring those two individuals.”

“No. You can just wait for the cop to get here.”

“Peter, do you have the number for the Chief of the Capitol Police?”

“Yes, Sir.” Peter instinctively knew what Sam’s next request would be and was already searching his cell phone contacts for the Chief’s number.

“Will you give the Chief a call and ask him to meet us up here as soon as possible?

“Yes, Sir.” Peter took a step back and called Chief Steigel.

The Police Officers, from the response team, arrived and the Response Leader looked at Sam and Peter and then at the operator with his friend.

“Sir, is there anything I can help you with?” The officer asked as he stepped up to the four people at the elevator.

“Yes, Officer, these men don’t have passes to be in the building” stated the aide.

“I wasn’t talking to you moron. I was talking to the President,” retorted the Response Leader.

“Yes, Officer, you can do something for me.” Sam responded. “You can take these two downstairs to some secluded location where they can no longer insult people the people in their presence. Then if you don't mind, find Senator McBain and Mr. Duffy and have them meet me in Senator O'Mahoney's office as soon as they can."

"Yes, Sir."

"Thank you, Officer." As the Officers got on the elevator with the two young men, Sam heard the aide ask;

"Oh, shit, was that Waters?"

"President Waters to you 'crap for brains' and watch your language, this is the Senate building not the bar you hang out at." countered the Officer

Sam smiled as he and Peter headed down the hall to O'Mahoney's office.

"Peter, if Senator McBain, Mr. Duffy and Chief Steigel happen to get here before I come out, will you please have them take a seat and wait for me? I would like to meet with them one at a time. I'm sure Senator O'Mahoney has a conference room we can use."

"Yes, Sir. I'll make that happen. Should I tell them what this is about?"

"No, Peter they can wonder and worry for a bit. I'm sure the Response Officer will have briefed everyone except the Chief."

"Not a problem sir. Do you want to report those two?"

"Not right now, but I will need their names. I'm looking forward to hearing the Chief's view of things on the hill."

"Okay, Mr. President, Chief Steigel will probably give you an ear full."

"Thanks."

Sam met with Senator O'Mahoney for about forty-five minutes. When he came out of the Senator's office, McBain, Duffy and the Chief of Police were waiting for him. Sam crossed the foyer to an empty office Senator O'Mahoney had offered him.

"Peter, Senator McBain would you come in please?" The two men entered the office. At the beginning of Peter's detail, Sam had stated that he would never meet with any representative or lobbyist without at least one witness even if that witness was his Secret Service Security Agent.

"Senator, do you have a young man named Christian Simpson working for you?"

"Yes Sir, and I understand he and his friend on the elevator were unaware of who you were earlier today and may have insulted you. I have spoken with him and it will not happen again."

"Is he an important asset to your staff?"

"Sir?"

"What does he do? Make Coffee? Run the copier? What is his job? Is his job important to your office? It really isn't a hard or trick question, Senator."

"Uh, he handles paperwork, does filing, answers correspondence and runs errands."

"So, he's like everyone else and is expendable?"

"Yes Sir, I suppose so."

"Who hired him and who pays his salary?"

"I hired him, and he's paid through the Office of Personnel Management, OPM"

"So, he's a civil servant. I would like to see his Standard Form (SF) one-seven-one to see his qualifications for the job he holds."

"Sir, there is no SF one-seven-one. I, personally hired him."

"Senator, if a person works for and is paid through OPM, then OPM must have a SF one-seven-one to insure the individual is qualified for the position. Someone, must have interviewed him for his position to see if he is the best person for the job and must have given you a list of possible candidates for the position you had announced. Peter ask Chief Steigel to step in please." Peter turned to the door and summoned the Chief.

"Chief, do you know how many people other than the representatives work in the offices here on the hill?" Sam asked.

"No Sir, I'm sorry I do not. The number changes with each election and with each new representative or Senator. Each one hires his or her own staff and aside from the badging requirements we don't know who works for who."

"Thank you, Chief, that must make it a little difficult to do your job of protecting the Representatives and the buildings and grounds."

"Yes Sir, it does."

"Senator, since you hired Mr. Simpson, and did, so without the OPM process of hiring Civil employees, I am going to direct OPM to terminate any employee who was not hired in accordance with their guidelines, beginning with Mr. Simpson. This includes severance of pay and benefits from the OPM payroll."

"You can't do that," Senator McBain exclaimed.

"Senator, I cannot fire this person. Nor can I forfeit his pay and benefits. However, there are regulations set forth by the United States Senate and House of Representatives regarding the hiring of civil servants. I can direct OPM to begin enforcing those regulations, effective immediately. Personnel in violation may leave voluntarily or be arrested for fraud and attempted fraud against the Government. If this person is important to your staff operations, you may keep them employed at your expense until such time as they properly apply to OPM and complete the proper hiring and training procedures.

"Chief, I want you to work with OPM to get a list of those who have not been properly hired. Remove their credentials and ban them from all Congressional offices and chambers until they can prove they have been properly hired by OPM. Bring in Mr. Duffy."

When Duffy entered Sam asked.

"Mr. Duffy can you tell me who hired Mr. Moore?"

"Yes Sir, Mr. Moore was hired by Senator Fulton of California."

"Is Mr. Moore on the civil service payroll?"

"Yes Sir, I believe he is."

"Can you provide me with a copy of his SF one-seven-one?"

"He doesn't have one Sir. In fact, you will have a tough time finding a one-seven-one for anyone on the hill."

"Thank you, Mr. Duffy. Mr. Moore won't be working for you any longer. Will you pick him up at the Police Desk and have him clean out his locker."

"Sir? Senator Fulton brought him back to my office before I had the message to meet with you here. Moore has been back on the elevator for nearly two hours."

"There lies the problem Mr. President. No one cares about the rules," detailed Chief Steigel.

Sam dismissed the others and asked the Chief to stay for a few minutes longer. Chief Steigel is a cross between Sheriff Buford Pusser, 'Walking Tall' and Hulk Hogan. Six Feet Six, with green eyes that cut through you like a knife. He was professional and courteous but at a glance you could tell he would crack your skull in a second if you messed with him.

“Chief, what did you mean by your comment about, no one cares about the rules, being a problem? What are the problems as you see them?”

“Mr. President, the problems my officers and I have, are too numerous to list and even if I did list them nothing would come of it. After all we are dealing with the representatives. Just like the affair today. At your request, we detained those two yahoos. Almost before Peter called for their names, Fulton was there for the elevator operator, Moore, and one of McBain’s other aides was there for Simpson. It’s just a big game to them. We do our job and the politicians cut us off at the knees and undo our work.”

“Chief, I want to hear more. Will you come back to the White House with me?”

“Do I have a choice, Sir?

“You do, but consider this – I will call you several times a day and will continue asking for a meeting until you meet with me. At our meeting, I will have all of the key players, the Attorney General, Speaker of the House John Woodward, the head of OPM, and the Vice-President. I think together, we may be able to resolve some of your problems.”

25
THE CAPITOL POLICE

As promised, Sam had all the key players in the Oval Office when Chief Steigel arrived. The Attorney General - Terry Jacobs, House Speaker - John Woodward, OPM Chief - Betty Gray, and the Vice-President. Sam made the introductions and the group got down to business.

"Gentlemen, I have asked you here today to address some issues I have regarding various dubious activities here on the hill.

"Peter and I had an encounter with a couple of young men yesterday in the Senate building. Maybe you heard about it through the grapevine as I'm sure news travels quite fast here. Betty and I talked at length after the incident and we are ready to take the appropriate action to right a very wrong situation. It appears that a great many people working as pages and aides to the representatives as well as other people in the employment of the civil service have never formally applied for their positions. They are appointed without process by the representatives. I don't know if these appointments are quid pro quo for the children of campaign supporters or friends of the family and I don't really care. This practice ends today. Betty is having her staff check each personnel file for an SF-one-seven-one. They are compiling a list of those without the proper documents and forwarding that list to the Capitol police who are taking their credentials and escorting them from the hill. If these personnel are required in the representative's offices, the representatives can pay for them out of pocket until the OPM hiring process can be completed.

Gentlemen this is not retaliation for my being insulted, I've been insulted more severely, by far better people than the two young men yesterday. This is enforcing the OPM regulations which have been put into place by past House and Senate representatives and signed into law by past Presidents.

The other and more important reason you are all here is that I have heard about incidents involving members of our respective houses and the Capitol Police. Chief Steigel, Peter has been telling me a few stories of things that have gone on around the Capitol, but they sound so outrageous that I can't imagine conduct like that coming from our representatives. I have been tremendously curious since our conversation in Senator O'Mahoney's office what you could have meant when you said your problems were too numerous to list, I would like for you to tell us your stories."

"Mr. President, I don't even know where to begin. I'm reluctant to share the Capitol Police stories. I have seen my officers and some past chiefs who had issues with the representatives, who are no longer members of the Capitol Police Department and to tell you the truth, most days, I like my job"

"Chief, I assure you, you will not lose your job for talking to us. No one in this Government or the country for that matter is above the law.

"The Representatives seem to think so, Sir. My officers have pulled over several of them for driving while intoxicated and after some discussion, the officer is dismissed, and the Representative continues his or her intoxicated drive to wherever they were going. The next day, the officer is terminated for disrespect to a member of the House or Senate. Nothing is ever done to the Representative."

"Is everyone listening and paying attention? I would like for you all to take notes as you listen to the Chief and feel free to ask questions. Terry, I want you to take exceptional notes because there may be some work here outside of the normal legal duties of the Attorney General. Mike and John if what the Chief tells us is true, I believe there needs to be some adjustment made to the thinking of the representatives. Chief, the floor is yours, what else is there?"

"Mr. President, there have always been incidents of corruption on the hill. In 1880, a three-story, fifteen room, green, limestone house was built on K street, by a land developer from Iowa, named Edmonds. Edmonds would throw lavish parties for the Representatives of Congress. Edmonds invited and later boarded prostitutes in the house to service Congressional guests and Lobbyists. Edmonds considered himself a lobbyist although he would never admit to it in public. After Edmonds died in 1901, Lydia Edmonds rented the house to a Senator from Maryland who was tough on corruption in the Government. The Senator was murdered some months later and Lydia moved back into the house. The Lobbyist seemed to like Lydia Edmonds' company and were frequently found mingling with the representatives until her death in 1912. The house was purchased by several lobbyists and the residence continued to serve as a central and secret meeting place for the corruption of Congress.

"In 1921, the house became the official headquarters of the Ohio Gang, a group of corrupt politicians and industrialists who surrounded President Harding. There were many shady and corrupt practices and deals made at the little Green House on K Street, most notably the Teapot Dome Scandal in Wyoming. Things haven't changed much since those days, the little green house was destroyed in 1941, but was readily replaced by the little red house on R Street or many C Street addresses where Representatives and Lobbyists reside.

"There have been incidents where the interns who live in the various dormitories will open their curtains and put on a show for the people on the street, who, in many cases are Representatives. On occasion those shows have been somewhat, shall we say, risqué. People have complained, and we have responded and cited the interns involved, only to have the Representative they work for telephone the next day telling us to dismiss the citation as a misunderstanding of what happened. In most of the instances, there was no misunderstanding, my officers witnessed the show and had photos and videos, but, all the charges and citations were then swept away under the Congressional carpet.

"There was once an incident where a new staffer brought a loaded pistol into the Senate building in their briefcase. Guns are banned, for obvious reasons, on all Capitol property, let alone the buildings occupied by our representatives. My officer discovered the weapon and detained the person. The officer asked why he had the gun and was told his father had given him the gun for protection. The officer read the man his rights and was charging him with possession of the weapon when the Representative he worked for stormed in and demanded his release. The Representative said the pistol was his and the staffer was merely bringing it to him. This put the situation in a very bad light for the officer. The staffer had already admitted the weapon was his and he was in violation of the gun ban on the hill. When the Representative claimed the weapon was his, it put him in violation of the gun ban.

"The officer wanted to charge and arrest them both, but, by order of his supervisor, he released the gun to the representative. The representative immediately gave the weapon back to the staffer and in front of the officer, told him not to bring it to work again. The officer was fired the next day. No reason for his termination was ever given.

"Sir, there have been representatives caught with alcohol in their offices and in Government vehicles, violating the bans on alcohol. Some have been caught having sex with their interns, pages, staffers and occasionally their wives and girl-friends, not just in their offices, but in conference rooms, bathrooms, hallways and even on the Capitol steps and at the various open monuments at night. Each offense was noted, but no charges or citations were issued. There have been many more issues, Mr. President; but, I think you get the idea."

"Yes, Chief, I do, and I think MS Gray, Mr. Jacobs, Mr. Woodward and the Vice-President do also. These sound like the some of the cases Peter was telling me about past occurrences. Are you still plagued with this kind of willful and blatant disrespect for the laws in the Capitol area?"

"Daily, Sir. I think you are the kind of individual who may do something about this. So, I took the liberty of making a copy of the call logs." Chief Steigel hands the logs to Sam, who looks them over and hands them to Mike, Terry, and John.

"Chief, I knew there were some shenanigans going on, but this all took place in one week."

"Mr. Woodward, that report is not for a week, that's yesterday."

"Gentlemen, I think you can see we need to do some house cleaning. Thank you, Chief. This has been very enlightening. Mike and John, I would like you to scrub the calls you were just given and reprimand those from your houses. Let your Representatives know, in no uncertain terms, they are not above the law and they will be held accountable if there are any further incidents. Terry, I want you to work with the Chief to determine what laws have been violated and what means of prosecution we have available. If nothing else, we can look at censure. Thank you, Gentlemen, you have work to do." Sam dismisses the others, but keeps the Chief for a moment. "What does your schedule look like for the twenty-eighth?"

"I can free my schedule for you Mr. President. What do you need?"

"Can you free the schedule for fifty or so of your officers also?" Sam proceeds to tell the Chief what he has in mind and the two men agree to meet again the morning before the next joint session.

26
LOBBY OR BRIBERY

It was February twenty-eighth and Sam's second joint session of Congress. After the roll was taken for this session only three Congressmen and two Senators are absent, but they had all called Sam to explain their absence.

"Ladies and Gentlemen, in the past thirty days, you have kept my staff quite busy fielding phone calls about my executive orders. Executive orders since the beginning of this country have been the President's method of correcting faults in regulations and making small adjustments in the law. In simple terms, executive orders are like spell check or autocorrect. If the President sees a fault or flaw he can use an executive order to fix it temporarily until the House or Senate can come together with a more accurate document. The other reason for Executive orders is to initiate military action through the War Powers Act. There have been many Presidents who used Executive Orders to exercise dominance over the House and Senate or to press an issue into effect which was stalled because of the partisan and one-sided nature of the two houses. Many of those Orders are borderline illegal, unconstitutional, and do not hold with our Oath of Office or serve the people.

"I saw many faults, many regulations which have loopholes and side steps which allow them to be manipulated and violated. The first two of which were the Campaign Contribution and Corrupt Practices Acts. I corrected them to close the loopholes and then blocked the side steps. Many of our recently elected or reelected must have agreed with me. The treasurer has informed me of two hundred-twenty-nine Congressmen and seventy Senators, who have transferred their campaign funds into treasury accounts. I thank those individuals for their honest support of these regulations.

"Ladies and Gentlemen, these Campaign Acts are law and have been laws for one-hundred years and more, the executive order which revives these campaign acts, is also law. You are not above the law! I will expect by our next meeting the treasurer's report will show five-hundred-thirty-five accounts and the GAO will show those accounts to be in balance with your reports of your campaign funds.

"This Government will not create laws for the people, by which the law makers are exempt. Neither do we, as lawmakers, pick and choose those laws we will abide by. Your position does not make you exempt from the laws of our Cities, Counties, or States. Some of you have been approached by Mr. Woodward and Vice-President Baker concerning your conduct. You are the hired Representatives of this country and by your position as protectors of our people and our constitution you should be held to a higher standard -- a standard which is above reproach. When we talk about our actions, we must always be aware of how the people we represent perceive those actions. When deals are struck to exempt Congress from the laws they pass for the people, the people draw conclusions and have opinions of those actions and their representatives. If you are stopped by the police, either here in the Capitol or at home, you will behave with respect. If you are stopped because you are suspected of having broken a law, you will behave with respect for the law enforcement officer who is doing his job, protecting you and the people of the community he or she serves. I hope I am understood. Perception is everything.

"Mr. Reynolds, since our first contact, you and I have had several conversations and discussions on many topics and I have come to respect your opinion. How do you suppose the people perceive you when laws are passed, and deals are made to exempt you from those laws?"

"Mr. President, since you and I talked shortly after you ordered a review of passed regulations, I have made a trip to the great state of West Virginia and talked to the people. If you put the people I spoke with in a single room and asked their perception, the answer would be in unison they feel everyone in Washington, except for the new Presidential Team, are crooked and are only in government to see how much money they can take from the people. I asked how they perceived the job I was doing. I was told in no uncertain terms that I should be looking for work, because there was a good chance I would not be reelected. I was wounded by the comments, because I feel I work very hard for the people I represent."

"Thank you, Mr. Reynolds and from our conversations, I agree, you do work hard for your people. By a show of hands, in the last thirty days, how many of you have talked to people in your States?" One-hundred hands were raised.

"I must say, I am not impressed. Only one-hundred of you out of over five-hundred have talked to your people in the last thirty days. How can you possibly know what you need to be doing for those people if you don't talk to them? Of those who have talked to your people, how many of you have asked what the perception of you is?" Sixty hands were raised.

"Here is a very solid example of our problem. Out of five-hundred-thirty-five representatives less than one-fifth talk with their constituents monthly and only sixty, care how those constituents perceive them. Let me take a quick sample of what those sixty found out when they asked about perception. Senator Taylor, what did you find out in Oregon?" Taylor remains silent and gives thumbs down gesture. "Senator Albright?"

"Mr. President, this is my first term. The people I spoke with from my district in Utah felt the dynamic duo and I were doing a good job. They also said they wished the rest of the, and I'll quote, "assholes in Washington" would get their act together. Their overall perception is the same as Mr. Reynolds,' they think we are all snakes."

"Thank you, Mr. Albright. By the way, how are you coming on the list I gave you last month. Please give me an update after the session. Congresswoman Dontae, did I see your hand up?"

"Yes, Mr. President, and the people I talked to from my district in Missouri were not a bit happy with the government, basically a reflection of the sentiment provided by Mr. Reynolds, Mr. Taylor and Senator Albright."

"Thank you. Four representatives, two Houses, four States and four basically identical responses. The perception the people have of congress, is we are all, as Mr. Albright's people expressed, 'snakes.' Yet, four-hundred-thirty-five of you don't need to talk to your people to find out what they need or even want from their government. Four-hundred-seventy-five of you don't care how you are perceived. You don't care what the people you represent think about you. Four-hundred-thirty-five of you need to, as Mr. Reynolds' people expressed it, 'be looking for work.'

“Ladies and Gentlemen, I have said it before, ‘This is unacceptable’ and I expect it to change and quickly.

“At this time, I would like each of the news reporters to come down to the front of the chamber. You can leave your camera operators and technical people, I only want the reporters.”

The reporters shuffled down from the balcony onto the chamber floor and faced Sam.

“Thank you, Ladies and Gentlemen, I have a request of the press. I would like to see the Capitol reporters print real news if that’s possible in today’s media. Ladies and Gentlemen, the days of yellow journalism in the Capitol are over. There has been far too much tainted news. News which many times these days isn’t really news and is sometimes made up and reported just to make money for your particular newspaper or broadcast network. I am probably the strongest political advocate for the Constitution and the amendments. I believe in freedom of speech and freedom of the press. There are, however, certain restraints which accompany those freedoms. One must show restraint and not preach the Satanic rites in the middle of a Catholic Church on Sunday. One must show restraint in not carrying a sign which says, ‘Death to’ some culture, religion or race while standing in a neighborhood which is predominantly occupied by that culture, religion, or race. Mr. Woodward, what would happen to me if I were to stand in these chambers and preach the downfall of our great country.”

“Sir, you would be impeached so fast you would be out of office before the session ended.”

“Thank you, Mr. Speaker. We can express our feelings, thoughts, and beliefs without advocating a violent reaction. You, reporters, are the people who need to remind us of those restraints. You are the ones who need to show us the truth of what is happening in the world. Real News, new that is not for sale to the highest profit margin. These restraints are not laws dictated by Government. They are the restraints of civility, and of respect. Would any of you go as guests to someone’s home and berate the host? I would hope not. I challenge all of you to report real news and if you do you will be welcome at these sessions and other press conferences in the Capitol. If you prefer to taint the news with yellow press, you will be banned from the Capitol. This is not a restriction of free speech. It is the restraint from subjecting the people of the United States to reporting of the news which has no basis in fact. You may return to your crews." The reporters shuffled back to the balcony.

"Now, I would like to have the lobbyist groups come to the front of the chamber."

There was bustling and activity and movement throughout the gallery as the lobbyists made their way down from the balcony gallery to the front of the chamber.

"Ladies and Gentlemen, I appreciate you all being here today and coming down to the front of the chamber when I asked. There is a forward in a book I once read which stated to the effect that groups who believe in America don't send lobbyists to Washington. Those groups that do send lobbyists, do so for their own benefit and agenda. This statement made me think about all of you. So, I started searching through Webster's dictionary and my thesaurus trying to find a word which describes what you all do. I looked at the definition of Lobby. Per the dictionary, ***a lobby is an attempt to influence public officials and legislators.*** An attempt to influence. Webster further defines a lobbyist as a campaigner, an asker, a supplicant, activist, or requester. Another synonym is beggar. You are begging our Congress to act on your request. I thought about that for a while and thought about all the diverse ways a lobbyist or requester might attempt to influence members of Congress.

"By a show of hands, as an attempt to influence a legislator, how many of you have treated a representative to an exclusive dinner, a trip or junket or given a representative a gift valued at more than twenty dollars?" About two thirds of the lobbyist raised their hands.

"Thank you, would those who raised their hands please move to my left?" The lobbyists again shuffled to where they had been directed.

"This group to my right, by show of hands, as an attempt to influence a legislator, have you ever invited any member of Congress to play golf, other than at a charity event, and paid the greens fees and cart rental.? Fine. Could those who raised their hands join the group on my left? I see there are about a half a dozen of you left. What groups do you represent?" The small remaining group answered with various groups: AARP, VFW. Wounded Warrior, Citizens for Children's Rights, Coalition for Battered Women, and Fraternal Order of Eagles. Thank you.

"The methods of lobbying set forth in our constitution and supported by the definition in Webster's dictionary as an attempt to influence legislation are these:

1. *Lobbyists can present signed petitions from the groups they represent identifying public opinion on the issue.*
2. *They can also present the issue to a congressional board or hearing, showing the relevance of their issue to the public.*
3. *They can present the issue to a convention of states to have the matter heard.*

"In the methods I listed, I did not see a single reference to junkets, dinners, gifts or rounds of golf. So, I was again perplexed about what it was our lobbyists did. I again went to my Webster's dictionary and thesaurus where I stumbled upon another word, one which more accurately describes the acts I just mentioned and which the group of you on my left have admitted to doing.

"The word I found that describes junkets, dinners, gifts and rounds of golf is Bribery. My dictionary defines bribery as: ***an attempt to corrupt or influence (one in a position of trust) by favors or gifts***.

"Okay, here again we have the word attempt. Only in this definition, the attempt is to corrupt or influence one in a position of trust. What could be meant by the term -- 'One in a position of trust'? It sounds a lot like the position these members of Congress are in. The people who elect them to their position, trust them to perform and represent them. Yet our 'Lobbyists' influence them with special favors and gifts. A free round of golf, a business junket to Bermuda, or something as trifle as a major campaign contribution. None of the methods of lobbying that I mentioned before, incur the use of bribery as a method of attempting to influence Congress. Those methods do not attempt to corrupt our Congress. Also, these are the methods set forth in the constitution these representatives are sworn to protect.

"In virtually every country in the world if favors and gifts, monetary or otherwise, regardless of size or value, are given to a person in Government, it is considered a bribe and both the person giving the bribe, and the person receiving the bribe, are sentenced to extended jail time. In some countries, the sentence for bribery is death, since bribery is considered equally heinous to murder, as it is a crime against all people.

"In the United States, these favors and gifts, political contributions, junkets, dinners, etcetera have been considered part of a lobby for too long. They are a bribe. They were considered bribes in 1853 when Congress passed laws making bribery of Federal Officers illegal. It is no less bribery, today.

"The Executive Order I signed prior to this session, reinstates the anti-bribery laws in this country and henceforth, those laws will be enforced. Chief Steigel, your officers may begin arresting the people on my left. They have freely admitted to committing the crime of bribery."

Chief Steigel signaled and fifty-armed Capitol Police Officers entered the chamber and surrounded the group of lobbyists. There was a great amount of commotion and shouting "You can't do that." from the lobbyist groups. Others threatened law suits for slander, illegal arrest, etcetera. Their outbursts were immediately quieted by the police officers reading them their rights.

"Mr. President?"

"Yes, Chief?"

"Sir, we have a dilemma. Since these people were not advised of their rights against self-incrimination prior to your questions, our prosecution may not hold up in court and will waste a great deal of time and taxpayer money.

Several of the lobbyists exclaim "Yeah, you can't prosecute us. We'll sue the Government and you personally, Waters."

Sam continues with the Chief. "Okay, Chief, I see the issue. How would you suggest we proceed?"

"Sir, I have never been in this position before, therefore, I'm at a loss for a viable solution. Sir, my officers have informed me, we have a greater dilemma."

"And what would that issue be?"

"Sir, the greater issue is -- we only have half of the perpetrators to the crime of bribery. We can charge this group with attempting to commit bribery, however this would be a much lesser Class E felony. If we have both the briber and the bribe, it becomes a Class A felony punishable by twenty-five years in Federal Prison."

"I see. To have a bribe, there must be someone to receive it." Sam looks over the members of congress. "I would suppose if I asked how many of you have accepted gifts, junkets, trips, dinners, special campaign contributions or any other form of bribe, none of you would confess that you have. Since, I can't very well use the taxpayer's money to prosecute the entire Congress, we will have to let them go. We will also forego prosecution of the lobby groups." The lobbyists began to making comments about Waters being a fool.

"However, Chief, I may have a solution that will not burden our Taxpayers. Photograph and record the names of these people and the groups they work for, confiscate their credentials which allow them access to the Capitol, then escort them off Capitol property. These individuals as well as the organizations they represent are barred from the House and Senate Offices and Chambers and all other buildings on the Capitol, for six months effective today. If they attempt to return prior to the first of September, arrest them on suspicion of bribery and prosecute them. Take them away."

"Yes, Sir." Chief Steigel and his officers escort the group out of the chambers and Sam allows the smaller group to return to the gallery.

"Ladies and Gentlemen of Congress, you are on notice. Article two, Section four of the Constitution clearly states:

The President, Vice President, and all civil Officers of the United States, shall be removed from Office on Impeachment for, and Conviction of, Treason, Bribery, or other high Crimes and Misdemeanors.

"If you are suspected of accepting a bribe you will be censured, investigated and prosecuted. If you are found guilty, you will go to jail. My election platform was respect and reform and I will provide the people with the results of that platform with or without your assistance. The days of Congress violating the laws of this country without due process are over. This concludes this session. We will have another joint session the thirtieth of March. Thank you."

The Congressional members stood as Sam stepped down from the podium not amid the applause of the last session, but into the dismal abyss of men and women who knew they may be serving on borrowed time. Some who had willingly accepted junkets, dinners, and other assorted bribes from lobbyists were now concerned about their position come the next election.

27
CONVENTION OF GOVERNORS

One of the first things Sam did on his first day in office was invite the State Governors to a Convention of Governors. Sam asked them to bring any issues they might have with the Federal Government to the convention. Sam also asked them to bring suggestions about how he can assist their states. Many of the Governors were skeptical about this convention. No President in the past thirty years had called such a convention. Many wondered what Sam was up to? What was his hidden agenda for calling this convention? How was the meeting going to play into that agenda? The convention opened on the third day of March.

Sam had requested Jerry Cummings to be the White House Press Secretary and Bill Kerr to be the head of public relations. Bill had graciously refused for personal reasons, but Jerry had accepted. Sam felt that the White House Press Person was much more than a 'secretary' so redubbed the title to White House Press Liaison. Sam asked Jerry to introduced him to the Governors.

"Good Morning, Ladies and Gentlemen. If you can find your seats, please." The Governors milled around until they found their State placard and sat down. "Thank you. Ladies and Gentlemen. Please stand for the President of the United States, the Honorable Sam Waters."

Sam entered the chamber to supportive applause from the Governors.

"Thank you. You may be seated. Good Morning, Ladies and Gentlemen. The reason I have invited you all to this convention is two-fold. First, I have invited you to discuss the various things we can do to help each other. I know the Federal Government has not always been your State's best friend or partner. At times, we have even gone so far as to be your enemy – when we have used Federal funds to coerce the States into compliance with some doctrine which the States opposed. One topic which comes to mind most readily was the fifty-five miles-per-hour speed limit which was in effect from the seventies through the early nineties.

"Secondly, I wanted you to know that I welcome your input on the issues which face your governments and make your positions precarious with your residents. I had previously schedule this conference for two weeks; however, I know you have States to govern and duties to perform, so, I will not delay anyone who may have to return home. I announced this convention to your Representatives and Senators, the Supreme Court, and my Cabinet members. You may feel free to speak with anyone of them directly with your issues. If there is anyone you would like to address personally, this is your opportunity.

"Ladies and Gentlemen, participation is the key to getting the most out of this meeting. I have set aside this week to be at your service and to attempt to resolve some of the issues you have. I can't fix what I don't know is broken. I will be checking back in with you as my schedule permits. Now I will open the floor to the Governor from South Dakota?"

"Thank you, Mr. President, I'm David Blake. Sir, you spoke of Federal coercion to make the States follow doctrine which is of little or no concern to our State. Almost every State Government has been threatened with a suspension of Federal Funding if we don't comply with the Department of Education's Testing Programs. Many of us believe testing is not a positive indicator of student performance or our teachers ability to teach, yet we must administer these mandated programs like the Iowa Basic Skills Assessment, or No Child Left Behind both of which cater to leaving our children on the verge of entering their adult world, college, and job markets without the necessary skills to compete.

"The Partnership for Assessment of Readiness for College and Careers test or (PARCC) test was the biggest insult to the States yet. The PARCC is given to grades 3-11 online but must be monitored within the schools. You cannot tell me that the big computer and computer software industry did not have anything to do with this test. Every school that accepts the PARCC program must buy enough computers, software and teacher and administrator training to give the test to hundreds of thousands of students nationwide -- and it is not just an assessment of high school students getting ready to enter college or career fields as the title would imply. It spans all schools; elementary schools, middle schools, Junior high schools, and high schools. Who gets the benefit? The computer technology industry, specifically the programs biggest technological supporter.

"Children are not test scores! There have been numerous studies and enormous amounts of research since the 1950s concerning the national testing of students. Researchers have determined that twenty-five to forty percent of all students suffer from varying degrees of test anxiety and these students score on average twelve to twenty percentile points below their peers. Forty percent of any test group severely skews the result. What do these tests measure? Absolutely **NOTHING!** They do not measure the child's ability to learn nor do they measure the ability of the teacher to teach. They do not measure all the students equally for their ability to learn or retain the information. The only thing the tests accomplish is to place undue stress and pressure on the students. If a teacher has been unable to teach the student to read or the parents have not encouraged their child to learn – how are they supposed to pass a test?

You cannot expect the average child from a ghetto or projects school to achieve the same score as the average child from an upper middle-class school or even the average child from the affluent upper class or private schools. It is not that the teaching or curriculum is any different. It's the prevailing undertone in each of these communities that dictates how well a child learns. Distractions from the street, peer-pressure and the community influence a child's ability to learn and a teacher's ability to teach that child.

Children are measured and evaluated every day based on their performance of the work presented in their classrooms. That should be sufficient to determine their ability to learn. Teachers are paid to educate, measure, and evaluate our children. If a student is failing – it is the teacher's job to provide that student with the tools to succeed. Those tools can be, but are not limited to:

Talk to the student –

Is there something in the information they do not understand?

Is there anything going on at home that may be an issue? Divorce? Death?

Are there troubles with their peers that may be an issue?

Talk to parents, same questions as above, and not just at PTA meetings

Talk to other teachers, do they know anything about the child?

Provide additional assistance (possibly after school hours).

Pair them with a more proficient student as a tutor.

It is ludicrous to continue testing our children to measure the performance of their teachers. In 2014, New Mexico began an online testing of students, the PARCC. Another test that replaces the existing assessment test? This test was developed by a coalition of states for evaluating children in grades 3-11. **What?** Did anyone look at the title of this test? **Assessment of Readiness for College and Careers**. What are we doing giving this test to elementary school students, grade 3-6? I do not think my eight-year-old grandchildren are quite ready to enter college or the workplace, unless of course our Government has also changed the child labor laws. Which, I would not doubt they have done or at least tried. I understand the test is different for students in each grade level but whoever thought up the name needs some serious help. New Jersey was the initial test bed for the PARCC. It was inconclusive and deemed a failure. In other states the test failed to achieve desired results. A couple of the States wanted to withdraw from the program but were not allowed to by the Federal Government. As the results have proven the test to be a failure, two of the original four tests have been removed from the basic test and revised and added as optional tests. What are you prepared to do?"

"Governor Blake, I would like for you to start here -- William Davies is my Secretary of Education. William, I want you to examine the mandates Mr. Blake has brought forward. He seems very well versed on the subject, so I want you to work closely with him and research these mandates thoroughly for their validity and usefulness. If you don't see a useful purpose, I want you to ask for a revocation from the House and Senate. I challenge everyone in the cabinet to get together with these Governors to find the issues with your departments. Research the laws, regulations and mandates which are creating the issues with the States and find a way to fix them. I realize I may not have done enough to fix the issue right now, but, I can assure you that it's a start and we will keep working on it for you. Is there anything else Mr. Blake?"

"Mr. President, as you just said, it's a start. At the beginning of your campaign when you were looking for contributions you made a comment I'm going to say to you now. We all hear you talk the talk, we'll see if you can walk the walk."

"Thank you, Mr. Blake. The floor is given to the Governor of Massachusetts."

"Thank you, Mr. President. My name is Madeline Burrows. Sir, there have been many times when our elected representatives in the House and Senate seem to act contrary to the views or desires of the state or the part of the population they are supposed to represent. We would like to be able to recall our representatives if they are not voting in accordance with the views of the state."

"Ms. Burrows, I completely agree that there must be some way, some method of removing a representative who is not performing responsibly in their position. As you may have seen in the news, I have reminded our representatives of their duties and oath of office. The problems with removing a representative are multi-dimensional.

"We have a means of removal by impeachment, if the person has committed a crime. But, what would the mechanism be to measure the representative's performance? What procedure would we use to determine whether a representative should be fired for failure to perform their duties?

"We can use the polls, but there is a problem with polls -- if the representative is of one party and the poll is taken in a primarily opposing party area of the district, the results could be tainted. Also, if a poll was taken of a random cross-section of the district, what percentages of the population would have to agree?

"We could take a vote, but again what percentage of the population would it take to remove the representative? If by popular vote only – it was the popular vote that put them in office; so, it can be assumed those same people would vote to keep them there. It is a quandary, but we can find a solution."

"Mr. President, what would be the possibility of a censure issued by the Governor?"

"That, Ms. Burrows, could be a possibility. I will get with the Speaker of the House, the Vice-President and the Justice of the United States and see what we can come up with along those lines that is legal, Constitutional, and effective. I have heard it said that getting anything passed in Congress is like making baby elephants – five seconds to conceive the idea and two years to get results."

The Governors laughed at Sam's comment as he promised not to take two years for the results and called on the Governor from Hawaii.

"Thank you, Mr. President. I am Ben Aikula. Being from the Islands and six hours behind Washington has advantages and disadvantages. The advantage is when we are awake, Congress is closed or sleeping. The disadvantage is when Congress is awake, we are closed or sleeping, and our Representatives have little or no input from our State. I am sure the Governors from Alaska and the West coast have many of those same problems. You have directed a joint session of Congress to be held on the thirtieth of each month. Would it be possible for the Governors to attend these sessions?"

"Mr. Aikula, I would be very happy to have you attend the joint sessions, however, I think your residents may not appreciate paying your airfare to fly to Washington D.C. once a month. However, I have a solution. I will schedule the joint sessions at a time when all the State Governors are able to attend via Vox Speaker Phone. Does this meet with your approval?" The Governors voiced their approval of Sam's idea and looked forward to the nest session.

The Governors spent the next two weeks discussing their varying issues and meeting with representatives and members of Sam's Cabinet. At the end of the conference Sam raised a question for the Governors.

"Ladies and Gentlemen. I want to thank you for coming and spending this week with me. I hope you enjoyed your time in the D.C. area and more than that I hope you found these days productive. I have one last question for you before you return home. What is your perception of me as your President. Mr. Blake?"

"Sir, you have given us something most of us haven't seen from the Federal Government or any past President and that is hope. You have talked the talk and I truly believe you will walk the walk. I think I can speak for most of the Governors. We are behind you. You have a good plan for the reformation of the country and we would be foolish not to follow your lead in the reformation of our states." The rest of the Governors echo Blake's comments and applauded Sam as he left the podium to walk among them and shake their hands.

28

TOO MANY CAREER POLITICIANS

Sixty days had passed since Sam's inauguration and Sam had done very little in the thirty days since the last joint session. Not that he wasn't busy, he had held the Convention of Governors and had worked with Senator Albright and Congresswoman Dontae on a couple of the items from their lists, but he hadn't issued any more Executive Orders or held any press conferences.

Senator Albright and Congresswoman Dontae had also been busy since they had taken the lists from Sam and were in the process of writing new regulations or amendments for the various issues on those lists. The two junior representatives, even though opposing parties and different houses had worked well together and had met with Sam, occasionally, on the issues to make them appealing to both sides of the aisle without distracting from Sam's intent which was to bring America back.

One of the items on Dontae's list was the ten percent corporate tax Sam had detailed during the Presidential debates. An item on Albright's list, also from the debate, was a bill permanently restricting any Senatorial or Congressional involvement in how the military conducted warfare. Both bills were on the floor of their respective houses at the end of March.

The joint session was scheduled for noon. Congress had assembled, and Mike had already taken the roll call. Everyone was present except Sam. Mike talked with Speaker of the House Woodward, and they agreed to take a joint vote on the bills before each house.

Mike gave the floor to Woodward.

"Ladies and Gentlemen, in the absence of the President, Vice-President Baker and I have agreed to have a joint vote on the issues on the floor of each house. The Vice-President has graciously allowed the House of Representatives to present first. Congresswoman Dontae would you please present your bill to the joint congress."

Prior to the last joint session, this item was a hot spot for the representatives on the committee for tax reform. After the session Dontae's 'New Lease' corporate tax bill with very minor suggested changes was approved in the committee and was submitted to the House for a vote the morning of the joint session.

Dontae, presented the New Lease HR 1223, bill to the joint session. Although, the House had been reviewing the bill for several weeks, this was the first time the Senate would see it. Dontae was sure it would not pass both Houses in this joint session. When she finished her presentation, Woodward asked by a show of hands anyone who had not reviewed the document. No hands went up. Cheryl Dontae looked at Ben Albright who just shrugged in disbelief and waved his copy of the document. Albright approached Dontae.

"Cheryl, this was in the inbox of every Senator five days ago. I thought maybe you had already blasted it through the House and it was up for our vote until I saw there were no House notes or speaker's comments. Then I thought you stepped out of line and gave us a preview copy."

"Ben, I wouldn't have done that, but I do know who may have. Waters."

"Ladies and Gentlemen, since everyone has reviewed the document. I will submit HR1223 to the floor for discussion. Is there any discussion?" A couple of Senators asked questions about the bill which Dontae quickly answered. "Any further discussion? No further discussion requested, I therefore submit HR1223 to this joint session of Congress for vote. Ms. Dontae would you call the roll for the House vote on HR1223?"

Dontae called the roll and the bill passed the house, three-hundred-four to one-hundred-twenty with ten abstentions and one absent.

"Thank You, Mr. Albright, I understand that you had a hand in this bill, would you please call the roll for the Senate vote."

Albright, called the roll and the bill passed the Senate eighty-five to ten with five abstentions.

"Thank you, HR 1223 has been approved by both the House of Representatives and Senate and will now go to the Supreme Court for Judicial review. Mr. Vice President the floor is yours."

"Thank you, Mr. Speaker. Ladies and Gentlemen, I would like to offer for joint consideration, a bill currently on the floor of the Senate. Mr. Albright would you please present SR 1018."

Albright's 'In and Done' Military involvement bill, also met with a lot of opposition prior to the joint session. Most of the older

Senators were opposed to giving up their control in military matters. However, after some debate, the committee only asked for a clause to ensure the military would take all possible measures to protect non-combatants without endangering our service men and women.

Albright presented 'In and Done SR 1018'. Again, everyone seemed to have a copy and the bill had been reviewed by both houses. Mike asked for discussion and instantly gets a flurry from the House of Representatives.

"This is absurd. Bills of Military nature are to be originated in the House. This is completely out of line and I challenge this bill."

Mike responded. "Mr. Hancock, has issued a challenge to SR1018 and has raised the question of the Bill's origin. Mr. Hancock, you are absolutely correct. The House of Representatives is the originating body for Military bills, which concern the formation of the branches of Service, their size and equipment and other budgetary and monetary issues. SR1018 does not intrude on the House's responsibilities. The Senate is responsible for passing laws governing this country. SR1018, is a law, which restricts congressional interference in Military matters in time of war or conflict, therefore, the Senate bill is well within their duties and responsibilities for the origin of this law. Mr. Speaker, would you agree?

"Yes, I fully agree that the Senate has not overstepped their responsibilities on this issue."

"Thank you, Sir. Is there any further discussion?" Several other Congressmen asked questions which Albright addressed positively, and the discussion concluded. Mike orders Albright to take the roll call vote for the Senate which passed ninety to ten. Mike then orders Dontae to take the roll call for the House vote. It passed two-sixty-five to one-hundred-sixty-nine with one absent. Mike announced the passage by both houses and ordered the bill sent to the Supreme Court for Judicial Review.

Sam finally arrived at two-forty-five. Mike announced him, and he took his place at the podium.

"Ladies and Gentlemen, I apologize for being tardy. There was some urgent business in the Middle East, a flare of radical extremist activity in Helmand. I hope you were able to accomplish some business in my absence. Mr. Vice-President, what have you been doing?"

"Mr. President, we presented HR1223 and SR 1018 and had a joint vote on both. Both passed and have been sent for Judicial Review."

"Thank you, Mr. Baker and thank you, Ladies and Gentlemen. Can you see by what happened here how far we can travel when we all work together on the same road for America and not just this, that or the other party line or agenda?

"For the record. I may have campaigned and been elected as an independent with no ties to any party, but, that does not mean. I'm against the parties. I believe the parties give our Government balance. However, when we get so caught up in our party values and agenda we forget who we are working for. Then it is time to bring in the independents or a third party to remind us of who we are. We are not, Republican or Democrat, Libertarian or Socialist, Green or Tea. We are first, and foremost Americans and we need to act like Americans and as elected representatives who work for the people of this great nation. We have to act for Americans."

The Congressional Members and the gallery applaud Sam's comment.

"This week I have asked Senator Albright and Congresswoman Dontae to write and propose an amendment to the Constitution. I would hope that when you hear my proposal, you will agree with me that it is time to resolve an issue which has plagued this country for almost a century. I want you all to agree to term limits for all elected officials and justices. I have thought long and hard on this issue. I know it should be offered as an amendment to the constitution. Just as Presidential term limits were established in 1947, all congressional term-limits should also have been set.

"The twenty-second amendment was designed to protect our country and Constitution from a dictator the likes of Adolf Hitler. Unfortunately, it relieved the country of the possibility of having one dictator in exchange for having five-hundred-thirty-five dictators. It is time to break the chains. It is time for term-limits for the House, the Senate, and the Federal Justices.

"We have just seen two new representatives. One from each house and from each party, work together to produce two documents on two very different and difficult subjects. Each document stood on its own merit without riders or numerous changes. Each were presented, discussed, voted on and passed both houses in this joint session. I do not know how much discussion these bills had, but I can imagine it wasn't much since both bills were presented, discussed, and voted on by both houses in less than two hours, forty-five minutes.

"Mark Twain once said, 'politicians are like diapers and must be changed often and for the same reason.' To some extent I must agree with Mr. Twain. We do need to change our representatives regularly to promote growth and keep the country from growing stagnant.

"I realize there must be some continuity, some glue to hold the Government together during the elections and transitions. Here's my proposal for your consideration:

1. *Amend the term for the House of Representatives from two years to four years with one-half of the House being elected every two years. Article one, section two of the Constitution sets the term of the House Representatives at two years and we elect or reelect the entire House -- Four-hundred-thirty-five Representatives every two years. A four-year term for representatives would stabilize the house and give some continuity. The only continuity they have now -- we reelect a clear majority every election.*
2. *No Elected Official will be allowed to serve longer than Twelve years total in any office or combination of offices.*
3. *Amend the Constitution to include term-limits of twelve years total for the House of Representatives, Senate, and Federal Justices.*

Under the twelve-year term-limit amendment, a Representative may serve:

Three Congressional terms

One term in the House and one term in the Senate

Two terms in the House and one term as President or Vice-President

One Term in the House and two terms as president or Vice-President

4. *Senators are elected for six years in accordance with Article one, section three of the Constitution with one*

third being elected every two years.

Under the twelve-year term-limit amendment, a Senator may serve

Two terms in the Senate

One term in the Senate and one term in either the House or President or Vice-President

5. *Federal Justices may only serve for twelve years cumulative total in any Federal justice position.*
6. *Federal Judges should be elected by the people just as our State, County and City Judges are. The President will nominate one candidate from each party, including Independent parties, for a Federal Judge vacancy. The Senate would confirm the nominations are eligible for appointment. The candidates would be added to the ballot for elections and the people would vote their choice. Popular vote wins the seat.*

"We have polled the people and they have indicated they want to see term-limits for Congress. Can we work together on this and make it happen?" There is scattered applause.

"Mr. Vice President and Mr. Speaker, I would ask the two of you to work this out together. Assist Mr. Albright and Ms. Dontae. Draw from the members of your houses those you feel can put the term-limits together in a constitutional amendment and work with them to get the proposal written, approved by both houses, through judicial review and out to the States for ratification by our next joint session in thirty days. Thank you, ladies and gentlemen, we will meet again on thirty April." The members of Congress again applaud as Sam exits.

Mike and Woodward worked together well, putting a term-limit package together. They had increased the term of Congress to four years with half being elected every two years. They had defined and fine-tuned Sam's proposal and had a document ready to be voted on. They put it up to the House and it failed to pass by four votes. Mike and Woodward took a second look at the amendment. It was correct in form and format, so it should have passed. Sam looked at the congressional vote and identified the problem. The House is split between new representatives and multiterm older representatives. Under the new term-limits, if ratified, two-hundred-nineteen representatives would not be allowed to run for reelection. Sam sent Woodward to talk to the senior Representatives and suggested Mike do the same in the Senate.

***

Sam held back some of his plans for the April joint session to be able to fight the fight for term-limits. It was April thirtieth and the proposed amendment still hadn't been passed by either house. Sam took the podium.

"Good Afternoon, Ladies and Gentlemen. Today, I want to make very clear my disappointment with this Congress. Some of you feel you can ignore the people. You feel you can ignore me and my agenda to put Government back into the hands of the people we represent. You feel you can fight a war of attrition with my plans and you will win, because you will be reelected and out last me like you have every other Presidents before me. I made a promise to the people of this Nation and I fully intend to keep it with or without your assistance. In case you have failed to notice, the press has been invited to every joint session. Your constituents see these sessions on regular broadcast news, not just CNET or CSPAN. Yes, you may win some of the battles with me, but I can assure you all -- you will not win against the people you represent. Mr. Speaker, please take a rollcall vote of the House of Representatives with State and District, on the proposal for the term-limit amendment."

Woodward complied with Sam's request and took the vote. The proposal passed three-hundred-fifteen to one-hundred-five with five absent.

"Thank you, Mr. Speaker. Mr. Vice President has the Senate been able to review the term-limit amendment proposition?"

"Yes, Mr. President they have."

"Mr. Baker will you please take a rollcall vote of the Senate, with State and District?"

Mike, also complied with the request and the proposal passed the Senate ninety-five to four with one absent.

"Thank you, Mr. Baker. Chief Justice Weaver, has the Supreme Court been able to review the document known today as the term-limit amendment proposition?"

"Yes, Mr. President and we can find no conflict with the Constitution. We recommend submission to the States for ratification."

"Thank you, Chief Justice. Please note it as such and forward the Proposal to the States.

"Ladies and Gentlemen, I thank you for passing this proposal. I would also like to see legislature on the ratification process which will prevent some of the errors of the past. The Sixteenth Amendment identified that we need a strict set of guidelines for the chain of events to prevent a proposal from bypassing any of the Congressional entities on its way to the States. If an error such as the Sixteenth Amendment occurs, we need guidelines to be able to recall a proposal from the States once it has been sent for ratification. We need to establish a system of tracking ratification documents other than a bin in the office of the National Archivist. Lastly, we need guidelines for the States restricting them from voting on a proposal which is not stamped by both houses and noted for issue and ratification by the Supreme Court.

"Thank you, Ladies and Gentlemen. We will meet again on the thirtieth of May."

There is no applause as Sam exits. Many of the career politicians turn their backs to him. Many others scowl at him and if looks could kill Sam would have faced the same fate as Caesar in the Senate of Rome.

Congress did not like being held accountable for their voting. Sam had made it more of an affront by requesting the roll call vote with each representative's State and District in front of the press. Many of the career politicians felt that even if the people did want term-limits, they didn't know what was good for them. The people had voted for career politicians or there wouldn't be so many of them. Now, this nobody comes in and calls the vote in front of the media. Who was going to vote against the proposal under those conditions. Sam had not made any friends today and he figured today was just one of many he would take a hit on.

29

THE FIRST HUNDRED DAYS

May thirty and time for another joint session. Sam was painfully aware that he wouldn't make many friends today. Mike was in Iraq; the Senate Majority Leader was working in his home State and the Minority Whip Jennifer Mitchell had the chair for the Senate.

Sam had completed his first hundred days in office and, although, he had made some great advances on keeping his campaign promises, he had done relatively little -- setting a record low for what had become the marker of presidential efficiency. Sam may not have set any records for quantity of items accomplished, but what he did accomplish was much more effective than his predecessors who had managed to do a lot on the surface but very little of which mattered to most of the people. Smoke and Mirrors -- a magic act to appease the public and lull them into a belief that government was working for them.

Sam's plan for his first hundred days was to curry favor with the two Houses. He didn't want to create too many enemies along the party lines. He needed to gain the support of as many of the junior Representatives as possible – he was successful. He also needed to gain a solid foothold among the career politicians – he managed to do that as well. To Sam and Mike, they were tremendously successful in their first hundred days.

Sam wasn't going to rush into things without a thorough understanding of what needed to be done or changed. He had a list of items he felt needed to be addressed and he was taking on those battles in their due time.

Sam, had gained ground with the skeptical Congress, with his ten percent corporate tax plan. Corporations normally file their taxes quarterly. The new tax structure had an almost immediate impact on the economy. The new bill had been a boost to the economy and small businesses were popping up all over the country and performing better than they had in the last fifty years. The deficit was slowly beginning to decline.

Today, however, Sam had received the notice that Mike's Helicopter had been shot down in Helmand and he was missing. He had been concerned about Mike's decision to visit Helmand. He and the Secretary of Defense had been on an International Diplomacy tour and visiting the servicemen and women who were stationed or deployed overseas. They had diverted their itinerary to the Middle East and Mike wanted to visit the troops at the front. Now he was missing, and Sam feared the worst. He had called Nancy as soon as he got the news and had assured her Mike was okay and that he was doing everything he could to insure a safe return. He had also called Kate and asked her to meet with Nancy and keep her company. Sam had seen many wives do drastic things after they received news of missing husbands. He didn't want Nancy left alone.

Senator Mitchell announced Sam and took the roll call.

"Good afternoon, Ladies and Gentlemen. I have just received word that Vice-President Baker was shot down over Helmand Iraq. His helicopter crash landed behind enemy lines and the last reports indicated he and the rest of the people on the craft were uninjured, however, when the extraction team arrived they were missing. There is a full search and rescue operation in processes and my prayers are with Mr. Baker and his people. May we take a moment in silence for each of us, in our own way, to wish these six souls a safe and speedy return home."

After the moment of silence, Sam continues.

"Thank you. Even with the bad news we must continue to take care of the business we were hired to perform.

"As you are all aware, three weeks ago I held a convention of Governors in this very chamber. The convention was very productive, and we successfully worked together on several Items. The Governors have agreed to follow the example set by this Congress in the past one hundred days and work for the people. The states had stagnated on the proposed twenty-eighth amendment on term-limits and hadn't ratified. The count was stalled twenty-seven of the thirty-three States required to ratify the amendment. The Governors agreed to push the ratification along and they also agreed to set term limits for their State legislators. They agreed to mirror the Federal Government's campaign laws and they are looking forward to the years ahead.

"When the Governors went home, they took with them an understanding of who I am and what I stand for. They agreed with my desire to have their States, mirror my programs. I pledged my support and the support of this Congress to any who need it.

"The Governors went back to their home states and fulfilled their promise to push the ratification of the twenty-eighth amendment to the Constitution. I received the Ratification documents from the Archivist five days ago and signed the Amendment into law.

"As I have encouraged you to do, I asked the Governors, what their perception of me was. The overwhelming response to the question was 'too early to tell,' however, they were united in believing that together we can reform and restore this great nation.

"I, then, asked the Governors what we can do for them.? How can Congress serve them better? Their response was almost unanimous when they told me they wanted to be more involved. I was told, and I quote 'we all have our representatives, but we wonder quite often if our voices are being heard.'

"Today, we are going to do things a bit different than usual. Today and for every joint session from this point forward, the voices of our Governors will be heard. First, we are rearranging the seating – will you all please stand? There is no longer a left or right side of the aisle or a division of the houses. In these Joint Sessions, you are not individual Congressmen and Women or Senators. You are Representatives of your State. If you will look around, you will find Vox speaker phones on the tables. Find the Vox or Voxes labeled with your State and have a seat." When all the Representatives were again seated, Sam began.

"Ladies and Gentlemen, this will be the future seating for joint sessions of this Congress and will hopefully carry on long after I am gone. We are supposed to be working for the States, Districts, and People we represent; it is time we started working together. Mr. Speaker will you please take a rollcall of the States?"

As Woodward begins the roll call the Vox phones come to life as the Governors come on line and answer 'present' as their State is called. When Woodward finished the roll call, all fifty states and six territories were represented.

"In January, mere days after assuming office, I gave a prelude for today's business. Today, Senator Albright and Congresswoman Dontae are presenting four bills to this joint session. HR2877, HR2878, HR2879 and HR2880. In 1937, in the middle of the Great Depression President Roosevelt signed into law as part of the 'New Deal' plan, the Social Security Act. Since then every President including myself, have made changes to the act. Senator Albright and Congresswoman Dontae and several other Representatives and Senators have worked with me to research, draft and now present 'New Deal Two'

"HR2877. the Federal Tax Act, sets all income tax at a flat rate. Article one, section nine of the Constitution states; *No Capitation, or other direct tax shall be laid, unless in proportion to the census or enumeration herein before directed to be taken.*

"This statement has been open to interpretation probably since it was written. In fact, section nine in its entirety has become volatile since the sixteenth amendment gave Congress the power to tax the personal income of individuals. Some say the section means there should be no taxes on personal income, only corporations and import and excise taxes. Others, interpret the section as saying if there is to be a tax it is to be laid or applied equally to everyone.

"HR2877 follows the later thinking and sets a Flat Tax of ten percent of every dollar earned. No one is exempt. There are no exemptions, deductions or other loopholes which keep anyone from paying their fair share. This amount will be withheld from the payroll of each employee.

"HR2878, The Social Security Act of 2025. In 1937, the Social Security Act would not have passed either the House or Senate without the addition of the welfare rider. HR2878 makes the Social Security Act a stand-alone act. Again, no one is exempt.

"HR2879, The Welfare Relief Act of 2025. This act makes the Welfare portion of the Social Security Act a stand-alone act. It also sets forth that welfare is temporary, not to exceed eighteen months of entitlement. To receive the entitlement the applicant must be drug free and submit to random drug testing. They must be actively seeking employment and they will pay taxes on the amount of income they receive.

"Lastly, HR 2880, The Howard Arbogast, Veteran's Care Act. This act has special meaning for me. Two weeks ago, I was doing some fact finding, talking to people around Mclean, Virginia. We happened to stop at a little coffee shop where I overheard a conversation between the waitress and one of her regular customers. The customer was a Veteran who had served this country for many years and fought in two wars. He told the waitress he wouldn't be able to come back into the shop and he would miss her company dearly. When asked why, the Vet replied his retirement and disability was not enough to support him in his current apartment and he was being evicted. He wasn't sure where he was going to live or if he would have a roof over his head and not be out on the street. This is where I entered the conversation. The Veteran's name was Howard Arbogast and he was three months behind on his rent. The total arrears in rent was only one-hundred-fifty dollars. Howard had lived in the same apartment and paid his rent on time for twenty-two years. Over the past ten years his rent had gone up about seven percent per year while his retired Military pay, and Social Security only had a combined increase of 5 percent a year. This year the increase was nearly twenty-five percent and Howard could not afford to pay the rent and utilities and be able to eat. He paid the old amount of rent but was left fifty dollars short of the full rent amount for the past three months. The apartment complex isn't new or elaborate and Howard has a simple efficiency unit, yet he cannot afford his rent. This is an unacceptable situation for someone who has faithfully served this country to be left with nothing. HR2880 will keep Veteran's benefits in line with the cost of living, reduce the number of homeless, and take care of those who have taken care of us. This bill includes all who serve -- Military, Police, and Firefighters.

"Ladies and Gentlemen, there are basically three types of government in the world today, capitalist, socialist and communist. I have again searched my Webster's dictionary and found these definitions:

Capitalism:

An economic system characterized by private or corporate ownership of capital goods, and by prices, production, and distribution of goods that are determined by a free market.

Capitalist:

A person who has capital invested in a business
A person of great wealth

Socialism:

A theory of Social Organization based on Government ownership, management, and control of the means of production and distribution and exchange of goods.

Socialist:

A person who believes in and practices Socialism.

Communism:

Social Organization in which goods are held in common. A theory of Social Organization advocating common ownership, management, and control of the means of production and distribution of products of industry based on need.

Communist:

A person who believes in and practices communism.

America is a Democracy which follows capitalistic values. We favor personal growth and private ownership of our businesses and corporations, because the economy grows as our businesses grow. We believe in free trade, so prices can stabilize at a more affordable level.

We are not a socialist or communist state that stifles growth by governmental or central control of everything.

Ms. Dontae will you please present the bills?"

As Congresswoman Dontae presented HR2877. The entire congress thought Sam had completely lost his mind. The House said he would lose everything he gained with the corporate tax and were firmly against the bill until Dontae presented the computer mockup which showed the economic growth because the average household would have more available income. This economic growth would substantially increase the number of businesses by creating a larger corporate base. They were surprised when it appeared to generate more residual money for Government to pay toward the deficit. When the House vote was taken, Congressman Heindahl of South Carolina voted against the measure.

Ruben Thompson, the Governor of South Carolina, immediately asked Sam for the floor.

"Mr. President, I apologize for the interruption of the vote, but we have a situation here that we asked about during our convention.

The State Government of South Carolina has been discussing a similar bill for the state for several months. Congressman Heindahl was aware of our discussions and the polls which were taken to survey the desires of our population. The Congressman has just voted in direct opposition to the public he serves and to his State Government.

"At the convention the Governor from Massachusetts, Ms. Madeline Burrows asked for a way to recall our Representatives when they are not Representing the people of the state. At the time you told us you would check into the possibility of a censure imposed or requested by the Governors.

"Sir, we have one of those instances at this moment and I would like to request a censure of Congressman Heindahl. During the time of censure, I would like Mr. Heindahl to return to South Carolina and explain his actions to the State Senate and Congress."

"Thank you, Governor Thompson. I believe in this forum we may introduce a request for censure on behalf of the Governors. Mr. Woodward, Chief Justice, Ms. Mitchell is there any objection to a Governor requesting a censure of a representative from their state when it is obvious the representative is working contrary to the wants and desires of the people?"

"No objection, Mr. President." The unanimous answer.

"Mr. Woodward at the close of this session would you please begin censure proceedings against Mr. Heindahl?"

"Absolutely, Mr. President."

The HR2877 vote continue and the bill passed both houses and was forwarded to the Supreme Court for Judicial Review.

When Dontae presented HR2878, which would give just one percent of the taxes to Social Security and remove the FICA and Medicare/Medicaid taxes, the Representatives initially rejected the whole idea. One Congressman stated HR 2877 was ridiculous and absurd. If only one percent of the tax collected through HR 2877, was applied to Social Security, the program would be completely out of money in a year. Dontae then showed where the one percent with the employer contribution requirement of one percent, when added to the funds already in Social Security and placed in a high yield account dedicated to Social Security would increase the balance by eight-hundred percent within three years.

The new act also placed a one-hundred-year ban on any use of Social Security for any other Government programs including Welfare. The Act passed in both houses and the Judicial Review and Sam signed it into law. The next October, those on Social Security received a twelve percent raise.

HR2879 was next to be presented. Sam renewed the New Deal Welfare system under its own act, The Welfare Relief Act. The Welfare Relief Act is a temporary fund to aid families, with some exception for single individuals, during periods of unemployment. The Act mirrored unemployment regulations to set the term a person or family could receive welfare. The total time welfare can be drawn is eighteen months and the person must be actively seeking employment and be able to pass random drug testing. The plan also provided vocational education for those without skills and Sam asked business owners to voluntarily provide the education. Business owners all over the country answered Sam's request, providing skilled training in construction for plumbers, electricians, and masons. Skilled training was also offered for mechanics. The Congress would distribute one percent of the HR2877 tax to the new welfare act for two years, after which the amount would be reduced to one half of one percent. If welfare could sustain itself at half of a percent, the distribution would remain constant until such time as a larger percentage was required. If the Welfare Act required additional funds, it would only be allowed to increase a quarter of one percent every other year. Other than needed increases in funding, the Act could not be changed or amended for one hundred years. Since the welfare act changed welfare to reflect unemployment the payments would no longer be taxed, however termination of benefits after eighteen months would be enforced.

***

HR2779 and 2880 passed unanimously through both houses and all four were signed into law.

30
WHISKEY TANGO FOXTROT

Mike was excited about the Senate resolution for military action and thought it was about time the Government allowed the military to take care of business without having their hands tied. The Government's mission is diplomacy and peace – the Military's mission is to wage war when Government's mission fails. The lines should never be crossed. Mike talked with Sam about a world tour of Military bases to meet with the servicemen and women and their commanders. Sam agreed with the idea and knew he needed to show some international diplomacy. A tour of Military bases would afford him the opportunity to meet with the world leaders, but this was not the time for him to leave Washington. They decided Mike would do the initial diplomatic tour and Sam would follow later in the summer. Mike left for Europe the next day.

Since this tour was both diplomatic and military, Mike had Nancy and Billy with him and invited the new Secretary of Defense, Marine Corps General Robert Chaffey, and his wife. Chaffey had been a great Marine Corps leader who was cut from the same or similar cloth as Marine Corps General and former Secretary of Defense James (Mad Dog) Mattis. Both men were brutally honest, no BS commanders who would lead their Marines from the front. Chaffey was dedicated and would become one of Mike's and Sam's closest friends.

Mike would not take his family into any Militarily hot zones, but he wanted them to see the world. Mike and Chaffey, along with their families, visited military installations and foreign dignitaries in a tour of twenty countries. Mike wanted to visit the troops in Iraq and especially Helmand, so he and Chaffey sent their wives home and headed for Riyadh, Saudi Arabia.

***

The two men had planned to visit several of the forward bases, but the local commanders advised them it wasn't a very good idea since most of the forward bases were in contact with the extremists who would love to pick off anyone in a suit who might be important to the Infidels.

Mike was adamant about the trip and let the Commanders know that he and Chaffey would be taking the tour, so they had better find a way to make it happen. Even though Mike knew the dangers from experience, he was dead set on seeing what was happening first hand. Mike and Chaffey agreed to limit their visibility and asked for uniforms and body armor for themselves and four of their security detail. The plan called for five helicopters, one for Mike and his security detail, one for Chaffey and his detail and three decoys. They would leave for the forward most fire base, code named One-Two Oscar, just before sunrise the next morning.

***

They arrived at the fire base at eight thirty and were briefed by the commanders as to the situation in Helmand. Mike met briefly with the combat Marines and requested a flyover of the Helmand area, particularly anywhere men and women were engaged with the enemy. After some discussion about the safety of the Vice-President and Secretary, the trip was planned. Once again, they would use five helicopters -- the flyover mission launched at fourteen-hundred.

The group reached the forward area in less than fifteen minutes and saw a Marine patrol pinned down by heavy enemy fire. From his position above the fight, Mike could see several enemy positions and ordered his escort helicopters to deliver suppressive fire into those positions. The helicopters began their assault and successfully routed the enemy, enabling the Marines on the ground to advance and destroy the threat. The escort helicopters were still engaged when two stinger missiles arose from the roof of an enemy held building and were flying straight toward Mike's and Chaffey's helicopters. The helicopter with Chaffey managed to evade the missile; however, Mike's helicopter was too close and only managed to dodge the main impact. The missile hit and disabled the tail rotor causing the pilot to lose control. Unable to maneuver the helicopter, it spun in what is called auto-rotation which carried it over a hill and behind enemy strongholds. The pilot was able to successfully land the damaged craft with no injuries; however, they were not in a very good position. They were behind the enemy lines in a rocky crag which prevented rescue helicopters from landing. They had no communication and night was falling.

The emergency call went out over the radio. "Mad Corps, this is Cover One. Red Dog is down. I say again, Red Dog is down. Over." Red dog was the codename Mike had chosen for himself because of his love for Irish Setters. The call would notify the command that Mike's aircraft had crashed.

"Cover One. This is Mad Corps, can you verify? Over."

"Mad Corps, Cover One. Red Dog is definitely down. All personnel appear to be uninjured, but the terrain will not allow extraction. I am low on fuel and cannot hold my cover position for much longer. Over"

"Cover One hold your position as long as possible, extract is inbound, ETA fifteen minutes. Over"

The auto-rotating crash had Mike and his group disoriented as to their direction back to friendly lines and the terrain was as hostile as the enemy. Mike signaled Cover One to fly home.

"Mad Corps, Cover One. Red Dog has signaled me to fly home. I believe they need the direction to friendly space. Over"

"Roger, Cover One, fly home. Relay your heading to Extract. Over."

"Roger, flying home. Out."

Mike watched as his cover helicopter faded out of sight, then gathered up the first aid kits, weapons and ammunition from the downed helicopter and started walking with his group in the direction Cover One had shown them.

As soon as the stinger missile passed Chaffey's helicopter, the Secretary was immediately evacuated out of the hostile area and back to the fire base, where his first duty was to call Sam.

"Sir, this is Chaffey. Red Dog is down, Sir."

"What happened, Rob?"

Chaffey explained the circumstances surrounding the crash and let Sam know Mike was okay. At least for the moment.

"Sir, Cover One reported everyone was unharmed, but when Extract arrived at the crash site, no one was there. All six souls were missing. Extract backtracked Cover One's heading to home, but night was coming fast and there was only forty minutes of twilight to search for Red Dog and his detail. There is no moon tonight, so aircraft search efforts are limited to infrared and we will continue with added helicopter and fixed-wing support in the morning. Ground units have insisted on patrolling the area and are on the move as we speak. Sir, I know Mike is your friend and Brother Marine, as well as the Vice-President. We will bring him home safe."

"Thanks, Rob. Please keep me informed."

Sam calls the Joint Chiefs of Staff into the war room.

"Gentlemen, if you haven't heard already, Red Dog is down in Helmand. We know he was okay after the crash, but have no idea where he may be now. If the extremists get to him they will make it a big public display to send a message to all their brothers that they are unstoppable. I want you to be ready to strike as soon as a video appears. Put a unit in or near every city, village, or campsite we know they have broadcasted from before. If anything happens to the Vice-President, there will be no-quarter. Are we clear?"

"Yes, Sir."

***

Twelve hours have passed since the Vice-President went down and disappeared. It is dawn in Iraq and the helicopters have been flying missions throughout the night with infrared sensors; but there is still no indication of where Red Dog might be. With the morning, the search intensifies.

The infantry Marines who were in the firefight, when Mike arrived on the scene and helped them, have been patrolling all night and are weary, but won't give up. They were about eighteen miles from the crash site when they ran into a group of extremists who seemed extremely interested in a small ravine. They were on a ridge to the East of the Marines, shooting down into the ravine and it was obvious someone in the ravine was shooting back. The extremists were so intent on the group in the ravine they didn't see the Marines approaching on their flank. The Marine patrol opened fire on the extremists sending them running for cover on the ridge. With the firefight raging, the Marine platoon leader saw a body in a U.S. uniform in the ravine below his position.

"Crap. Sergeant, they got Red Dog." The sergeant looked in the direction the Lieutenant was pointing and saw the uniformed person pulling himself under a ledge out of the fire from the ridge above.

"No, sir look. He's safe under that ledge." The Sergeant radioed to Command. "Mad Corps this is Over Watch Three, we believe we have found Red Dog or at least some of his group. They are pinned down in a ravine at coordinates five, eight, six, niner, four, three, six, one. We are attempting to extract and are engaged with the enemy. Request air support, Over"

"Over watch Three, keep the Red Dog group covered. Your fast movers are inbound. ETA two minutes. Over."

"Roger. I will pop green smoke at Romeo, Echo, Delta. Enemy is on the opposite ridge."

When the air support arrived, there was green smoke rising from the enemy position opposite the Marines. The harriers and helicopters promptly target the smoke and blast the area with machinegun and rocket fire destroying the enemy and showering the people in the ravine below with rocks, dirt and debris. Marines in combat situations will often code a message in case the enemy is listening. In this instance -- they were. If there had not been green smoke from the enemy position, the Marines would have popped a red smoke grenade. The result would have been the same -- the aircraft would have leveled the same ridge.

The Marines worked their way down the rocky slope into the draw below and found Mike and the others. One of Mike's security detail had been shot in the shoulder and the co-pilot of Mike's helicopter had broken his leg when he slipped off some rocks in the dark.

"Man, am I glad to see you guys!"

"Not half as glad as we are to see you Red Dog. Are you ok?"

"Yes, but I'm not sure where we'd be if you hadn't come along when you did. We've been playing cat and mouse with those guys all night. The night was so dark, and they made so much noise, they were easy to evade; but, they kept us from being rescued. We could hear the choppers in the distance and knew we weren't where they were looking. The extremists caught up to us about dawn and pinned us down here in this ravine. It was only a matter of time before we ran out of ammo and they would come off the ridge and capture or kill us. Thanks Marines."

“Sir, no thanks necessary. We were just doing our job. Semper Fi!”

“Do or Die! Let’s get out of here, Lieutenant.”

“Roger that, Sir.”

“Mad Corps, this is Over Watch Three. We have Red Dog and he is unharmed. We need a medevac for two wounded and an evac for Red Dog and Over Watch Three.”

“Roger, Over Watch Three your medivac and evac are in route. ETA eight minutes.”

Secretary Chaffey was relieved when he heard the radio call from Over Watch Three saying they had Mike and he was unharmed. He immediately called Sam with the News.

Sam, had been in the war room and had not eaten or slept since receiving the news of Mike’s helicopter being shot down. Now he was relieved, tired, and hungry. He went to the kitchen for a sandwich and talked to Peter about the incident with Mike. When Sam returned to the war room he called the Russian President and the leaders of the Arab countries and let them know his plans. He then called the United States’ UN Ambassador, Mary Rufelo, and briefed her on the situation. Sam told her to let the UN council know they were ending the strife and extremist activity in the Middle East today – to either sanction the action or get out of the way.

Sam hung up the phone and addressed the Joint Chiefs.

“It’s time to end this thing in the Middle East once and for all. Unleash the Dogs.”

“Yes, Sir,” the unanimous approval.

The next morning the UN sanctioned the action to end hostilities in the Middle East and Chaffey and the Joint Chiefs unleashed the dogs of war.

31
THE PRESIDENTIAL WIVES

Nancy was talking to Kate about the wonderful trip she had with Mike in Europe. She talked about the grand balls and gala affairs held in their honor and about meeting all the different foreign leaders and their families. What she avoided talking about was the news that Mike's helicopter had been shot down.

After the session Sam went to Mike's house to see if there was anything Nancy needed.

"Sam, I appreciate your care and concern, but I'm fine, really. Mike and I were married while he was still a grunt and volunteering for every hot spot in the world. He's been missing or out of communication before and has always come home. You said he was with the Marines in Helmand. I know they will keep Mike safe and out of danger.

"Now how did your session go?"

Sam described the session and the passage of the four bills.

"Sam, is the welfare bill the one you were working on with Ben and Cheryl?"

"Yes, why do you ask?"

"Sam, we have a problem."

"What kind of problem, Kate?"

Kate and Nancy were concerned that the New Deal Welfare Act didn't address single parents. They both believed the Act was needed and had merit; however, they felt it needed some fine tuning. They sat down with Sam to discuss their feelings.

"Sam. Nancy and I feel the welfare act doesn't provide for people who are suddenly left as single parents. You know how hard it was for John Taylor when his wife died a few years back. He lost half of his household income and was left to raise his three kids by himself. If the people of Buffalo hadn't come together to help him he would have lost his house." Kate began.

"Yes, Sam," Nancy continued "there are a lot of people out there, who, like John, are widowed or women who were married right out of high school and have no skill sets, but suddenly find themselves divorced with no means of support for themselves and in some cases for their children."

"I understand your concerns and Cheryl Dontae recognized those also. There is a place in the act for those situations, but welfare must remain temporary in nature. If we remove that, we will be right back where we started and those on welfare will be on it indefinitely and it will again be a lifestyle rather than a temporary assistance program. I have set up training resources for the unskilled through the volunteer workforce training program. The act is signed into law as is. What would you like me to do?" Sam asked.

"We know you looked at every possible angle, but isn't there some kind of program you could set up for these cases?"

"Kate, you asked before I decided to run what First Lady Katherine Waters could be known for? This would be your time to shine. You and Nancy design a program for single parents and people like John. Research it to see how much it will cost to run. Get with Cheryl and Ben to do a feasibility test and write a proposal for the Congressional budget committee. Then if approved by Congress, which most first wives' programs are, you two can start building your organization, fair enough?"

"Fair enough! I knew you would have a solution, you're so smart."

"and you're such a wise ass."

"Nancy, we have some work to do." As the two wives started to leave, Nancy turned to Sam.

"Sam, please bring Mike home safe."

The next day Sam was able to tell Nancy, they had found Mike and he was safe and on his way home.

***

Kate and Nancy, asked Sam for a copy of HR2879 to see exactly how it is written for single individuals, how it is written for families and into which category single parents fall. Sam was right, Cheryl Dontae had addressed single parents and provided for them to be considered under the family regulation. The eighteen-month limit still bothered Nancy.

"Kate, it takes twenty-four months to complete most vocational school courses, but the welfare act only helps with eighteen months. What are people supposed to do for support during the last six months of school?"

"You're right, Nancy, but so is Sam. A time line has to be drawn to keep welfare from becoming a lifestyle again. Maybe that's where our program comes into play. If people, single, single parents, or families are taking part in a vocational studies program, not the volunteer workforce training program. Then 'the Presidential Wives' Vocational Assistance Program' will provide aid and support for the last six months of vocational training."

"Where did you come up with that name?"

"I don't know it just popped into my head. Hahaha. Let's bounce the idea off Ben and Cheryl and see what they think."

***

Sam had already given a heads-up to Ben and Cheryl, so when the wives called, they were ready. They listened to the idea and agreed it sounded like a great complimentary program to the welfare act.

"Mrs. Waters, can I suggest a name change for your program?"

"Sure Ben, but, only if you call me Kate."

"Alright, Kate. I suggest you call your program 'The Presidential Wives' Vocational Education Program.' From the way you described your idea, you are not just aiding, you are providing training and education for the last six months of vocational courses."

"That's true, Thank you Ben."

"Kate, you and Nancy, know that many vocational schools and two-year colleges and junior colleges have placement programs with local businesses. You may want to meet with the heads of those schools to see if they would place the better students in paid internship positions while they finish the last six months of the courses."

"That's a wonderful idea, Cheryl. That would help reduce the burden on the program's funding. Thank you for coming and giving us such helpful input. We will talk again as Nancy and I get ready to finalize the program for submission to the budget committees."

The response from the two representatives encouraged Kate and Nancy to define how the program would work and to research the possible costs. They were excited about the possibilities and decided to talk to the two-year institutions in the D.C. area to see if they would be receptive to their ideas and Cheryl's suggestion about early placement.

Two weeks later they had put their program together and were ready to meet with Ben and Cheryl again. The two representatives brought some of their fellow representatives to listen to the wives and give suggestions. The two wives were prepared to give a full presentation to Ben and Cheryl, but were not expecting the dozen representatives who showed up to hear the plan.

The ladies nervously presented their program to the group, who gave some constructive suggestions to help refine and fine tune the program. After the presentation, the representatives helped Kate and Nancy draft a proposal for the budget committee and draft a bill for Congress and the Senate to make the program law.

Kate and Nancy were amazed to hear it would become a law. They would have been happy just having a program like the Ford Centers. The name would change one more time. The Presidential Wives' New Deal Two, Vocational Education Act of 2025. The Act was presented to both houses and passed with easy majority votes. It passed Judicial Review and Sam happily signed the wive's education act into law.

32
THE SUICIDE COMMITTEE

Once a month for the past year Sam had held a joint session of Congress and the representatives of both houses had come to expect the unexpected. Sam's ideas and actions had been radical at times, but they had worked, and Sam was able to declare positive advances in about every area of his first State of the Union address.

Sam had toured Europe, Asia and the Pacific rim with Kate and the kids and made many friends among the foreign leaders. He had met with the Russian President and they had discussed how well the action in the middle east was progressing. Both leaders hoped for a new relationship between countries.

Sam had a good first year and he was hoping for a better second year. With the growth in small businesses, unemployment was down. The New Deal Two, Welfare Act and The Presidential Wives' New Deal Two, Vocational Education Act of 2025 were a great success and welfare enrollment was down sixty-five percent. The country was closing the gap on the deficit and beginning to repay much of the debt. Yes, it was a good year and a good start for Sam and Mike. Their approval rating was seventy-eight percent. Possibly lower than it could have been because of disgruntled Welfare recipients, but even they had begun to feel some pride in being able to return to the workforce.

The biggest battle this next year would be congressional pay and allowances. Sam knew congress wasn't going to be very thrilled to take a pay reduction, especially after having conceded campaign contributions and term-limits. When Sam and his family returned from the goodwill tour, he began researching Congressional Pay and the pay increases of the past fifty years.

There was still a problem with Government spending. For every dollar Sam was able to gain ninety cents was going out. Sam would have to advance his timetable to plug the hole in the bucket. He called on Dontae and Albright.

"Cheryl and Ben, you have been a great help to me and we have had a fantastic year. I need your help again this year. Are you up for a challenge?"

"Of course, Mr. President." Dontae answered enthusiastically.

"Anything, Sir." Albright's straight forward answer.

"What I'm going to ask you to do isn't going to win you any favors from the senior members of your houses and you will probably have to work harder on this request than you have on any other bill so far. I know I will lose a lot of support and the Houses aren't going to like me much. After I tell you what I want, you may not like me either."

"Never happen, Sir." The unified answer.

"I want a bill which reduces congressional pay. I mean everyone. House, Senate, Justices, Senior Military, Me, Mike and the cabinet -- everyone."

"Wow, sir That's a tall order. What do you have in mind?"

"Ben, right now we have two schedules of wages for civil service: The General Schedule or GS and the Executive Schedule for department heads, Congress, the House, Senate, Cabinet and me and Mike. Military Generals also fall into the Executive Schedule. There is a separate schedule for the military and that makes sense because, they have all the special duty pay, but that schedule should cover all the military including the Generals. Since you and I are civil servants the GS schedule should cover all of us. Do you kind of see where I'm going with this?" Ben and Cheryl nodded agreement.

"Let's work together and find a solution to cut some of Government's spending from the top instead of continually cutting programs we may need. We have a joint session in three weeks. I want to present the bill at that session."

"Sir, you know Ben and I are behind you one-hundred percent and the list you gave us last year made perfect sense to get the country back on its feet. But, this could be politically damaging. You are going up against some very powerful individuals who are not going to go down easy and if you lose the support you've gained so far. You may lose a lot of your ability to fulfill your campaign promises. Are you sure you want to take that chance, Sir?"

"I know Cheryl. I was going to wait until after the election when many of the good ole boys would be gone; but I have to act now, so the new blood will come into a consistent pay system."

"Okay, sir, we're on it."

"Thank you both, you will never know how much I appreciate you. If you need anything, you know the number."

Cheryl and Ben left the oval office talking about Sam's request.

"Do you think Waters has totally lost his mind this time, Ben? This seems like the craziest thing he's asked of us yet. He has made real strides on both sides of the aisle. But, to drop this kind of bomb, he's going to lose at least two-thirds of both houses if not more."

"I really don't know, Cheryl. He has come up with some crazy ideas before and I wondered as we were working on them, what I would do in his shoes. Sam is going to be a tough act to follow for any President for the next hundred years.

"So far everything has had a purpose and his ideas have not only worked but have worked very well. I don't know about you, but I must admit, I've often wondered what I do that justifies a six-figure income. Especially as a base salary when many of my constituents are lucky if they make forty-thousand a year with over-time. Let's just do our jobs and see where this goes."

***

Ben and Cheryl worked through the week on Sam's request and were having trouble trying to bring all the schedules into just two working pay scales. They had brought several other Senators and Congressmen and Women into the project and although they were not fond of the idea of taking a pay cut – they believed the President would do what was necessary for the good of the country. They started calling themselves the Suicide Committee, since they all believed Sam to be committing political suicide and they were all drinking the Kool aid.

Ben called Sam and asked for a meeting on the pay bill. They scheduled the meeting for Friday at one o'clock. On Friday, seven Senators and fifteen Congresspersons, the whole suicide committee, entered the oval office.

"Well, I must say I wasn't expecting this, should I call the Vice-President and Cabinet for reinforcement."

"Sorry, Sir. We drafted some friends to help with the pay bill and since we're having trouble putting it together we thought it best we all meet and get a better understanding of exactly what you are looking for in this bill."

"That's okay, we will need all of the support we can get on this one.

"Ladies and Gentlemen, here's the problem. We have far too many pay scales to manage effectively, and too many people trying to manipulate them for their own agenda.

"I encourage you to look back at the last fifty years and note how many pay increases have been passed. Then look at the Constitution Article II, section one and the twenty-seventh amendment for guidance. These are the two most violated articles of the Constitution. Congress and the past Presidents have passed and given pay raises almost every year for the past fifty years, it is time to correct a major fault.

"I have a choice, I can have the Government Accounting Office, GAO, perform an audit of all congressional pay increases for the past hundred years and adjust the pay accordingly – or I can waive that action in lieu of instituting a new and enforceable pay system. Are you with me, so far?" The committee nodded their acknowledgement.

"Good. So, how do we fix the pay system? We need to first identify which parts of the current system works best. I have spoken at length with the people at the Office of Personnel Management, OPM, about which systems require the least amount of labor on their part and which are easiest to manage. Throughout OPM the consensus was that the GS schedule was the best and had the most flexibility. The Defense Finance and Accounting said the same thing about the basic Military scale.

"Aren't we all, Civil Service employees? And aren't our Generals, all part of the military? Then, why are there so many pay scales. All Civil Service should be on the same schedule and all Military should be on the same Military schedule.

"The annual salary for the top-level GS-15 step ten, this year is one-hundred-fifty-thousand dollars. If we add GS Levels up to GS-22, the scale would cover all the executive schedule levels plus the Vice-President and President. Each of the new Grades would have a wage base five percent higher than the preceding level. For instance, a GS-16 would be those personnel currently in Level 5 of the Executive Schedule and the annual salary would be one-hundred-sixty-two-thousand dollars. Pay for GS 21 and 22, the Executive Offices, could only be changed every four years per the Constitution regarding Presidential remuneration. Pay for GS 16 through 20 could only be changed every two years in accordance with the 27th Amendment.

"Now, are we on the same page? Do I still have your support or am I on my own on this?

"Sir, I will admit, I have had my doubts about some of your ideas. I have been pleasantly surprised when they not only worked well, but had highly measurable results. Sir, we, like most people shun the idea of taking a pay cut, but we are with you. I think we all feel this bill will kill your support in both houses, however, we have agreed to stand with you and present a bill for this issue. We will look into Article II of the Constitution and the Twenty-seventh Amendment and if we find anything in the interpretation that differs from yours we will meet again to discuss them."

"Thanks Ben, I appreciate that and that's all I ask. I would never expect or ask you to just go with my opinion."

"To tell you the truth sir, hearing you lay this out, I'm surprised no one has done it sooner."

"Cheryl, sadly to say, in most cases your fellow representatives were too busy lining their pockets and voting more raises to even begin to remember whose money they were spending. Of course, the Supreme Court which is supposed to perform judicial review and should have caught the oversight, slightly overlooked the fault, because it affected their pay as well.

"Thank you, Ladies and Gentlemen, for this meeting. Now, I think we have work to do."

***

Cheryl Dontae approached Sam before the joint session.

"Mr. President, I'm afraid we don't have the support for the pay act we were hoping for. Many of the senior representatives are against giving any credence whatsoever to approving it. With their disapproval comes the expected fall out in the junior reps. and they are following the lead of the others and won't vote to approve the measure. Ben is having the same conflict in the Senate. I think there may be a filibuster planned."

"Thank you for the heads-up, Cheryl. I will deal with the Representatives and we will get this act through both houses and the judicial review today. You have worked very hard on this project; would you like to be the one to present the bill you've worked on?" Cheryl agreed and after the roll call, Sam took the podium.

"Congresswoman Dontae would you please present HR2987 The Congressional Pay and Allowances Act of 2026."

Cheryl did a great job on the presentation and passed the floor back to Sam. Sam asked for discussion and there are several heated banters between some of the new blood and the good ole boys. One senior Congressman began a long-winded dissertation on anything and everything, but the bill that was presented and Sam cut him short after an hour.

Sam was determined to get the pay bill through the joint session. He knew if it went back to the two houses it would fail and die. When Sam, stopped the Congressman's filibuster attempt, there was a commotion on the floor as the other Representatives expressed their displeasure at Sam's interruption.

"Ladies and Gentlemen, Ladies and Gentlemen, if I may have your attention, PLEASE. There is no need to filibuster this measure. I ended Congressman Daniels rant when he veered away from the issue at hand. Here are the facts on this regulation.

"I gave Congresswoman Dontae and Senator Albright a task. That task was to find a system for Congressional pay which would uphold the letter and intent of the Constitution and the twenty-seventh amendment which you are all sworn to support and defend. Albright and Dontae, with the assistance of other Congresspersons and Senators, have created the document which has been presented. I knew when I issued the task, it would create one great hullabaloo in chambers. I also knew it would create animosity and discord between you and me. Yet, I still issued the task. I had a dilemma, a problem which needed to be addressed and fixed.

"For most of the past fifty years Congress and the past Presidents have ignored the Constitution which restricts pay increases for the President and Vice-President to once every four years and with no raise given during their term in office. They have also ignored the twenty-seventh amendment which restricts Congressional pay increases to every two years with no increase awarded until after the new representatives have taken their seats.

"I have noticed that Congress and the Presidents have justified annual and sometimes semi-annual pay increases by calling them Cost of Living Adjustments or COLA.

"I looked to OPM to provide me with a definition of COLA. What OPM told me was that COLA is a temporary increase to a person's salary and the COLA amount should be terminated at the next regular salary increase.

"I thought about that definition as I researched the pay increases of the last fifty years. I found that the COLA increases may have been terminated, however, the new pay rate was computed into the new pay schedule, so the adjustments included the previous COLA amount making the claimed COLA pay increase, a raise, and not a temporary COLA. Since these increases were no longer considered COLA, they were all illegal and unconstitutional.

"I had a choice:

"I could work with members of the House, Senate and other Government agencies to provide a bill which would develop a starting point for future pay, allowances and raises. Possibly, helping to restore some of the deficit, because the bill would create more available dollars for the budget.

"Or, I could sign this Executive Order." Sam held up a folder. "This order enforces Article II of the Constitution and the twenty-seventh amendment and rescinds every pay increase awarded during the past fifty years and calls for the restitution and or repayment of one point seven trillion dollars in illegal pay made to Congress and the Presidents. It also, adds the charge of embezzlement for all those who willingly took advantage of the illegal pay by voting in favor of the raises.

"Now, you have a choice:

"You can agree to pass the House Resolution and settle this issue respectfully, and quietly take the reduction in pay.

"Or, you can fight me on this and I will sign this Executive Order and instruct OPM to begin collection action of two thirds your pay until your part of the illegal pay debt is collected. I will also instruct the Attorney General to begin an investigation into who among you have voted for the illegal pay increases.

Congresswoman Dontae, please take a roll call vote of the House."

The bill passed by a single vote, Congressman Woodward,

the Speaker of the House voted in favor of the bill and broke the tie in the House. Sam breathed a sigh of relief as he heard Woodard's vote and ordered Senator Albright to take the roll call vote from the Senate. The bill passed the Senate sixty- five to thirty-five.

The Suicide Committee had written the bill with exacting detail and even added paragraphs pertaining to the submission of congressional travel and per diem. It upset a lot of the older members and Sam, as expected, lost some ground with the senior representatives. He had cut Congressional pay almost in half and it was four months before Sam was able to get a bill passed in either house. The mid-term election was only five months away and Sam knew he would be fighting an uphill battle to get anything done until then.

He hadn't had a vacation since he took office nearly two years ago, so Sam, decided to take Kate and the kids back home for a week. He took the boat out fishing on Lake De Smet, but, of course, there were fifteen other boats in a circle around them and Peter was in Sam's boat in his three-piece suit; but it was a great week anyway.

33

BACK INTO THE FRAY

Sam returned from his vacation in Wyoming to find Mike in an absolute frenzy.

"Mike, what happened to get you this riled up?"

"A bill was presented to the Senate while you were out of the loop. Senator Dumphrey, should be Dummy, from California, decided on his own to introduce an LGBT bill for the Military. When I asked what he was doing, he looked at me and said since we have gays at the top of Government we should have them in the military too. I'll tell you Sam, it was all I could do to keep from coming out of my chair and smashing the little man's face."

"Dumphrey is one of the senior Senators who isn't eligible for reelection this year right?"

"Yes, Sir. He should be gone after the election."

"Mike, we knew the LGBT, gay marriage, abortion and all of the other church issues were going to come up sooner or later. We just stick to our guns and we don't let them into the chamber."

"I couldn't very well stop him and when I tried he threw accusations about you and I being gay, and our marriages are just a scam on the American people. Like I said, I just wanted to throttle the guy."

"Liable and slander are still against the law in America, right? Call for a Senate investigation of Dumphrey for slander. He defamed you and me in a public forum which was recorded for the archives and I imagine CSPAN and several other media agencies had their cameras rolling.

"Start a Senate hearing to investigate Dumphrey. Censure and bar him from the Senate Chambers while the investigation and hearing are conducted. His term should expire before the hearing and he won't be a problem any more. Next issue."

"Sam, you still don't have any support from either house since your pay Act passed. Some are calling for your head for using coercion to force the vote. What is your plan to finish the year?"

"Mike, I really don't know if there is anything I can do which will turn the houses around. They are deadlocked and boycotting me. I've tried talking with some of the Senior representatives individually and they aren't willing to listen. We have a scheduled joint session on Friday and we are going to straighten this thing out. What I did was right, and they all know it. I may have upset them but it's time they saw what the rest of America sees daily.

"What else is there?"

Mike updates Sam on everything that happened during the week he was gone. The business for the week was business as it had been for the past four months. Nothing was done!

***

Mike opens the joint session with the usual roll call and introduction of the President.

"Ladies and Gentlemen. It would appear we have a problem. For the past four months since the passage of HR2987, on Congressional pay, you have boycotted my plans for reform in this country and not completed a single order of business on any issue. You have denied the Congressmen and Senators who supported HR2987 even the minutest hope of passing legislation they feel is needed.

"You are upset. Your pay was reduced by nearly half. How much less would your pay have been if the illegal raises had not existed to begin with? Your pay without the illegal raises would have been one third the amount you were receiving, and you would have been none the wiser for it and we would not have this issue and boycott.

"Albright, Dontae and the rest of the committee who worked on the pay act, recognized their current pay level was attributed to the illegal and unconstitutional activity of the past and they created a great new pay schedule that works for everyone. Yes, the representatives of the house and Senate had to take a pay cut! But, so did everyone else. Me, the Vice-President, the cabinet, the Military Generals all had our pay reduced. Why is it that, only you, who are responsible for supporting the Constitution, who are responsible for insuring the proper appropriation of funds, are the ones whining the loudest about stopping an illegal activity and rescinding all the illegal raises of the past fifty years.

"Can any one of you, explain to me why you need a six-figure income at the expense of the American people? Please, I'm waiting for an answer. If you can give me one good reason you need such an income I will gladly have this joint session vote to rescind HR2987."

"Sir, we need to pay for travel to and from our districts and pay our staffs at home." Congressman Stover answered Sam's question.

"Thank you. Mr. Stover, says you need to travel to and from your home districts and pay your staffs in those districts. Am I understanding you correctly, Mr. Stover." Stover nodded his agreement. "Mr. Stover, do you file a travel voucher when you return from your district?"

"Yes, Sir, we all do."

"Okay, a question to you all. When you file for your travel, do you claim any travel which wasn't in the line of duty."

"No, Sir, that would be illegal." Stover answered and was echoed throughout the chamber.

"Thank you. So, let me get this straight. You all need the big salaries for your travel to and from the states you represent; but you file travel vouchers which reimburse you for that travel like any other business in America does, so, your travel is basically free. I don't see that as a reason for the big salary: but you mentioned another expense you need the salary for.

"You have offices in your home states. Mr. Stover, since you have been so good as to answer so far, I will ask you, how much do you pay out of your pocket for your state office?"

"Well, Sir, Rent is about thirty-four-thousand dollars a year and I have a staff of three full time and two part-time employees who are paid at the GS-3-4 level."

"Mr. Stover, does the Government pay for any of these expenses?"

"Yes, Sir, they are part of the appropriations for all congressional officers."

"Have you claimed any of these expenses as deductions on your personal income taxes?"

"No, Sir, that would be illegal and tax fraud."

"So, Mr. Stover, when I asked how much you pay out of pocket, the figures you gave me are not your out-of-pocket expenses, but those from the pockets of the American Taxpayer. Am I correct?" Again, Stover nodded acknowledgement.

“As Mr. Stover admitted, if you claim any of those expenses as personal expenses, it would be illegal. It would seem to me, you don’t need the large six-figure salary for either the travel expenses, which are reimbursed to you or your home office expenses, which are paid for by the taxpayers. Can anyone help Mr. Stover out here. Anyone?”

“We have expenses for speaking engagements at events all over the world, in fact I have been asked to speak at a three-day political rally in Greece next week.” Stated Senator Williams.

“For a minute, Mr. Stover, it looked like your peers were going to let you flounder on your own. Mr. Williams, concerning this speaking engagement in Greece – will you be speaking on each of the three days?”

“No, Mr. President, my speech will be one hour on the second day. I will be a guest for the rest of the time.”

“Is this engagement in the line of duty to your District? Will you be speaking about the issues we have been addressing here in chambers? Or will you be speaking to help Greece with issues in their Senate?”

“Sir the answer to all three of your questions is no, however this engagement will boost goodwill with the nation of Greece.”

“Mr. Williams, I am aware of the engagement’s location and content. Will you answer a couple more questions for me? Is the sponsor or host of this rally paying your travel to and from the event in Athens.”

“Yes, Sir.”

“Are they paying your lodging costs while you are there?”

“Yes, Sir.”

“In that case, Mr. Williams why should the American Taxpayers from your district pay you a six-figure salary, so you can jet to Europe for a speaking engagement you are being paid handsomely for by the host. Are you planning to file a travel voucher when you return to the Senate?”

“No, Sir, that would be illegal and fraud.”

“How do we determine if the speaking engagement is personal or in the line of duty? If the event coordinator is paying a speaker’s fee and the representative accepts that fee, it's personal. If the Representative is sent or volunteers to speak about an issue of public interest at no cost to the event, it's Government Business or line of duty.

"There are some of you who frequently visit your district. Those who, while on their home visits, often talk with their constituents and have even removed their jackets and worked shoulder to shoulder with the folks in the district. They have worked with farmers, city workers, industry workers and several other different types of laborers. Not all the people who are helped have great and glorious jobs. Mucking out a pig, horse or cattle stall is not very prestigious, but some of you have done it. When these representatives return to Washington and file their travel vouchers, they don't include their travel around the district. They are entitled to because they are performing the job for which they were hired, but, still, they only file a travel voucher for their travel to and from Washington, D.C. Ladies and Gentlemen, these representatives are to be commended for being the watchdogs of the American people's money.

"Mr. Williams and Mr. Stover pointed out some very interesting items during my questioning. Falsifying a travel claim or a tax return for office expenses paid for by the Government is illegal; but taking an unauthorized and unconstitutional pay increase is not. Filing a travel voucher for a paid speaking engagement is fraud and illegal, but voting yourselves one of the aforementioned unauthorized and unconstitutional pay raises is not.

"Ladies and Gentlemen, you seem to have a very warped and twisted view of what is <u>right</u> and what is <u>wrong</u>. So, I will straighten this out for you.

"HR2987 makes all pay raises NOT in accordance with Constitution Article II, section one concerning pays for the President and Vice-President or the Twenty Seventh Amendment, concerning Congressional pay - ILLEGAL.

"HR2987 also establishes a pay system that reflects a truer value of the duties you perform for the people you represent and sets a standard for Congressional pay, allowances, travel and retirement.

"Ladies and Gentlemen HR2987 is legal and the right thing to do for the American people who have been slaves to the Government for too long. I don't care if you support me or not. I do not care if you support the Junior Representatives or not. The Senior members of Congress in this chamber are waging a war with me that they cannot win, and I don't care. The reason I don't care is simple -- I know that two-hundred-twenty-seven Congressmen and thirty-three Senators will not be spending Christmas in Washington D.C. and after the first of the new year there will be a brand-new-breed of representative sitting in your seats. Fresh minds with fresh ideas of where we need to go with the reform of our Government and this great nation. I look forward to this new breed which will replace the stagnant Good-Ole-Boy mindset of the representatives who sit before me today.

"In two years another large group of you will not be eligible for reelection. Your seats will again be filled with fresh thinking minds who believe in this country and what it stands for.

"So, for the first two-hundred-seventy-five representatives, you can leave your offices having done nothing for the people you represent this year. Or you can go out with a bang and finish this year leaving an impression, an example, and even a legacy for those who follow you. What's it going to be?"

Sam closes his notes and looks out at the Representatives who are giving him the first honest standing ovation since he took office. He steps off the podium and mingles with the representatives.

The next four months produced more positive action than the previous four decades. The House and Senate passed legislation restructuring the Internal Revenue Service to better support the new tax laws. Legislation was passed supporting the second amendment right to bear arms and created harsher penalties for those who perpetrate violent crimes. There were restrictions placed on Military expansion and reduction to protect the interests of the United States. The Senate passed regulations for education – removing the testing requirements of students as an evaluation of teacher skills. The House passed new regulations concerning the use of Government property – including office spaces, vehicles, and furniture. A week prior to the election, Sam called a special joint session of Congress.

"Ladies and Gentlemen, will the representatives who have reached their term limits please come forward. I would like to sincerely thank all the representatives who will be going home in a few short days. We have not always agreed or seen eye to eye on which road we needed to take for the people of this great nation, however, together, we have accomplished some great things for our country. Thank you for your many years of dedicated service to our nation and God's speed and protection for your future endeavors." Sam closes his notes to another standing ovation and steps onto the chamber floor and personally says farewell and thank you to all the representatives who will not return after the election.

Sam would not be around for the election results.

34
UTTER CHAOS

Peter was promoted to the Position of White House Security Chief and took great pride and pleasure in the job. He had never felt the country was in good hands and had spurned the idea of bringing a child into an unstable world. He and his wife, Julia, had talked many times and hoped with each new President that things would change, and they might be able to start the family they both wanted. Sam was the first President who had come into office with purposeful agenda for the people and the country. Peter and Julia were going to have a baby boy.

It was election day for the Midterm elections and Sam had gone home to Buffalo to show his support and cast his vote for the local candidates. Julia had been in labor when Sam was scheduled to depart for Wyoming and Sam told Peter to stay with his wife, there were other agents who could escort him for the three days in Buffalo. Peter reluctantly agreed and assigned another agent for the detail.

"Peter, I want a full account of your new baby when it arrives, and we will have a cigar to welcome the boy when I get back."

"I still wish you would let me go with you, Sam. I just don't feel right not being there. I don't know what it is but there is something, a feeling, something ominous."

"Peter, I'm going to Buffalo. You've been there. I don't think you could find a sleepier town in America. Nothing is going to happen, and I'll be back in three days."

"Yes Sir, and I will call you as soon as the baby arrives. Have a good trip."

***

Sam visited a couple of rallies in Cheyenne, Casper, Gillette, and Sheridan before heading to Buffalo to vote and return to Washington. He had not scheduled the Sheridan stop prior to leaving Washington but the rally was prime time for Carl Talbot an independent candidate for the Congressional seat for Northern

Wyoming. Sam knew Carl and wanted to show his support and endorse him for the position.

The Rally had gone well and even with the last-minute change, Sam's Security detail had done a great job of pre-screening the crowd in and around the auditorium on the Sheridan College campus and ensuring the safety of the President.

As Sam was leaving the rally, a young man bolted out of the crowd and began firing two semi-automatic pistols into Sam's entourage. The Security detail reacted and brought the gunman down but not before he had shot Sam and three of his Security agents.

The scene was pandemonium and chaos. Several agents had grabbed Sam and pushed him into the bulletproof Limo, without realizing he had been hit by one or more of the bullets. There were more than a few seconds before they were aware of Sam's injuries and they sped to the hospital. Several of the other agents were trying to help the agents who had been shot, others were trying to deal with the crowd and still others were chasing down and capturing the gunman – Allen Bryan Cage. The news spread immediately that the President had been shot.

Kate was in Buffalo with Toby and Lauren waiting patiently for Sam, when their Security detail rushed them to the waiting limousines and sped toward Sheridan – she was told as they merged onto I-90 that Sam had been shot, but his condition was unknown. Mike was at his home in Kaycee when he received the call and immediately sped toward Sheridan General Hospital with his detail. Nancy would follow as soon as she could find a babysitter for Billy. Terry and Mary Jacobs were also home in Buffalo when they got the call about the shooting. All the notifications were made within one minute after the shooting. Kate, Mike, and Terry all met at the hospital.

Peter called Kate and said he would be on the next flight out of Washington, but Kate told him to stay with Julia and the baby. The Damage was done and there wasn't anything he could do if he came.

"Okay, Kate. Is there any word on Sam's condition?"

"He's still in surgery and we won't know anything until one of the doctors comes out to tell us something. They've never had this kind of thing here so all of the doctors and surgeons in Sheridan County are here trying to save everyone's life."

"Please let me know as soon as you hear anything. Our prayers are with you."

"Thanks Peter, and I will call you as soon as I have anything new."

***

It had been two hours since the shooting and Sam's arrival in the emergency room. No one had come to report on Sam's situation or to give any kind of update to the group that filled the waiting room. Kate had overheard one of the doctors tell a nurse at the desk that one of the Security detail didn't make it.

Another hour and still no news. Kate was trying to put up a strong appearance for the children's sake, but the hours without knowing were beginning to wear on her – she started to cry.

A doctor in blood soaked clothing finally came out and asked to speak with Mike.

"Mr. Baker, I'm afraid the President is in very critical condition. The bullets fired by the gunman were cut laterally like a pie causing the bullet to peel into seven or eight pieces on impact. We have removed seven pieces of the bullet which hit the President, however, one of the pieces is lodged dangerously near his spine just below his shoulder blades and he is too weak right now to attempt to remove it. Is his wife here to sign the medical releases?"

"Yes, she's there on the sofa with the kids."

"What do you need from me or Kate?"

"Well, we need to put the President into a medically induced coma, so he won't move. If he moved in normal sleep, he could move the fragment and either make it impossible to remove or causing damage which would render Sam a paraplegic for the rest of his life or worse it could kill him."

"What are the options doctor?"

"Sam needs a surgeon more experienced in this kind of thing, than we have in Northern Wyoming. While he is in the coma he could be flown to Bethesda Naval Hospital without any risk of moving the fragment. Then you can bring in the best surgeons in the country and with the better equipment, they could perform the operation and save his life and his legs."

"That can be arranged. Is there anything else?"

"Yes. There is a good chance the President won't be mentally capable of performing his duties after being in the coma and it will take months or even years for him to totally regain his health, both mental and physical. You may want to have the Justice of the United Sates swear you in as President."

"Thank you, Doctor. I appreciate the update and your candor and concern. I will mind the store temporarily, but Sam isn't out of the office yet and I will not take an office which isn't mine. We will see how everything goes with the surgery and his recovery and make any adjustments at that time."

The doctor talked with Kate about the coma procedure and the medical consent and release forms to place Sam into the coma. She talked with Mike and Terry about the legalities then agreed it was in Sam's best interest and signed the papers. Sam was put into the coma and transportation to Bethesda, Maryland was arranged.

***

Secretary of Defense Chaffey came through the door of the hospital like he was taking a hill in some far off militarized zone. He walked straight to the Nurses station and asked if the President was ready to be moved and asked where the ambulance was that would be taking Sam to the Sheridan Airport.

"Come on, Ma'am we have a man's life to save and that man happens to be the best President this country has had for more than a century. So, get the lead out of your behind and get him ready to go."

Chaffey had ordered a jet out of Andrews Air Force Base to take him to Sheridan to be with Mike and Kate and help organize Sam's move to Bethesda. Peter was at Bethesda coordinating Sam's movement from the airport in Baltimore to the Hospital and the implementation of the surgical team. Sam was flown out of

Sheridan at midnight and was in the Bethesda Medical Center two and a half hours later. He survived the trip and the surgery and only time would tell if he would be able to return to the White House.

Sam would spend the next three months in a coma. The surgeons felt the coma would help him heal internally from the multiple surgeries to remove all the fragments. When Sam awoke from the coma he was in recovery and physical therapy in the hospital for the next two months. He would spend the next seven months in a mechanical support that would help him learn how to move and walk again without injuring himself. Sam had always been physically fit and active – it would be a long and difficult process for him to live with, but he would live.

35
THE AFTERMATH

It was November thirtieth and Mike would be holding the first joint session since Sam's Goodwill tour, during their first year in office. Mike had done well for those three months, but this was different. Mike and Sam had a comradery, a friendship which had surfaced during their campaign and endured to the present day. If they didn't see each other they would call and discuss issues and plan campaigns to get the support needed for the reform agenda. Now, Sam wasn't available to call for guidance if the issue wasn't clear. He wasn't available for comment on how to deal with the representatives. Now Mike was alone and facing a fight Sam had avoided, gun control.

As has been the case with every shooting incident for the past fifty years or more, there was outcry in the Congress for increased gun control after the assassination attempt. Even among the newly elected representatives, the age-old dispute over gun rights lingered. Sam was in a coma at Bethesda Medical Center and Mike was up to his ears in the paperwork of those representatives wishing stricter gun control laws. Mike paced the floor in the oval office until Chaffey came to remind him of the session.

"I know, Thanks Rob. I've just been going over the gun rights and restrictions that are going to plague me in this session. I have no idea how to handle the Congress on this issue. Part of me wants to go with the vote and pass the gun restriction laws, because Sam is my friend and so were the agents who were killed in the line of duty never seeing it coming. Then the other parts say to stand my ground."

"Sir, it isn't really a hard decision. You have seen Sam in this position on a great many occasions and how he handled the representatives. This is a Constitutional issue. You just have to ask yourself one question – what would Sam do?"

Thanks, Rob that helps, please tell the speaker and Senate Majority leader that I am on my way.

***

Sam had not been wrong when he told Cheryl Dontae she may become the Speaker of the House. After she was reelected, she was the Senior Representative of the majority party in the House and therefore became the Speaker. Ben Albright, who had two more years on his first term became the majority leader of the Senate.

When Mike arrived, Ben Albright had taken the roll and introduced Mike as the President. Mike carried two bulky boxes to the podium then addressed the Congress.

"Thank you, Mr. Albright. Ladies and Gentlemen, let's get one thing straight. Sam Waters is still the President although he is temporarily out of place. I will temporarily act as the President until Sam returns, but I am not the President, nor will I be addressed as such unless Sam does not return to the office and the Chief Justice administers my oath of office. Are we clear?"

The chamber applauded Mike's small speech showing their approval.

"With that out of the way let's see if we can accomplish some business while the President is out so he doesn't think we sat on our hands for three months.

"Mr. Helm could you please stand, sir? Many of you know Mr. Helm, he is the chamber custodian. Mr. Helm would you please bring the trash can I asked for earlier?" Helm left the chamber and within a minute returned with a large rolling trash receptacle.

"Since the assassination attempt on the President and the killing of two Federal Secret Service Agents, I have been inundated with proposals for bills, laws and mandates for gun control regulation.

Amendment II of the Constitution states 'A well-regulated Militia, being necessary to the security of a Free State, the right of the people to keep and bear Arms, shall not be infringed.'

"Ladies and Gentlemen, the right to bear arms is an inalienable right of every person in this country. It is the right of every person to be able to defend their family and their home against intruders and those who would do them harm. The Second Amendment **does not** bestow upon us the right to keep and bear arms, that right is inherent. The Second Amendment keeps Government from infringing upon the rights we already have by being humans.

I have read through the documents in these boxes and have found that every one of them violates the oath of office of the preparer. We are the defenders, the first line of defense against those who would attempt to change or corrupt the Constitution to fit their own agenda. We cannot continue to attempt to suppress the freedoms of law-abiding citizens who legally and responsibly own guns, because, a criminal has used a weapon in the commission of their crimes.

As such, I banish these seditious documents and we shall hear no more on the subject." Mike takes the two boxes of documents and dumps each in the larger trash can being guarded by Mr. Helm.

"Thank you, Mr. Helm. You may take this can to the shredder and return to your duties."

The Senior members of the two Houses were aghast when Mike threw their documents in the trash. The Junior Representatives applauded the action, realizing the Vice-President would continue to act on the campaign promise of respect and reform.

36
A NEW ELECTORAL

It was December, Sam had been in a coma for two months. The families had truly missed him at the Christmas and New Year functions. For the past two months, Toby and Lauren had been bounced between Mike's, Terry's, and Chaffey's homes while Kate spent many or her days and nights at the hospital with Sam. The kids would come to the hospital on the weekends and show their sleeping father their week's work from school. Mike had been performing exceptionally well in the temporary position of President, but would gladly give the job back to Sam in a New York minute.

Mike had postponed the December joint session as Sam had done the year before to allow the representatives to have a full Christmas holiday and bring in the New Year with their families.

***

January twenty-ninth and the eve of another joint session. Mike had developed a greater self-confidence than he had before the November session and he knew Sam's agenda for the reform. Mike was ready to tackle some of the challenges in that agenda and was looking forward to January when the new members of the House and Senate would outnumber the career representatives. He felt he could start to move forward. He called Ben Albright.

"Ben, I need the Senate to propose an amendment to the Constitution. We desperately need to amend the twelfth amendment."

"The Electoral Amendment, Sir? I was wondering when we would get around to that change. I have already been working on it with a couple of the senators. We have been on it since the swearing in and can't quite figure out how to change it to be equal for all states, since it is representative based. I know you wouldn't have called me if you didn't have something in mind to fix the electoral college."

"Ben, you have had the Senate bench since the election while Sam's been in the Hospital and I've been acting as President. I would like you to assemble as many of the Senators as you can in chambers tomorrow at one and arrange for the rest to be on Vox. I'll give my idea to the entire Senate and you can put your heads together to make it happen."

"Okay, Sir. See you at one tomorrow."

Ben and the few Senators who had been working on the electoral college issue were excited to hear Mike's plan. Some of the remaining career Senators, although they had come to respect Sam and Mike and their ideas, don't think they should mess with the Electoral College. They believe it could create a bigger mess than they already had. They were skeptical that any change might result in disaster in the next election.

Mike looked at the Electoral College, which he felt had been out of date for many years. Originally designed to balance the election and give lesser populated States an even playing field with the more populated States, the number of electors was based on the number of representatives and the number of Representatives a State had was based on the population of the State -- basically one representative per seven-hundred-thousand people. The electoral college might have been a promising idea if, during the westward expansion, the population had stabilized equally in all states. Instead, as the country grew, the population gravitated to only a few States which made the electoral as biased towards the lesser populated States as the popular vote. The electoral vote is dominated by the States with the highest number of Representatives and because those States also have the highest population, Mike wanted to change the rules.

At one o'clock, Ben announced Mike and he took the podium.

"Ladies and Gentlemen, today, we are going to give States like Wyoming with only three electoral votes, a voice in the election. I know this is a Constitutional amendment subject and we won't settle it today, but we can start the wheels turning.

"We all know the electoral college has always been part of the Constitution. The Electoral, as used today was proposed as an amendment, ratified by the states, and first used in an election in 1804. The men who drafted the twelfth amendment did not change the way the electoral college worked, but refined it to fit the country of that period. They saw in our nation's growth a system for elections, which needed to be monitored and revised from time to time. This is where Government started to go astray, the representatives stopped monitoring those items which needed updating as we grew a nation from coast to coast with over three-hundred-million people.

"After only thirty years, some representative realized the electoral system no longer fit the country as it was growing, but no one has seen the same problems since. In the last two-hundred years no one has recognized that the Electoral system was outdated and no longer fit the country. The Electoral system hasn't been changed since 1804, however the country has changed immensely. In 1804, the country's westward movement was just beginning. No one knew where the population centers were going to be one-hundred years hence, just as we don't know where the country will be one-hundred years from now.

"This we know! One, we cannot throw out the Electoral College in favor of the popular vote, since that would bury the smaller states and they would have no voice at all, not that they have much voice now. Under the current electoral system, the presidency can be won with as few as twelve States. If we remove the electoral system in favor of the popular vote we reduce the number of States to five. Five States controlling the outcome of an election. Under a popular vote system, the high population centers would control the elections forever and the less populated States would never have a voice.

"Two, we cannot continue to use a system which is outdated and antiquated. The current electoral system should have been revised or at least reviewed every ten years as the country and population grew.

"I've been thinking about this a lot since the President and I were elected. Sam and I were very lucky when we won California. If we hadn't, the vote would have gone to the House of Representatives who would have voted the party line and Johnson, or Grainger wouldn't be standing here asking you to amend the constitution. They would be playing golf. Many of you wouldn't be here either, because the good ole boys and career politicians would still be here.

"We need to level the playing field not only so each State has a voice in the election, but also every person who votes. We also need to level the field so every candidate, party member or independent, has a fair chance of winning.

"As I said, I have been considering this for some time and here are my thoughts:

"Every State and the District of Columbia gets three electors. Not three per candidate, just three. One must be the Governor the other two are one from each of the two major parties. With one-hundred-fifty-three total electoral votes there will never be a tie and the candidate with the most electoral votes wins. Period. No minimum required amount to win.

"The Electors must vote the popular vote. No exceptions. They can't vote opposed just because they don't approve of the popular candidate as we've seen in the past.

"There will always be a winner, so the vote will never have to be decided by the House of Representatives.

"Since, Hawaii, Alaska and the Pacific Time zone states are three to six hours behind the East Coast, they should be allowed to vote on the Monday, prior to the election Tuesday. Their results may not be released until after the polls close in the Eastern Time zone. This allows those extreme western states to have their votes considered. In the past candidates have won the electoral and been announced before the polls have closed in Hawaii and Alaska. This has been extremely unfair to the citizens of those states.

"This still isn't the best system but it's better than what we have. I'm asking you to use this as a guide to develop an acceptable system and one which will work for the betterment of the election process. Thank you."

The Senate worked diligently to design an election criteria and electoral system which was up-to-date with the country and would hopefully appeal to the high population areas as well as the less populated. They use Mike's basic plan of having a standard number of electors per state, but increased the number to five per state and three to the District of Columbia.

The Senate added a clause related to the Presidential Debates in which the Senate would be responsible for and would direct the Presidential debates. All candidates who appeared on the ballots of at least twenty-five states would be allowed to participate.

The Governor would not be required to be one of the electors. The Governors would be responsible for appointing the electors and ensuring the electoral vote was consistent with the popular vote. The Senate removed the – one from each part requirement, leaving the Governor free to appoint any two people to be electors.

The Lieutenant Governor would be one of the electors and the elector charged with ensuring the electoral vote was consistent with the popular vote.

Pacific and Pacific Coast States will vote on the Monday prior to the election Tuesday.

The candidate with the most electoral votes after all states are counted will be considered the winner of the election.

Since the proposed amendment is the brain-child of the Senate and every Senator had a hand in creating the document – it passed unanimously and was forwarded to the House of Representatives. A few of the Congressmen questioned why the electoral college needed to be amended but the vote was still decidedly two thirds in favor of the proposal. The proposed amendment passed the Judicial Review by the Supreme Court and was issued to the States for ratification. Mike was sure it would be ratified quickly, and he was a little surprised when the ratified amendment was laid on his desk for signature just twenty-six days after being issued.

37

A NEW PERSPECTIVE

Sam was given the medication to bring him out of the coma, but it would take several hours. Kate went to Mike's house to check up on Toby and Lauren and catch a short nap while waiting for the medication to take effect.

Sam came out of the coma earlier than expected and looked around the room. As soon as Peter saw Sam's eyes he rushed to the bedside.

"It's good to have you back, sir." Peter stated as Sam's eyes seem to focus on him.

"Who are you and where am I back from?" was Sam's dry reply.

"Sir, I'm Peter, your Secret Service, Chief of Security. Don't you recognize me?"

"I'm sorry Peter, I don't know you, in fact I'm not sure who I am or why you insist on calling me Sir."

"Just a minute Sir, let me get your doctor."

"Peter, would you really leave your President alone in this room? Maybe there are crazies on the hospital staff who would like to finish the job that was botched in Sheridan." Sam looked at Peter and a huge grin appeared on his face.

"Damn, Sam you had me going there for a minute. We have been afraid you may have lost some mental ability with the bullet fragments, loss of blood, and the three-month coma."

"I've been out of position for three months." Sam interrupted. "Has Mike been doing okay? I have to get over to the White House!"

"Sam, please relax. Yes, you have been out for three months and, Yes, the Vice-President has picked up your playbook and been doing fine. I think he will be even better since the new group of Senators and Congresspersons have taken their seats. Now, I must make a few phone calls to some people who will be very glad to know you are awake and doing fine." Peter took out his phone and called Kate, Mike, Terry, and Chaffey. He then paged the Nurse and Doctor.

Sam was out of his coma and appeared mentally ready to return to the White House, but when he tried to get out of bed his legs buckled under him and it was all Peter could do to catch him and keep him from crashing onto the floor.

"Sam, please just take it easy and follow your doctor's orders. The Vice-President has kept you in the White House for the past three months against the biddings of the Congress and the Justices. Trust me your job isn't going anywhere."

"Thanks Peter, you are a true friend. Could I get you to do something for me?"

"Anything, as long as it doesn't involve smuggling you back to D.C. and the White House. You'll be back soon enough."

"Nothing like that I promise. I want you to have Ben Albright bring me everything he can find on the Federal Reserve Act and the Fed. As soon as I'm out of here we're going to tear down the Federal Reserve."

"That's a tall order, Sam, but I'm with you and I'm sure a lot of the people will be celebrating in the streets when that monster falls."

When Mike arrives at the hospital Sam asks for a minute alone.

"Mike, I need you to start recruiting support from the Senate on a bill to break up the Fed. Are you up to the task?"

"I am, but are you sure you are? I can see you are mentally ready for that fight but what will it do to you physically. I mean, you've just come out of a coma and can't even stand on your own yet. The Doctors said it will be at least two more months before you can return to work and then you will need a mechanical device to help you walk."

"Mike, two things. One, I'm a Marine. Two, don't forget number one. We are taking down the Fed when I get back to work whether I can stand on my own or not."

"Okay Sam. You're the boss."

***

Mike was still reeling from Sam's request as he took the podium for the January joint session.

“Ladies and Gentlemen, I have some very good news. President Waters is out of his coma and is doing well. He has all of his mental acuity, however, being bed ridden in the coma for the past three months has left his muscles a bit weak, but he wanted to let you know he will be back to work as soon as possible.” There was boisterous applause from the floor.

“Would all the new representatives please stand? Chief Justice would you please have your judges administer the oath of office to these new representatives.”

Congressman Clemons from Arkansas speaks out.

“Mr. Vice-President, we were already sworn in.”

“Thank you, and you are?”

“Sir, I’m Congressman Jerod Clemons from the first district of Arkansas.”

“Well, Mr. Clemons. Everyone in this room had been sworn in prior to President Waters’ first joint session. In fact, Mr. Waters and I had been sworn in only the day before that session. This is a time to reaffirm your oath, and understand what that oath means – not only to you but to the people you represent.

“Chief Justice, please continue with the administration of the oaths for the new representatives.”

The Justices administered the oaths and Mike broke down the oath as Sam had done two years earlier and he explained the cost of an absence. He received applause after the ceremony was completed.

“President Waters had been hopeful that after the midterm-election, he could continue to make progress in reforming Government and America. The exiting Congressmen and Women, Senators and Justices had made some great strides prior to leaving office, but there was still a lot more work to be done. Are you all ready to continue making progress on the President's plans?” There is applause from the floor and the gallery.

“I don’t know your personal reasons for running for office, but I do know that I will hold you to the oath you just affirmed. Sam Waters will also hold you to that oath, not because he and I are power mad – but, because it is the right thing to do for the people of the United States. Now, it’s time to go to work!”

“Mr. Vice-President, a word please?” Dontae asked

Mike turned to Cheryl Dontae in the House Speaker’s seat.

"Sir, a lobby request for funding climate control was presented to the House today. Because, I understand how you and Sam feel on the subject, I benched it until after I talked with you. I think this session would be a good place to address the issue and get us all on your page."

"Thank you, but it's not my page, Cheryl, it's what is best for the country." Mike turns back toward the chamber.

"Ladies and Gentlemen, Speaker Dontae has just informed me of a petition by the clean air lobbyists. I hope we can resolve this issue in a way that brings to light reasons for this Government to avoid the climate control trap and keep it from recurring year after year.

"Ms. Dontae, how much money is the petition asking for?"

"Sir, the petition was for one billion dollars. Down from the trillions of past requests but still a large sum."

"Have any of the Climate groups been able to produce any proof that the scientists are coming together in a common position on the issue?"

"No, Sir."

"There is reason the President and I oppose climate control issues and will continue to veto any funding. As one group of Scientists are touting climate change an equal number of Scientists are calling it a fake, a great hoax. The basic reason for the split is that the earth cycles. It doesn't just rotate East to West creating day and night, but turns North and South as well but at a much slower rate. The North and South poles gradually rotate toward the Equator. As one side approaches warmer climates the ice caps melt. While the other side of the Polar caps, the side which is moving toward the poles the temperatures are freezing. The problem is that the thaw and freeze are not a one to one ratio. Thus, oceans rise, the earth changes, then stabilizes for several thousand years building massive ice structures around the poles but constantly in motion – one side thawing and one freezing.

"Here's another example of why Science can't or won't agree – about twenty-five million years ago the entire American Southwest was at the bottom of the ocean, yet now it is predominantly dry and arid high mountain desert. What caused the change? There weren't any factories or automobiles using fossil fuels to pollute the air and damage the ozone, but the change happened anyway, because the earth cycles.

"The President and I agree that we need to research and develop alternative fuels because they make good sense. We can't keep depleting our natural resources. We also agree that if science can unify and speak as one voice on the subject -- we will listen.

"Are you beginning to see the issue the way President Waters and I see it?

"Ms. Speaker, Have the people been polled to get a fair idea of where they stand on the issue?"

"To date sir, the people are split, however, the greater consensus says prove it, then support it."

"The petition from the global warming lobby, requested a billion dollars. Can anyone in this chamber tell me how much a billion is?"

"Sir, a one with nine zeros?" Questioned Congressman Goodhue of Arizona.

"Yes, that is correct, but it is much more than that. Most of us have a hard time comprehending a million of anything let alone a billion and trillions are completely out of conceptual reality. So, let's start with a bit of reference: a trillion is one-thousand billion and a billion is one-thousand million. Instead of looking at a billion as a one with nine zeros – look at it this way:

One Billion Seconds ago, it was nineteen-eighty-nine

One Billion Minutes ago, it was one-sixteen AD.

One Billion Hours ago, it was a little over one-hundred-thousand years ago, our ancestors were cavemen and dinosaurs walked the earth.

One Billion Miles is one-thousand-eighty-four round trips to the moon (One round trip being five-hundred-four-thousand miles).

"Here's another reference that is probably a little closer to home and easier to see in terms of dollars and cents.

There are a little over three-hundred-million people in the United States. If we took one-billion dollars and divided it equally between each person in the country from one-day old to one-hundred years old, each person would receive a little over three million dollars.

So, let me ask you, do you think giving the climate group or any group for that matter, one billion dollars for any research project would be considered spending taxpayer money wisely?

"Mr. Vice-President, we spend billions of dollars on various programs to support the people, why don't we just give them the money?" Questions Mr. Goodhue.

"All of you take a moment and think about what Mr. Goodhue just asked. We've seen time after time where a lottery winner will quit their job the next day. If every person in the country were given three million dollars, who do you think would show up for work the next day?"

"I see your point, Sir." Stated Mr. Goodhue.

"Are you sure? Imagine if we gave everyone three million dollars and they all thought they could live very well on the money. No one goes to work. No food is produced because there is no one to produce it, no farmers, no processors, no canneries, no one. Stores are all closed because, there are no people to work in them plus the delivery drivers aren't making deliveries. Within three days people are breaking into stores to get whatever food was left in them. The Gas stations are all closed so no one can get gas for their vehicles. Transportation, if it hasn't stopped for lack of gas, grinds to a halt, because there aren't any drivers. The whole country is stagnant. After six months, any of our enemies can take over the country without firing a shot, because we have either killed each other for food and water, or are starving to death and willing to surrender for table scraps. Most of our younger children have starved to death and anyone with an ounce of anything is welcome. That's why we can't just give the people the money and that's why we must be very frugal with the money they give us."

"Thank you, Sir. I guess I had never really thought about things like that." Responded Goodhue

"When you are discussing spending a billion of dollars to fund some program, ask yourselves – Where is that money coming from?

"The Government only has the money which is paid into it by people and small businesses who are working and paying their taxes. For years we have given breaks and created loopholes for the wealthy, the banks, corporations, and industries, so they don't have to pay as much tax as the average working person. I have just demonstrated what a billion dollars divided equally throughout the population of the country would be like. So, when you consider how many working people there are in the population, ask yourselves who is paying that three million dollars per person into the government for that billion-dollar program.

"Where is the money coming from? I hope those of you on the budget committee now have a greater understanding of why we need a balanced budget."

After the session, the House Budget committees made a poster of the billion-dollar example and it became the tool by which all standards were set.

Many had no idea of how much a billion was other than, like Goodhue, a one with nine zeros. The reference to each person in the country having over three million dollars had the greatest impact and the entire House of Representatives began reviewing every expenditure with a fine-toothed comb.

Cheryl appointed a committee to review the annual omnibus appropriations bill for any oversights which would waste taxpayer money.

38

CRIMINALS AND CONGRESSMEN

Sam had been making great progress in his physical therapy and was a month ahead of his rehabilitation schedule. His Doctor said he could return to work by the February joint session in ten days. Until then, Mike was still performing the duties of the President.

Mike, was reading through a couple of pieces of legislation when Terry entered the office.

"Good morning, Terry. What can I do for you?"

"Mike, we have a problem."

"I rather figured that Terry. What is the problem?"

"The CIA and FBI have been investigating the Shooting in Sheridan. The inquiries have uncovered some disturbing links to a couple of Representatives. I know we have been working hard to regain the trust of the people and I fully understand the damage implications of this nature could have on that trust, but we need to take very aggressive action against the people behind this."

"Okay, so what have you got so far?"

"About eighteen months ago, FBI Director Stevenson, came to me and told me the FBI was investigating a couple of key people in the Government regarding a sex trafficking ring that was operating in the nation's capital. Homeland Security and the FBI have been monitoring several people who appear to be using the services of this organization, however at that time they had not been able to get close to anyone inside. Although we have been working together on this, it seems we each only had a small part of what appears to be a much larger picture.

"About eight months before the President was shot, the CIA's intelligence branch picked up some chatter we believed to be the radicals planning an assassination attempt somewhere here on the eastern seaboard. That intel led us to place surveillance on one Allen Bryan Cage, who lived in Georgetown Commons here in D.C. Cage was the shooter in Wyoming.

"The intelligence implied an assault on the President's entourage, but the exact location wasn't determined. The intel suggested the purpose of the shooting wasn't to directly assassinate the President, a stray bullet hitting the President was a caveat. It seems the young shooter was hired, given the weapons, and trained to make a hit on any group exiting a building at a select location and time. It just happened the President's team in Sheridan, was a target of opportunity and not the objective. The purpose was to create fear in the people like we have seen throughout Europe as the terrorists continue to wreak havoc with bombings and mass shootings. Now, it seems, terror has come to the United States and although we try to keep it in a low profile, every one of these incidents raise the stakes in the war on terror and makes our enemies even bolder. With the shooting of the President they are becoming even more brazen. Here is the most protected person in the entire world and this young man could get close enough to take out several of his security, shoot the President, and be a threat to our country.

"During the surveillance of Cage, he was followed to Greece, where he attended the conference at which Senator Williams, Congressman Prushing, and Congressman Dobbs were guest speakers. We have surveillance pictures of the two Congressmen meeting with Cage. Sometimes all three would meet, sometimes the Congressmen met individually with Cage, but always at the same park and around the same time of day when traffic would be heaviest and hinder listening devices. The surveillance team would get bits and pieces from conversations but nothing concrete. At first, the FBI thought Cage might be setting up a bribe for some budget legislation. They were pursuing the bribery charges when Mr. Donnally from the CIA intervened and informed them that there were international indications there was going to be a major terrorist attack in the United States. The CIA was also lacking a lot of details but had also been following Cage's activities. The FBI originally thought the threat was U.S. based, but the CIA added that it was being planned by an international organization with ties and contacts in the illegal arms community and the radical extremist factions, but, these weren't confirmed until just before the shooting."

"You stated that Cage was under surveillance by two agencies. If they were watching him, how did he manage to elude the surveillance long enough to put eighteen rounds into a crowd and murder five people in Sheridan?"

"Mike, it seems both agencies, lost him in Greece. He entered a street market and disappeared. The next time they saw him was when he was captured at the shooting.

"Cage, told his interviewers he had come back to the United States through Canada and walked across the border in Montana, bought a two-hundred-dollar car and drove to Sheridan. We had no way of tracking him after he disappeared in Greece. Sorry, Mike."

"Cage, also told the FBI interviewer that he had no idea the President would be the one coming out of the auditorium. If he had known, he would not have fired. He has also given up valuable information regarding all the group who hired him. We will clean this house, Sir."

"Mike, we have been trying to get something on this organization for a couple of years. We have lost several agents and have suspected we had a mole in the agency, but our investigations turned up another scenario.

"Since the Iran-Contra scandal, the agencies must detail their activities to the budget committee to ensure their funding. They have been frequently asked if they have any undercover or covert activities in process. If they don't answer the questions, their funding requests get vetoed which in the past has put agents at risk.

"While investigating the possible attempt on the President, the FBI quite literally stumbled upon their leak. Both Congressmen, Prushing and Dobbs are on the budget committee, and both have been ruthless in their questions regarding our undercover activity. When the FBI came across the connection between Cage and the Congressmen, it opened some doors that had been blocked before. They began investigating Dobbs' foreign travel and found his travel to be timed exactly with that of Cage although Greece was the only time we photographed the encounter. We have a similar file on Prushing." Terry handed the field and intelligence reports to Mike.

"Mike, I apologize. I had the FBI and CIA side-step and omit some things from their report to the House, so we could divert funds and agents from the Middle East to the Cage case and were able to get an agent inside without alerting Dobbs and Prushing. That's when we found the depth of the organization and the full connection to the Congressmen. We now have detailed names and places where this organization is doing business and we are ready to close the net, but we need your permission, since we are dealing with representatives."

"Terry, I want you to go with me when I visit Sam this afternoon. I think this should be his call and you can answer any questions he may have. I'm sure he will tell you to burn them down, but we must be sure all our ducks are in a row. I don't want any of this falling through the cracks because we missed some detailed technicality. By the Constitution you cannot arrest a representative while in the performance of their duties during a session, or while traveling to or from the session, therefore, this session ends with Sam's return on February twenty-eighth. Representatives fly home to work on issues right after the session. I would suggest that you prepare to make the arrests as they exit their vehicles at their homes.

39
A HIGHER LEVEL OF CONFIDENCE

Mike and Terry visited Sam at Bethesda and Terry briefed him about the two congressmen and their clear connection to the shooting and to international crime.

Looking at Sam, Mike said; "Sam, I'm completely in the dark as to what action to take against Dobbs and Prushing. This is truly an affront to the American people and the districts who supported them. Can you give me any suggestions?"

"Mike, there have been criminals in government since seventeen-seventy-six when the Continental Congress refused to pay the Continental Army and again in the eighteen and early nineteen-hundreds when they all congregated at the Little Green House on K Street.

"Although, there has always been a criminal element in our Congress, very few have been prosecuted. It is time for us to show the people we will prosecute those guilty of criminal activity regardless of their position in Government and gain a higher level of confidence in the government.

"Announce to Congress that I wish to see everyone when I return on the twenty-eighth. I'm fairly certain everyone will be there, but I don't want any exceptions. How firm are the charges against Dobbs and Prushing?"

"There are several witnesses and we have the testimony of the man who shot you."

"If all the witnesses are of the same caliber as the guy who shot me it may be hard to bring the two outstanding pillars of the community to trial. We need to tie them directly to the organization."

"Okay, Sam. Should I start a censure in the house?"

"Not just yet, Mike. But I think it's time we require our nation's highest governmental positions to hold a Final-Top-Secret security clearance. I want Stevenson and his FBI folks to develop a bulletproof security clearance qualifying procedure. Background Investigations (BI) reveal the obvious, but do not reveal the hidden. I've known guys who shined on their BI and couldn't be trusted with the schematic to change a lightbulb. While others had credit debt and other obvious character flaws who would never, even on threat of death, give up this country. In addition to the BI, I want to see a good Psych evaluation and a multilevel litmus test.

"We will present the Executive Order on the twenty-eighth and follow it up with a senate bill.

"The Representatives will be tested in the House Chamber immediately after the joint session before heading home. They can fill out the documents for the BI between sessions and give them to the FBI when we reconvene in March.

"Get with Albright and the two of you work out the wording for the bill. Make sure the Senate is aware of the investigation but not of the players. That should help get the bill passed in the Senate. I would imagine the two Congressmen will oppose the House vote.

"Mike, tell the FBI and CIA to hold off on any arrests until the BIs and test results are back. Tell them to work closely with Interpol. Work with the local governments and police where this organization is set up but don't give them too much information. We've seen before where the local governments were part of the organizations we were after. Get some concrete hard evidence we can use to bring these scumbags down. Make sure you don't lose them. If their travel itinerary deviates from their home town tighten the net but not so close as to spook them. They may make the case for us, because we know something they don't. They don't know we're after them."

Mike and Terry left and followed Sam's suggestions. They informed the FBI and CIA of Sam's instruction and set the wheels in motion for the security clearance initiative for Congress. The Executive Order was drafted, and Sam signed it as his first official duty upon returning to the White House and moments before the joint session on the twenty-eighth of February. On the fifteenth of March the Senate passed the Congressional Security Clearance bill, the House passed it three days later and Sam signed it into law on March twentieth. As expected Prushing and Dobbs voted against the bill. They also failed the psych evaluation and litmus test. On twenty-five March both were arrested and charged with conspiracy to assassinate the President and multiple international crimes. They were tried and convicted, and they are serving seven consecutive life sentences in separate maximum-security prisons. Cage is serving twenty to life at a federal work farm. The crime organization headed by the two former Congressmen was crushed by international police departments, who worked together to bring down the organization and jail all its participants.

40
TAKING DOWN THE FED

Sam has researched the Federal Reserve and the Act which created it. He also researched the rumors which state there was no gold stored in Fort Knox and found them to be untrue. Although, the Vaults do not hold the twenty-five-thousand tons of gold it had at the end of World War II, it still holds several thousand tons of bullion. Sam also found U.S. gold reserves in other locations.

Sam called a meeting with Mike, Rob Chaffey, Cheryl, Ben, Treasurer – Tom Carter, and Federal Reserve Director – Gene Anderson.

"Gentlemen and Lady, we need to dismantle the Federal Reserve System and I need you to help me put together a plan for doing that which won't cause a complete breakdown in our banking network or throw the stock market into an international panic.

"I know this is a big challenge and I hope we can succeed in finding a solution. The Bankers did an excellent job of putting the Federal Reserve Act together in 1910 and made it almost unbreakable, but I believe that nothing is completely bulletproof. We must try and find a hole in the way the Fed works -- some loophole in the mechanism which will work in our favor and help the people. And we must find the way before the Fed can create another recession or worse. You can bet that once the Bankers and Corporations know we are going to dam their river of tax free income, they will do everything in their power to muck things up."

"Sam, I know you have been reviewing and researching this since you came out of the coma, but are you sure this is the right time for this? The changes you have made to the tax system for corporations and the people have been working to improve the economy and we have been paying off a great many of the Nation's debts so this could be disastrous."

"Yes, Cheryl, it's time the Fed came down. The Government has been involved in the Federal Reserve lie long enough.

"We have implied for the past century that the Fed was part of the Government. The Federal Reserve System is not a Federal entity. The government does not control it, nor does it have to answer to the government. It is a private Corporation and who do you think is on the Board of this corporation? The Big Banks and Corporations. The President appoints the Head of the Federal Reserve, but that person is just a figurehead, a show piece to give the impression that the Federal Reserve is part of the Government. They have no real input into the workings of the Fed. The Board controls the Fed and how it works. Are there any other concerns?"

Gene voiced a concern.

"Sam, as you said, the Fed has been controlling America's money for over a century and backing Government spending, which is why we continually bailout the big banks and corporations. If you break up the Fed, there will be a huge debt owed to those Banks and Corporations. The Banking Cartel will fight you every step of the way and won't surrender their hold on America's finances without a major fight. There's a good chance the banks and corporations are going to dump and run, which will cause a crash in the stock market. Then they will close a couple of central banks which will cause a panic in the public which in turn could cause a run on the banks like 1929."

"Gene, I am very aware of the scenarios of breaking up the Fed could cause. I have researched the Fed from top to bottom and the essential point is – the Federal Reserve is a failed concept for everyone except the Bankers.

"The Federal Reserve System was formed to stabilize the U.S. economy and has failed miserably in that mission. The great depression (1929-1939) began a mere sixteen years after the signing of the Federal Reserve Act and should have been the greatest reinforcement that the Fed could not do the job for which it was commissioned. The roller-coaster ride the economy has been on for the last century should further attest to the fact that the Federal Reserve System is a failure and should be abolished. Furthermore, the U.S. Dollar has lost 90 percent of its value since the beginning of the Federal Reserve.

"The Federal Reserve was not the sole problem for the condition America was in two years ago, but it is a major contributor.

"My research has pointed to a few solutions, but I need all your help to make them happen. Are you ready for the fight?"

"What's the plan, Sam? Mike asked, and the others nodded

and voiced their agreement.

"Okay, here we go. First, Cheryl, I need you to do three things:

"You will need to find the document in which FDR banned personal ownership of gold and gold coins in 1933. Although, people are buying and selling gold all the time, we need to be sure the FDR ban was reversed or rescinded. We don't want the banks to bring up an outdated law we are still obligated to enforce.

"Then I need you to put a bill together putting the United States back into the gold standard of currency.

"I walked through the Congressional offices the other day when I returned from the hospital and saw the 'What is a billion?' posters and thought that was a great idea. So, the third thing I need you to do, and this will mean getting the help from all your representatives and budget committees. I want you to change every request for money to the next lower denomination. If the request is for a trillion you vote on approving a billion, billions to millions, and millions to hundred-thousands. We need to get our budget backed by the gold standard.

"Unfortunately, reestablishing the gold standard of currency will initially devalue the dollar because there is so much paper currency out there, but we should be able to recover in brief time.

"Mike and Ben, I need you to research the Federal Reserve Act, line by line. The original act allowed government to borrow money from the reserve but limited it to an amount easily repaid by taxes. The amendments of 1914 removed that restriction. I want you to find a way to reverse those amendments to the reserve act and again place restrictions on what the government can borrow from the Fed. If there is an amendment to the original act find a way to reverse or rescind it.

"Tom, I need you to issue a directive to the Mints to stop production of money for ninety-days. Absolutely, no new currency. After the ninety-day moratorium the mints will only produce twenty-five percent of their current production for another one-hundred-twenty-days. This gives us seven months to reestablish the value of the dollar and strengthen the economy. My hope is that by the end of the seventh month we will no longer need the Mints to make mountainous volumes of paper money.

"I know the Mints take in millions of dollars daily which are scheduled for destruction. Issue a notice to the banking community that the Mints are only accepting severely defaced and damaged bank notes. Older currency must be recirculated.

"These two actions will significantly reduce the amount of paper currency available.

"Mike get the Senate on board so when you get the gold standard bill from the House you are ready to vote on it."

"Sam, how will these actions help break up the Fed?"

"Gene, I'm glad you asked and I'm sure the others are probably wondering the same thing.

"FDR banned individuals from owning gold, so the Government would control all the Country's reserves. This was Big Bank's idea for getting control of all the money in the country.

"The next thing FDR did at Big Bank's bidding, was remove the country from the gold standard of exchange and issue the Federal Reserve Notes we use as currency. Meaning the Federal Reserve then controlled all currency.

"The original Federal Reserve Act of 1913 had restrictions and limitations to keep it from becoming the monster you see today. Unfortunately, once the Act was signed into law, it could be amended, and the restrictions removed, in 1914, a mere six months after the act was law, Congress did just that.

"The actions I have asked for will in essence reverse the decisions of 1913 and 1914 and put the country back on a level playing field with the Banks, by rescinding the FDR ban and putting us back into the gold standard of exchange. Then we must regain the value of the dollar. The only way to do that is to stop making money. We only have a little over eight-thousand metric tons of gold and the exchange rate is around one-hundred dollars per ounce.

"We can only have dollar per dollar currency to the value of the gold exchange. That's total currency, that which the public has on their person, under their mattress, and in banks and that which Government has in its treasury. It's simple math, if you have twice as much currency as there is gold value. The currency is only worth half as much – the more currency the less it is worth.

"We cannot continue to make money without it being backed up."

"The Bankers will expect to be paid for the trillions of dollars they have spent funding the Government."

"Yes, Gene, that is probably true. So, here's how we deal with that debt.

"As I told Cheryl, The Federal Reserve System is not a system at all. It is a private corporation that regulates all things monetary in the United States. The Federal Reserve Building and the thirty-six Federal Reserve Banks were paid for and built with tax payer dollars. The Federal Government spent tax money to build facilities for a private corporation without the people's knowledge or approval. This Private corporation has been housed in these facilities without paying rent for the last twelve-hundred-months.

"The Government has rented facilities over the past century at many locations around the country. Gene, I want you and Tom to get the square-footage of the Federal Reserve facilities and the dates they opened. Then prepare an invoice for the past rent for each facility owing from when the facility opened to the date of the invoice. Those invoices must also include the cost of construction.

"Tom, I want you to also work with Rob and get all of the gold reserves out of the basement of the Federal Reserve Bank in New York and into one of our depositories. Fort Knox, Denver, or West Point.

"Cheryl, Gentlemen, the clock is ticking. I only have twenty months left of this term of office and even if I run for reelection, there is always the chance I may be defeated. I would like to see where this battle is headed before the end of my term."

***

The meeting adjourns, and the players begin their tasks. Within a week, Cheryl had completed the research into the FDR items and had found both to be in effect -- she wrote two bills to rescind them. The House unanimously passed the resolution to allow individuals to buy and own gold, but there was much debate by the remaining older Congressmen and Women over the country's return to the gold standard. They feared a major depression, one which would be greater than the Great Depression of 1929. In the end, after six-weeks of debate and a presentation by Sam at a joint session, the bill passed the House and Senate.

The dollar instantly devalued to eleven cents, but within the month had climbed back above the twenty-two cents – the value before the change back to the gold standard. The depression never happened. Although the stock market fell significantly, it rebounded quickly. The housing market, crashed, however the banks agreed to refinance at updated terms based on the value of the currency, meaning a formerly priced two-hundred-thousand-dollar home was still worth two-hundred-thousand-dollars under the gold standard. The difference was, the banks had to have the money in bank secured deposits to be able to make loans or finance mortgages

Tom had issued the money production and destruction orders and the Mints and banks were complying. Then Tom sent the invoices for the Federal Reserve facilities construction and rent for the past century. Gene personally presented it to the Board of Directors.

The Fed was beginning to lose its hold.

41
IS FOUR YEARS ENOUGH?

Sam must make a choice this year. With nineteen months left in office he must decide whether to run for reelection. Campaigns will begin in a year and Sam isn't sure he wants to continue the fight. He had talked about the idea of a reelection campaign with Kate and the kids and Kate was firmly opposed to the idea.

"Sam, when you were in the Marines and deployed I knew you might be hurt or killed. Even though I worried every day you were gone I still understood that it was your job and you had to do what needed to be done.

"I never anticipated having to pace a hospital floor waiting for news of a surgery to remove bullet fragments from my husband, the President. I never had to sit by your bedside while you were in a coma wondering if you were going to wake up. There are no words for what that did to both me and our children psychologically. So, NO, you are not going to run for reelection."

"Kate that was a fluke. The kid even said if he had known it was me he wouldn't have fired the weapons."

"And you believe that? What about the next nut case? What if the next time isn't a random act of violence to put fear in the people but an honest assassination of the president, You?" Kate punched Sam in the chest and started crying.

"I know Baby, it was a terrible thing for you and the kids to endure, but we've come so far and there is so much left to be done. You know I can't leave a project unfinished."

"I know Sam, but I'm going to stand firm on this. If you run, the kids and I are going home and will be waiting for you. If you are reelected, the door will be open and a light in the window when you are done in 2028. We won't be in the White House with you."

***

Sam had a lot to think about. He knew Kate would follow through with her statement. He also knew there was a lot to accomplish and there wasn't enough time in his remaining term to get it all done. Who would take his place, and would they feel as devoted and dedicated to the country as he was. Yes, there was a fresh bunch of representatives with fresh ideas and plans for the future of America, but, there were also those who would work against everything Sam had accomplished.

Not just the remaining long-term Reps, but the money which creates the desire and lust for power. Sam had been victorious over the money and the power it brandishes for two years. He had gained ground and advanced forward against overwhelming odds: but can he win the battles he has left. Will his remaining term be enough to engage the final battles?

Sam's election and the following years had made headlines around the world and many countries had new Independent candidates emerging and challenging the standing parties. These new Independents, like Sam, swore away from belonging to any party including the regularly accepted independent parties. And they were winning. People were speaking out and making their voices heard by the millions worldwide.

Sam and Mike continued to tour the world on missions of good will and always made sure to congratulate the new independent leaders in England, Canada, the Ukraine, and several other countries throughout Europe and South America.

Sam had accomplished many of the things he felt needed to be corrected but there were still issues which needed to be addressed. The country and government were getting back to being of, for and by the people but it was a continuous battle against the corruption that seeps into the foundation, taking advantage of the weak and unscrupulous persons in our government.

Will Sam run for reelection or pass the torch? We'll have to see!

www.ingramcontent.com/pod-product-compliance
Lightning Source LLC
Chambersburg PA
CBHW060806310726
48980CB00002B/248

* 9 7 8 0 6 9 2 0 5 9 6 9 2 *